The Judas Son

630-PAKE

The Judas Son

Michael Pakenham (signature)

Michael Pakenham

To Frank + Gloria with
best wishes.
10.08.01

To order additional copies of this book, contact:
Xlibris Corporation
1-888-7-XLIBRIS
www.Xlibris.com
Orders@Xlibris.com

Contents

MRS BOND
WITH ALL MY LOVE AND THANKS.

I LOVE THEE WITH THE BREATH,
SMILES, TEARS, OF ALL MY LIFE! -
AND IF GOD CHOOSE
I SHALL BUT LOVE THEE BETTER AFTER DEATH.

ELIZABETH BARRAT BROWNING

Also by Michael Pakenham

Fiction
The Bitter Web

Biography
The Polish Exile

PROLOGUE

HE came to kill his father at twenty-five minutes past ten at night.

Richard never heard a sound until the library door swung open. He was standing there dishevelled and grinning, the shotgun pointing at his father's chest. "Hello father, don't move unless you want that diseased heart of yours blown into bloody pieces. What's the security situation?"

It was as if an iron fist had thumped into Richard's stomach. Any remaining hope he had had was dashed. The realisation that his only son had been the perpetrator of such a horrendous crime left him speechless.

"Come on you rotten bastard answer me."

The hatred was all too clear. Richard swallowed hard, found his voice, which was not as steady as he would have liked. "There is no security." He gave a wry smile, "I didn't think I would need it—certainly not to protect me from my own flesh and blood. I am the only one in the house. Your mother is not here either thank God. I dread to think what she would feel if she could see you holding a gun at my chest."

"Yes, I saw her leaving the house. I'm glad, makes my task easier. So you guessed that I killed Sarah?" There was no compassion in his voice. "But you haven't done a thing about it. Feeling too bloody guilty were you to show my letter to the police and your political cronies? Of course you fucking well were! No man wants to admit he's been such a lousy father that his son is forced to become a murderer. Shit! You wouldn't like that father. You would be scared witless in case your friends turned their backs on you." He laughed mirthlessly. "Well I'm going to solve all your problems; I'm going to kill you just as I said in my letter. Stand up and turn round slowly. Bastards like you deserve to be shot in the back."

Richard didn't move. "You will never force me to turn round. If I am going to die I die looking you straight in the eye. Live with that if you can."

There was not a flicker of emotion on the young man's face. Suddenly Richard felt desperately afraid. He meant nothing to his son.

James smirked at him. "Oh I can live with it father, by God I can. I will relish seeing the fear in your eyes as I slip off the safety catch and you wonder how long you have to live before I bring your miserable life to a close. I'm told most people shit themselves when facing certain death. I doubt you will be any different."

Richard had to ask the question. "Why, why has it come to this?"

"Jesus father don't you know? Well let me tell you. You have ruined my life. Ruined any chance I had of living within your rules and your society. You refused to even entertain my girl friends. You despised me. Oh how you despised me father. I became lost, isolated, so very alone. But now I have met a girl, who you would really despise. Perhaps hate would be a better word. She has told me about the other side of the Irish conflict, very different from yours. And do you know what? I believe her. Now I'm going to strike a blow for the Ireland she loves. A free Ireland, free of British rule."

A cold hand touched Richard's heart. Instinctively he knew he could not reason with him or persuade him he was being manipulated. It was too late. The damage had been done. He was within an ace of dying. He glanced hopefully at the open french windows and quickly discarded the idea. He would be gunned down almost before he moved. He was trapped. But he would not die a coward. No way would he give James that satisfaction. He came round the desk fast, shaking with fury. "You little bas......"

"No further father! Stand right there! I have the gun. I'm in control at last. Just sweat with fear. Gaze at your killer, the product of your sperm and mother's womb. Did you ever think it would come to this? Did you ever think that she would give birth to a cancer that would one day destroy you? Poor darling mother, your rock, your lover. How she will suffer when she finds your blood stained body. She will not be able to live without you, soon withering away with grief. It will not be long before she joins you in Hell. After that I will be the only Hanmore left. No doubt a traitor to the British Establishment's eyes, but to the Irish Republican Movement I will be a hero. Look hard at me father. Can you feel my hatred? Perhaps even smell it? Reflect on it before you die. There is little time left now, just a few seconds before I experience the most exciting moment of my life so far."

Stunned by the hatred opposite him Richard could only stare at the two small dark holes pointing at his chest. He was surprised now how calm he felt, almost elated that he was not going to shit himself or beg for mercy. All he had left was his self-esteem. It was not much—but it was something. "Go on then James, if you have the guts pull the trigger."

James raised the gun to his shoulder…………..

Chapter One

Total desolation.

SIR Richard Hanmore staggered out of the dining room into the high ceilinged hall and painfully made his way to his favourite armchair by the Adams fireplace. As he sank into its softness the tightness in his chest reminded him that the doctors had said that stress could kill him. He looked at the dirty piece of paper he was holding in his hand and gave a resigned shrug of his wide shoulders. Perhaps this was his death warrant.

The letter had arrived in the morning post just after his wife, Blanche had left for London. It had been twelve worrying weeks since they had last heard from their son James and now he held the reason why in his shaking hand. How he needed Blanche by his side to share the pain, and he cursed the fact that he'd encouraged her to go to see their daughter Sarah.

He furiously brushed away a tear and stared up at the painting hanging over the fireplace. It was of his grand father standing proudly outside the family home at Crumlin, a small village a few miles south of Belfast. Richard had inherited the old man's love of Northern Ireland and his desire to see peace come to the troubled island. He had worked tirelessly to reach this goal, and what was his reward? A heart attack, which had forced him to resign as Northern Ireland Secretary. He threw his son's letter onto the floor and cursed aloud. The boy had always been difficult. Lack of attention from his parents had been James's excuse, but should the lack of parental love lead to such treachery?

He thought of his mother, who had warned him years ago not to let his driving ambition come between him and his children. She had never hidden her criticism saying, 'You and Blanche are building up trouble and when things start to go wrong you'll only have yourselves to blame.' However, she understood his dilemma, juggling his time between fighting for peace in Ireland and bringing up a young family, and did everything she could to help. It had not been enough.

His eyes darted round the large hall. He never imagined he could feel so wretched in the house he loved. Never in the twenty eight years since he had bought Rosehall had he felt so insecure and in need of company. There was no one in the house apart from Jose and Maria, Blanche's Spanish couple. A few months earlier he would have had his security team to talk to. How he had hated having them around him, and yet now he would give anything to have one of them beside him. He could still have had them—albeit in smaller numbers. But on his resignation from the Government he'd refused the offer of further security much to the concern of the Prime Minister's Office and Scotland Yard. He remembered telling the PM that he thought it a waste of public money guarding half dead old crocks. James's letter made him realise that he might have been a trifle foolhardy.

A sharp spasm of pain scythed across his chest and he involuntarily sucked in his breath. His heart seemed to trip into another gear, beating alarmingly against his ribs and a headache pounded at the back of his brain. Dear God was this the warning the doctors had spoken about? He knew what to do in the circumstances. "Just get to the telephone and damn quick." The doctor had warned. "Any hesitation could mean death."

Was he destined to die alone without Blanche by his side? Another stab of pain ripped across his chest. He involuntarily focused on James's crumpled letter on the floor. "My death warrant!" he thought.

His head spun. "Call the ambulance you damn fool."

He started to move towards the telephone. Every painful step making him gasp for breath. Half way across the hall he realised he wasn't going to make it. His heart felt as if it was bursting through his rib cage and a mist began to form in front of his eyes.

The pain forced him to his knees. Through watering eyes he could make out the telephone so tantalisingly close and yet so far.

He made a feeble attempt to rise to his feet but the pain was too intense, embracing his whole body. His legs were numb, his body too weak. He groaned more with frustration than pain and toppled over onto his side like a discarded doll.

As his cheek touched the cold stone of the floor he lost consciousness.

Blanch stood by the sofa in the sitting room of Sarah's small house close to Putney Bridge. She wondered why on earth she had come to London. It was the first time she had left Richard alone since his heart attack and she could feel her unease growing.

She did not want him to die at 58. She had hoped for years of contentment after his retirement. My God she deserved it. She had supported him throughout his political career. To be fair she had loved it as much as he had but she had so hoped for peace. Then the premature breakdown in his health had ruined her dreams. Had the price been worth paying? Should any man be put under such pressure, or lose a son because of his ambitions? Blanche shrugged. What did it matter. It served no purpose dwelling on the past. It made no difference to her love for the man she had married years ago. Quite simply he couldn't die.

To add to her unease was the certain knowledge that it wasn't going to be an easy meeting with Sarah. As far as her daughter was concerned anything that happened to James was his parents' fault, and Blanche feared the sting of Sarah's tongue.

Time and again Sarah had shown her disapproval over her father's treatment of James and time and again she had been forced to be the mediator between them. It was not a role she enjoyed and she had made her father all too well aware of her disgust. But Blanche knew he would always be ashamed of his son. It made her weep.

She looked out of the sitting room window at James's car and wondered why he hadn't taken it with him. It had mystified Sarah as well. Blanche hoped it meant that at any moment he would walk through the door and they could start again. She gave a resigned shrug of her shoulders. Who did she think she was trying to kid? James didn't want anything to do with his parents. She had known that for years. Her guilt ran deep. She felt the first tear trickle down her cheek. She had been crying a lot recently and it annoyed her not being in control of her emotions.

She nervously tapped her fingers on the window sill. How long had it been? It had been twelve painful weeks. At first she had not worried unduly. She was used to his disappearances, but none had been longer than two weeks. After a month she was angry. By twelve weeks panic had set in. It was the uncertainty that was beginning to take its toll on her normally robust constitution.

Oh James, James where are you? She thought.

Blanche flopped down onto the sofa, impatiently gathering up the sheets of an old Guardian newspaper, which lay scattered there, wondering how her daughter could live in such chaos. There was a pair of laddered black tights on the back of one of the two chairs; a pile of dirty washing on the brown carpet and two tea stained mugs clustered together on the floor by her feet.

She looked at her watch. It was two minutes to one.

"The key will be under the flower pot on the right of the front door,' Sarah had informed her on the telephone the day before. 'Now remember that. I move it around you know, to try and fool the inevitable burglar.'

Blanche wondered who on earth would want to risk losing their freedom by breaking into a place which had nothing to steal.

'I'll be with you as near to one as I can be,' had been Sarah's parting words. Blanche couldn't help smiling. Not much chance of that. When had Sarah ever been on time?

A rusty spring creaked under her weight and she grimaced at the hardness of the seat. She must remember to chivvy her daughter into buying a new sofa. Why on earth she wanted to live in such apparent squalor defeated Blanche. It wasn't as if she was short of money.

Picking up the magazine she began to flip idly through the pages. They were full of discussions with women having trouble reaching orgasms, or the inability of the average man to stay faithful to his wife. 'They're all shits once you have let them into your knickers,' screamed a large heading on page ten. Apparently written by a woman who had had three husbands and just been deserted by the third. Perhaps she had never had the mind blowing orgasm page twelve was suggesting that everyone should have enjoyed in marriage.

Blanche wondered how many of the younger generation read such utter tripe. She and Richard hadn't needed to search the pages of magazines to discover the mysteries and variations of the sexual act. If the contributors to Cosmopolitan were to be believed they had been one in a million. Orgasms for Blanche had been the natural culmination of sex with Richard. She hadn't needed the writings of a sex therapist to tell her how to achieve one. My god sometimes just his tongue had been enough to drive her into convulsions.

She had once explained to Richard, 'Orgasms with you are like swimming quietly in the sea naked, and then suddenly being hit by a gigantic roller which picks you up, frightens you to death, and then hurls you screaming to the safety of the warm sand.'

Blanche threw the magazine on the floor and glanced at her watch. Twenty minutes after one. 'Ah well Sarah darling some things never change' she thought. Normally she would not have minded, but nothing was normal any longer and she had a sick husband at home. What on earth was she doing away from him? What had possessed her to leave him alone with only their Spanish couple in the house? Irritably she brushed away a fly, some sixth sense telling her she shouldn't have come. She imagined she heard Richard calling for her. Her mind was playing nasty tricks making her feel trapped. She got up and paced round the room continually looking at her watch. It was no good she couldn't wait any longer. She must get back to Rosehall.

She jumped up from the sofa, fumbling in her bag for a pen to write a note explaining why she had left. She tore a leaf out of her diary and sat down at the small writing table by a window, the sunlight sparkling on the diamond ring Richard had given her the day he had exchanged contracts on Rosehall. She smiled, remembering his words. "This will be our little bolt hole."

A house with ten bedrooms, five acres of garden and a thousand acre farm was not what she'd have called it, but after a few years in politics she'd grown to understand what he had meant. Time together became a rare commodity and Rosehall provided the solitude and beauty they needed to unwind. Even though after Richard had taken up his cabinet post the police and their personal security men still shadowed them everywhere.

Rosehall. Just thinking of the name calmed her a little. She loved it, felt secure in its surroundings. It was all she had ever wanted. And then along came the children. Nothing had been the same again. She had almost resented them. God she had been selfish. Perhaps this was His way of punishing her.

She reluctantly pulled her mind back to the present and with a shaking hand she began to write quickly. She did not wish to be delayed by Sarah's arrival. She put the completed note by the telephone and let herself out, hurrying towards Putney Bridge and praying she wouldn't hear the familiar voice of her daughter hailing her. A few hundred yards on she found a taxi.

"Waterloo please driver."

"Certainly Lady Hanmore."

Alarm coursed through her. Just her luck to choose a driver who recognised her. Oh God, she thought dismally as she collapsed onto the seat. Would it be the usual question of 'what's it like to be married to a man who risks being murdered every hour of the day and night?' Or the statement that seemed most common, 'Well I'm labour myself but your old man hasn't done a bad job. Mind you I think he's a fool, given the risks involved and you with children.'

Blanche pushed herself against the back of the seat, wishing to disappear. But the cabbie said nothing and as they crossed Putney Bridge and turned right into the Kings Road her nerves began to settle. She sent up a silent prayer of thanks for his silence. As they crawled up the congested street she stared vacantly at the crowds walking in the warm sunlight. Was James out there desperate and wanting help?

Was he wandering the streets high on drugs or lying in a gutter unconscious from too much alcohol? Or perhaps lying naked by some stinking whore? She shuddered as she remembered Sarah telling her of James's appetite for such girls. But he could just be dead. Rotting away somewhere never to be found. Dear God please dear God not that. In spite of the heat she shivered. To think the worst would destroy the last of her resilience. She had to be positive.

She watched two young women risking their lives as they weaved their way across the street. Several angry blows of the horn only made them laugh and raise two fingers at the offending motorist. Blanche noticed their short denim skirts and high heels, their bottoms undulating as they ran. Perhaps that was the sort of girl James could have moved in with. It was, she thought sadly, as positive as she could be.

The taxi was forced to stop at the light by Peter Jones and she closed her eyes only to see James's reproachful eyes staring at her. Involuntarily she cried out.

"You alright Lady Hanmore?" The cabbie asked, his voice showing concern.

"Yes, yes," said Blanche weakly, "Just felt a little faint for a second, but I'm fine now. Thank you so much for your concern."

"Not at all Lady Hanmore. No problem at all.

Touched by his kindness Blanche felt like unburdening him with her troubles. Perhaps he would see everything in a different perspective and give her back some of her lost confidence. But it was only a fleeting thought. It would be ridiculous for her to talk to a stranger. She closed her eyes as the lights changed and forced her mind to go blank.

The next thing she knew he was speaking to her again. "Nearly there now."

She glanced at her watch. She could hardly believe it. She had been oblivious to the passing of time for fifteen minutes. With difficulty she pulled herself back to reality. "Just stop outside the Station will you driver. I think I'm in need of a short walk."

"Okay. I'll just pull round this corner." He stopped and jumped out to open the door. It was something he didn't often do, but he was a little concerned by her obvious agitation.

As Blanche's feet touched the pavement she stumbled and but for his outstretched hand she would have fallen. "Are you sure you are alright?"

She smiled weakly, "Yes, really I'm fine, I promise. It's just the heat that's all. I don't like this humidity. I'll be glad when I get back to the country where the air is so much fresher. Now, I've taken enough of your time. How much do I owe you?"

"Five quid exactly." She gave him six. He smiled and gave a little bow. "Thank you Lady Hanmore, and if I may say so I think you should take it easy when you get home. You look proper pale to me. No doubt you have been worrying about that husband of yours, and quite right to. I was only saying to my wife the other night that he was a candidate for a heart attack. You can't work all the hours God gives you and expect to be in the peak of health, especially as you get older. So take care the both of you."

Tears welled up in Blanche's eyes. The kindness had been so unexpected. "Thank you, thank you very much, I'm sure Sir Richard will live for many more years to come. You are a kind man."

He watched her walk down the road until she disappeared round a corner. He couldn't stop thinking about her obvious distress. He shrugged as he got back into his cab. He pushed the money into a pocket and started up his engine, it wasn't for him to worry about his fares. But this one…well she had been different and he couldn't get her out of his mind. He decided it was time to go home. He switched off his light and drove slowly back towards his home, thanking God that his life was so simple.

Blanche bought Harpers and Queen at the book-stall in the main concourse of the Station, thinking it might take her mind off her problems. But as she settled into her First Class seat she left it unopened on her lap and thought of the taxi driver. There had been something about him that she envied. He had seemed so confident, so in control. In fact the two emotions she was lacking at present. How she would have liked to have changed places. She smiled a little wistfully as she imagined him going home to a house or flat where his wife would be waiting with a hot mug of tea and no doubt a plateful of something delicious to eat. Perhaps their conversation would revolve round his fares of the day or the growing traffic congestion of the London streets and the pol-lution that the environmentalists said was threaten-ing his life. However she had a feeling that tonight might be different and that their conversation would revolve around her and Richard, both agreeing that they were bloody glad his job was a cabbie and not that of a politician risking his life and health for an ungrateful public.

She jumped as another passenger entered the compartment. She scowled at him as he smiled at her. She was hot and tired. It was seven hours since she had left Richard. Hours that she should not have been away. If he died her grief would be boundless, her world bleak. Angrily she brushed away a tear and hid her face behind the magazine. An article on rowing caught her eye. There was a paragraph on the skill of rowing in a coxless pair. It struck her how like the oarsmen she and Richard were. If one oarsman failed the boat went nowhere. Blanche glanced again at the man sitting in the window seat opposite. Once again he smiled and once again she scowled. She wanted to be alone. Damn him for his presence.

Chapter Two

Winchester Station.

THE drive back to Rosehall had always given her butterflies in her stomach. But tonight it was not happiness that caused them but her deep concern about Richard. She found her hands almost too stiff to hold the steering wheel and she wondered if she was capable of driving the few miles to Rosehall. She told herself not to be stupid. Of course he would be perfectly alright and besides a woman like her did not panic. She had been brought up to control such emotions, but God it was difficult to be calm when her whole body was aching with anxiety. She thought, 'Pull yourself together you stupid woman.' But the feeling of unease was not going to go away. She would just have to live with it until Richard's smiling face dispelled all her anxieties. The wrought iron gates of Rosehall could not come soon enough.

And then at last she was there, steering her green Rover 216GTI through the gates and onto the long drive. She could see the tranquil façade of the regency house looking reassuringly comforting ahead. Soon, very soon now, she told herself, she would be home and her worries left behind. For the first time in almost seven hours she allowed herself to smile as she drove up to the front door and braced herself for the usual eruption of dogs as soon as they heard her wheels on the gravel drive. Her two border terriers, Fiennes and Shackleton were always the first to come bowling over to the car, their stubby tails working overtime. Following along in a more sedate manner would be Scott, Richard's venerable black labrador. It was a routine that had gone on for all the years that she and Richard had lived at Rosehall, even though time had dictated a change of dogs. Those that had died were buried in a quiet corner of the garden adjoining one of the fields, with their headstones lovingly inscribed. Blanche had always felt it was one of the great injustices of life that the life span of dogs was so much shorter then that of humans.

Today there were no dogs, only Doctor Morgan's car. Her heart sank. Dear God her premonition had been right. She almost fell out of the car as she saw the ashen face of Jose standing on the front door steps and her legs felt weak as she stumbled towards him.

"He's dead, I know he's dead." She made no attempt to hide her hysteria.

"No, no, Lady, he's alive, but not well. Doctor Morgan is with him now."

"Is it his heart Jose?"

The Spaniard nodded. "Si, si, it is his heart."

She rushed passed Jose into the house. She knew it must be serious. John Morgan's reluctance to visit his patients was well known in the village. His maxim was, if they could walk they could get to the surgery. She swallowed hard. Oh God the pain was coming. She came to halt in the hall panting violently. She knew what was about to happen. Ever since puberty, fear had stimulated her sexually, at times to such a pitch that she would erupt into an orgasm. It was erotic and perverse, leaving her sapped of energy. She had never been able to control this force that propelled her into such a state and this time it was going to be no different. She forced herself towards a chair and dropped into it just as the orgasm erupted. Through misty eyes she saw Jose looking at her with horror as she gasped for breath, the pain so exquisite that for several seconds she was swept along on a tide of sexual excitement, divorcing her from the crisis at hand. When the spasms ended she was sweating profusely, but as on previous occasions her mind was crystal clear, the only reminder of the orgasm was the wetness between her legs.

She smiled confidently at Jose and said reassuringly, "I'm alright Jose, just a momentary crisis. Now tell me quickly what happened before I go upstairs."

Pointing dramatically at the floor a few feet from where he stood Jose blinked, shook himself like a wet dog and stammered, "Maria and I found the master lying here asleep. We were very worried, his breathing was loud, very loud and how do you say it, unevens." Jose's eyes filled with tears. "It was then we thought him dead. So we called doctor like you said, who told us master was not dead, just very ill. We helped doctor carry him up to his room."

Blanche touched the little man on the shoulder. "Well done, you and Maria did well. Sir Richard is in capable hands and I must go and see him now. You go back to the kitchen and tell Maria that Sir Richard is fine."

She watched him retreat towards the green baize door that separated the kitchen from the hall, his shoulders hunched despondently. She allowed herself to feel a moment of affection for the man she had plucked out of poverty with his young bride. She knew they would both die for her. Each year she offered them the opportunity to return for a few weeks to Jose's family farm in the hills above Valencia. Each year the reply was the same. "We have no desire to go back until we have to. There is nothing for us in Spain except poverty. The farm cannot support ten children."

As the green baize door swung closed Blanche shook her head and headed for the stairs. On the landing she turned left along a wide corridor, its pale yellow walls hung with half a dozen Winifred Austen sketches and three family portraits of Hanmore ancestors in various states of disrepair. Hanging in the dining room of the Irish house, being constantly covered in cigar smoke exhaled by a room full of men hunched over large glasses of port had done the canvases considerable damage. Richard had always meant to have them cleaned, but there had never seemed to be time, so they had stayed in their slightly decadent state, which both he and Blanche had grown to enjoy.

She hurried past the subtle lines of the Austen sketches and the flushed faces of the ancestors and turned right into Richard's and her bedroom. Large and bright, its walls were hung in a stunning Chinese wallpaper depicting dragons of various colours lurking amongst masses of bamboo shoots. Richard had voiced his disapproval when Blanche had suggested such vulgarity and she had admitted it was only devilment because she had known her mother would be horrified. 'We will change it once she dies,' Blanche had promised. But by the time she'd died Blanche and Richard had grown attached to the dragons lurking in their bamboo and had seen no need to change the paper. 'They saw us in, so they might as well see us out,' Richard had laughingly said to Blanche. Even in her present distressed state of mind she couldn't help smiling at the multicoloured faces as she hurried towards the large bed in the middle of the room.

He was propped up on three silk white pillows, his face as ashen as the material. Scott and the two terriers, who had been lying forlornly on the rug by the bed, leapt up to greet Blanche with their usual exuberance. She pushed them away impatiently only having eyes for her husband. For a second she hesitated, almost too frightened to move in case her obvious distress upset him, but then her emotions over road any other thoughts and she rushed to the bedside with a cry. "Oh my darling, God, my darling. I'm so so sorry I left you. I thought you would be fine. Can you ever forgive me?"

The 6' 4" frame of John Morgan towered over the bed and he spoke before Richard could answer. "Do not blame yourself dear Blanche. You need not feel ashamed of leaving him. It was not you who caused this relapse, not one little bit."

She looked at him questionely. "What does that mean?"

Morgan looked down at Richard. "It was not another heart attack It was a combination of several things that caused him to black out, but shock was the main contributor. His regular pills should be

enough to calm his heart beat down and hopefully
there will be no more shocks." Morgan hesitated.
"However that sadly seems unlikely so I think trips to
London or anywhere where you might be away for
some time should be off for the time being. I think
you are both in for a very worrying time."

Blanche's hand flew to her mouth. "Oh dear God
not James!"

It was Richard who answered her in a weak voice.
"I'm afraid so. Under the circumstances I decided
to tell John of his disappearance and this is the reason why." He held out the crumpled letter.

Blanche took the piece of paper with shaking
hands and threw a look of sheer terror at John Morgan. She thanked God he was in the room. She
trusted him as did all his patients. She had discovered he was the opposite of his gruff exterior. 'A
gentle giant with a big heart,' his wife would say to
those who complained about his manner and
Blanche agreed. She held the gaze of this large man
now playfully kicking at Fiennes, who was pulling at
the trousers of the thick tweed suit which Morgan
wore every day of the year whatever the weather. He
had been her doctor for twenty-five years and she
trusted him almost as much as she did Richard. He
had been like a rock to her in times of stress. 'And
God,' she thought, 'there have been plenty of those.'

"You must read it," Morgan said soothingly, knowing how distraught she had become. "Your son is not
dead...."

"Though it would be better if he was," interrupted Richard.

Blanche felt a shock wave course through her. It
must be very bad. She lowered herself onto the bed

beside Richard, took his hand with her free one and began to read.

Dear father,

No doubt by now you and mother are wondering what has happened to me. Well I'm not dead as maybe you would like, or certainly will do by the time you finish this. What I am going to say will I know shock you to the core. And fucking good thing too. In fact I think you will feel sick as well, but it is nothing more than you and mother deserve. Please don't make the mistake of taking this as a joke. It is not. I have for years tried to please you, worked my arse off at school and on the farm so that you could be proud of me. YOUR ONLY FUCKING SON! And what have you done? Made me feel small, made me feel your contempt. It has bitten deep father. FATHER! What a joke that word is. You have been a dreadful father, cruel even." Blanche sucked in her breath. *"Now at last I have found a cause I can embrace and at the same time hurt you hopefully more than you have hurt me over the years. By good fortune I have discovered the other side of the 'bloody Irish problem' as you call it. I have become aware that during your years as Secretary of State for Northern Ireland you lied to me about the IRA. For God sake father what is wrong with a country wanting to be free of the invaders and the rule of corrupt governments of whatever hue? Why should the Unionist call the shots? Why should they strut their power on a piece of Ireland? Why shouldn't the Catholic minority have the same rights and freedom as these religious bigots?*

*I have been convinced that the IRA will tri-
umph in the end. It may take many more years
and many more deaths but they WILL WIN! The
brutal RUC will be disbanded, the sadistic soldiers will go home and Ireland will become one
nation. Rest assured father this will indeed happen. Ah, now I really can feel your fury! Did you
ever expect a son of your to talk like this? I hope the
pain my words cause you eat deep into that rotting
heart of yours."*

Blanche gasped. "Oh this is wicked! How could James
write such terrible things. Poor Richard!" She was
near to tears. Wanted to throw the letter away, but
she knew she had to read on. She swallowed hard
and lowered her eyes.

"*The IRA have given me a life line—yes, that's what I
call it. It is an organisation I am proud to serve and it will
enable me to forget I am a Hanmore—a name so despised
by Republicans. They know I'm ashamed to be your son.
Ashamed of you as time and again you condemn them on
television. Oh, how wrong can you be? So I no longer want
to be known as your son. I do not want to inherit your wealth.
I don't want to be part of the cosy, sickening society you
belong to. I want to forget you. Shit how I wish that. But
you will always be part of me and I'm condemned to bear
that burden for the rest of my life. You drove me into loneli-
ness. So fuck you father. May you soon die and rot in Hell
where you belong.*

Blanche felt utterly forlorn. For several minutes
she stared at the letter in her hand before letting
out a moan and throwing it to the floor. "How could
he do this to you! "How could he!" Mascara ran down
her tear stained cheeks. She sobbed, "I never thought
I could say this about one of my children but per-

haps you are right. He would be better dead." Her head sank onto Richard's chest. "This is so cruel, so very cruel," she cried.

He could smell the familiar scent of crushed roses. Even now it reminded him of their wedding day in June 1958. 'If only the happiness had remained as well,' he thought. He stroked her hair absently and murmured, "Not good is it?"

Looking up she saw the pain in his eyes and asked, "Where does all the hatred come from?"

He opened his mouth but no sound came out. It reminded her of the time he had regained consciousness in Southampton General Hospital after he'd suffered his heart attack at one of his weekly constituency surgeries. He had been in physical pain then but the look in his eyes was the same now. She had hoped she would never see that look again. She felt she had to say something positive. "Perhaps it's not genuine. Perhaps he wrote it under duress or perhaps it's a forgery."

Richard at last found his voice. "I think not. We have to face the fact that it is from our son. No one could ever fake his writing. Our only hope is that it might have been written under duress as you suggest, but frankly I think not. Our son Blanche is bad. Very, very bad I fear."

She nodded in reluctant agreement and caught Morgan's eye. "Do we deserve this? Have we been so bad as parents. Tell me John, the truth now. Have we?"

Morgan shook his head. "I don't know enough about your relationship with James to answer that. Only you and Richard can know the answer. But if it gives you any comfort I cannot see either of you treating him so badly that he could resort to what I can only call treachery."

Blanche smiled at him. "Thank you for that small crumb of comfort John. Now can I ask you to leave? I think we need to be alone for a little while."

"Of course. Tell you what, I will go down and get Maria to rustle up a cup of tea for us all. I think we could do with it. Just give me a shout when you want me to return. And Blanche, don't blame yourself too much."

"Thank you John. I will try, but James wouldn't write like this unless he had been seriously damaged by his childhood. This has the makings of a very dangerous situation and at the end of the day the blame rests fairly and squarely on Richard's and my shoulders." She choked back a tear.

Morgan quickly left the room appalled by the misery he had just witnessed. He could deal with the heartache of death and the terrible consequences to families of life threatening illnesses. But when it came to dealing with the effects of psychological cruelty he readily admitted he was a novice. He was half way down the stairs when he heard Blanche's long drawn out wail of distress. For a fleeting second he was tempted to return, but decided it would serve no useful purpose. Better to let Blanche and Richard pour out their distress and guilt in private. There was little he could do to help.

ChapterThree.

Six months earlier.

HE propped himself up on an elbow, the warm musty smell of the prostitute filling his nostrils. Her breathing was heavy in sleep. James was grateful for the silence and reached for a cigarette from his discarded trousers on the floor by the bed.

Not for the first time in such situations his frustration boiled. He gazed with disgust at his drooping penis. Once again an erection had eluded him, his inadequacy all too visible. The girl had whispered she understood, but they all said that. Fuck that! He knew she would soon be sniggering with someone about his impotency. It was four weeks since he had started to pick up prostitutes and three weeks of humiliation and self-disgust. Then a week ago things had changed. A fit of temper had found a solution. It had not ended the frustration but it had brought about an exciting climax—God what a climax! He began to shake in anticipation, his body wracked by the tension building up. Hold back, he told himself. Let the adrenaline flow. Draw deep on the nicotine and breath in the foetid air that stirs your loins. Embrace the sordid surroundings and the excitement will be all the greater. Flick ash over the side of the bed. Why did none of the whores provide ashtrays? They were all the same. Living in grubby rooms with threadbare carpets. Rough sheets of various sickly hues and soiled condoms in a wastepaper basket. Sometimes there were cheap erotic pictures hung on the bedroom walls and always the smell—ah that smell—pungent was the way he would describe it. He breathed in deeply. It turned him on.

He inhaled the last of his cigarette and silently cursed the man he blamed for all his troubles. They had fought ever since he could remember. It had been a terrible childhood. Thrashed on his seventh birthday for smoking a cigarette his sister had given him. Thrashed for still wetting his bed when he was eight and thrashed for crying whenever he went back to school. And finally dispatched to Australia without even a 'would you like to go.' If he was honest it had been better than living at Rosehall and he'd reluctantly returned after a year to take up a place at Cirencester Agricultural college hoping that his relationship with his parents could improve. What a stupid fucking dream that had been. His father was as dismissive as ever. He cursed under his breath. All he had wanted was love and understanding. His father had never known the meaning of those words. God how he hated the man. As for his mother, well she'd never done a fucking thing to stop the unfair attacks. He despised her for that.

Then four weeks ago, after yet another row with his father, he'd fled from Rosehall, vowing never to return. His father had scoffed and told him he'd return within a week and his mother had cried and begged him not to leave. He had to admit the parting had been more painful than he would ever have thought but his resolve had held firm. He had never glanced back as he sped down the drive and headed for London and his sister's flat. He'd known she didn't really want him, but knew she would not refuse him. Her sympathies were entirely with him.

The girl stirred. He gazed at her flat stomach and thick black pubic hair. She was not unattractive. He liked them pretty. He'd discovered it gave him an extra thrill to ruin their beauty. He'd wait for as long as it might take her to become fully awake. He liked them to see the first blow coming and hear them cry out in fear. The thought made his groin stir. He wondered what had made her become a prostitute walking round Shepherds Market at nights risking her life. Perhaps she had come from an unhappy environment like himself. Rotten parents, perhaps a drunken father who would beat her mother. Or perhaps she had just been bored with family life and come to London to make a fast buck. Whatever, he would make sure she didn't return to the streets in a hurry.

He ran a hand through her hair. It was soft, reminding him of Sophie. He'd met Sophie a month into his first term at Cirencester. He'd been sitting at a lecture wondering what the hell he was doing when he'd become aware of her sitting next to him. He'd turned and scowled. She'd laughed and said, "You frighten me to death." He'd hesitated, then smiled. He remembered the moment well.

They had made a strange couple. Sophie Ballard had despised wealth. She had been the only child of impoverished parents struggling to make a living in the harsh environment of a Yorkshire Dale farm. She had been a fragile figure standing 5'3" in her bare feet and weighing a slight eight stone. Her auburn hair had been cut short and her green eyes had smouldered with resentment. She'd had nothing but contempt for her fellow students. To her they had been the rich elite of farming.

Poverty was the word she'd known best. Her parents had struggled all their lives to make ends meet. She'd never stopped telling him that she admired their resolve and that it was a triumph they had survived. She'd hated the degradation that had been forced on them and when he'd asked why they hadn't just left the farm she'd snorted contemptuously and pointed out that he wouldn't understand but they were so in debt to the banks that if they walked away they would have nothing. They were in fact prisoners on their own land. Her political views had been left of centre and she had looked upon Cirencester as a relic of a by-gone age but her father had begged her to take the opportunity that had come her way and because she loved him she'd agreed to go.

They had grown close. They both had needed friendship. They had talked a lot. And then one day she had told him about her father. Incest. That had been a shock. It had been difficult for him to grasp that she could love such a depraved man. She had drunk too much at the time, but her voice had been steady and devoid of emotion as she recounted her experience. He remembered every word as if it had been only yesterday. "My father raped me when I was nine. My mother was drunk every night by six and I was the only person he could turn to for love and companionship. At first I didn't really know what was going on, in fact even thought his behaviour was normal. But as I grew older and went to school I realised what he was doing was wrong. I nearly hated him then, even briefly thought of running away. But where would I go? I might end up in a home. I didn't want that, so I stayed and a strong bond developed between us. It wasn't deep love or lust but I enjoyed the physical contact and I knew he needed me. He was so gentle, so loving and so grateful. And then when I was fourteen I had my first orgasm. There was no turning away after that. I needed him as much as he needed me. I think that was one of the reasons he got me into this fucking awful place—he felt we were becoming too close.'

James shuddered. She had told him her mother knew. She hadn't cared. As long as she had a bottle in her hand she had been happy. He remembered asking Sophie if she and her father still made love. She had nodded and he'd felt sick. They had never spoken about it again. He had never made love to a woman and was terrified of ever having to do so. It would have been no surprise to either of them if the relationship had broken down. But it had been the opposite. She had understood him and had been sympathetic to his festering hatred. She had known he was weak, but had not cared. He had been the perfect foil to her belligerent nature. For his part he had admired her strength, and thrived on her affection. It had never quite been love, but it was as close to it as he'd ever got. It didn't matter to him that his father thought she was unsuitable and very rough. In fact it had given him great pleasure to see the disgust on his face the few times he'd taken Sophie back to Rosehall

The end had come like a thunderbolt out of the sky. He'd never understood how he'd withstood the trauma. She'd died on the Dale farm. Illogically he'd blamed his father. He'd stormed round Rosehall shouting abuse at his father and ignoring his mother. Alone in his room at nights he'd cried himself to sleep.

James hit the side of the bed. The memories hurt. But the roller coaster was going too fast to jump off. At the beginning of the Easter holidays she'd called to tell him that her father had given her a sheep dog puppy. She'd been so excited. It was something she'd always wanted. A dog she could work with the sheep on the hill. She'd been so sorry, but she'd decided not to come to Rosehall as they had planned. For a little while at least all her time had to be with the puppy. On the fifth night she had been opening the door to let the puppy out before going to bed when the telephone had rung. Without thinking she'd pushed the puppy out into the farmyard and rushed to answer the phone. Ten minutes later when she'd gone outside to retrieve the puppy it had disappeared. She'd closed the farmhouse door quietly behind her and rushed out into the yard.

Four hours later her father had woken up in front of the dying embers of the fire in the small sitting room. Befuddled by sleep he'd staggered up to the bedroom he shared with Sophie. He had not been unduly alarmed she hadn't been in bed and had lain down to wait for her. When he next woke the first rays of the sun were coming through the window. An hour later he'd called the police.

By the time they arrived Sophie's mother was having hysteria and her father was wandering around the farmyard in his pyjamas calling her name. It took another two hours before an eagle-eyed constable spotted a bobble hat floating on the top of the foul smelling slurry pit. Sophie's father confirmed it was hers. It took another hour before the fire brigade finally emptied the pit and discovered Sophie's body lying on the concrete base, the puppy cradled in her stiff arms.

James wiped away the tears as he remembered the telephone call from Yorkshire. His life was in tatters, and he knew he'd never recover. Inside he was still bleeding and so very bitter. Why, why did it have to happen to him? He was cursed. He was sure of that, and his fucking father was to blame.

He slapped the girl on her face. She woke with a start and stared up at him. "Ready to try again big boy?" she said sleepily. He slammed a fist into her side.

"What the fuc....!"

He drove his fist into her face splitting her upper lip, the blood running onto the pillow. She cried out and went to jump off the bed, but he was too quick for her and hauled her back. Sitting on her stomach he began to hit her face with clenched fists She begged for mercy. He hit her. She cried in pain. He hit her again. She fought to get out from under him and he pummelled her stomach. The madness was in him. The more she cried, the more she moaned the more he hit her. Soon her face was a bloodied mass. He might have killed her but for the feeling of an erection growing. Elation. He rolled off her and threw her onto the floor where she lay moaning half conscious. He stood over her, his legs apart and masturbated over her bleeding face. "Damn you, damn you!" he cried, "Why can't you be Sophie!"

Sarah hadn't slept. It was four in the morning when she heard the key turn in the lock. Throwing on her dressing gown she raced to the top of the stairs and saw him standing there, unsteady on his feet and looking very dishevelled. When he saw her he shuffled his feet and looked down at the carpet. In a truculent voice he asked, "What are you doing up at this time of the fucking morning? Just got rid of the boy friend have we?" He heard her sharp intake of breath and the laugh died in his throat as he saw her ashen face. "Something wrong Sis?"

She came down the stairs and stood very close to him. She could smell the cheap perfume on him and she almost threw up. She knew where he'd been. He'd confessed his habit to her a few days earlier. "Listen you pervert, father had a massive heart attack about four hours ago. I've been waiting for you ever since. Why did you have to stay out so bloody late! Mother wanted us down in Southampton hours ago, so grab a bag and let's go."

He put both hands on her shoulders and gazed into her eyes. "Let me tell you something that may shock you, but I'm not coming. Wild horses wouldn't drag me to that man's bed. I'm going to get some much needed sleep." He pushed past her and started to climb the stairs.

"James, for God sake he's your father!" she cried. "This isn't the time for your childish antics. You must come."

He turned on her, rage flowing through his body. "Childish antics, by Christ! How dare you accuse me of that. Father has never cared about me and you know it. Why should I rush to his sick bed now and hope he gets better. To be frank Sarah I hope the bastard dies. In fact give him a message if he is well enough to hear you. Tell him I hope he rots in Hell!"

Her eyes widened with shock. She understood her brother's feeling of being badly treated, but he was family and they had to stick together in times of crisis. It was totally alien to her to think otherwise. "You can't do this to him James, he needs you. Please come if only for me."

"Not a hope in Hell!"

She turned then, determined not to let him see her tears. She had never imagined the damage had been so deep. Without another word she picked up the bag she had packed earlier and fled out of the door.

As the door slammed behind her it dawned on James what he'd done. The last vestige of the adrenaline pumping through his veins evaporated and it was replaced by the thought that he'd probably fucked up on a relationship that he could not live without. He sat down on the stairs, tiredness wrapping him in its embrace. Shit, he hadn't meant to say such dreadful things to his sister. He needed her. He knew he'd never have gone to Southampton but he could have handled it better. He stared down at the empty hall and wondered how much damage he'd done. Fuck, he was useless. He'd become a sexual deviant, dependant on violence for his kicks, and without thinking he'd hurt the one person who had stood by him. There was no excuse. He'd have to beg for her forgiveness.

He dragged himself up the stairs to his bedroom and turned on the light before throwing himself onto the bed fully clothed. He was too tired to undress. He would sleep with the light on. The darkness frightened him. There were too many ghosts. The girls

he'd abused, his father and mother and of course
Sophie. He cried out. None of this would have happened if she'd still been alive. He sobbed as the room
stared back at him silent and empty. The light kept
the ghosts away, but it didn't calm his fear that one
day he'd kill a girl for sheer enjoyment. It would be
the next step. It was like a drug flowing through his
veins and the more he took the more he wanted to
experiment. He was on a slippery slope and he knew
that he couldn't blame all his troubles on his shitty
parents. He'd suspected for some time that he had
a faulty gene. His recent behaviour confirmed this.
No amount of parental love could have saved him
from the dark pit he was falling into. There was a
solution that would solve all his problems. He had
toyed with the idea before, but now full of guilt, fear
and self-disgust this solution seemed to be the answer. What better time to end it all? The house was
empty, he knew there were pills in Sarah's bathroom
and plenty of whisky in the kitchen. All the ingredi-
ents he would need. But it needed guts and he wasn't
sure he had enough. He lay for sometime thinking.
Who would miss him, his parents? A fleeting tear no
doubt. Friends? He hadn't got any. Well Sarah? Perhaps, but after his behaviour tonight she might be
glad he'd gone. No one would miss him for long. So
do it. End the misery and the pain beating at his
brain. It really was time.

He jumped off the bed and ran along to Sarah's
bathroom. He knew the pills would be in the cabinet over the bath. He smiled as he discovered a full
container of Nurofen. That would be more than
enough. He hurried down to the kitchen, aware that
if he stopped his frail courage might desert him. Two
bottles of whisky winked at him from the hob. He

hesitated, his guts churning. This was the moment and he felt sick. He emptied the pills onto the hob by the whisky and wondered how strong a cocktail was needed to kill him. He must get the dose right, the last thing he wanted was to end up as a vegetable. Shit, take no chances, grab a handful of pills. Were there twenty or thirty? He didn't bother to count. Washed down with as much whisky as he could drink would surely do the trick. He laid them on the hob and reached for one of the bottles of whisky. He unscrewed the top and his nostrils breathed in the strong scent of the light brown liquid. He ran a hand down the side of the bottle. As smooth as Sophie's skin, he thought. He began to pick up the pills. One by one he laid them in the palm of a hand. They danced before his eyes, their whiteness so innocent. Very deliberately he put each pill into his mouth. 'Chew you bastard, go on chew the fucking things!' he thought. The paste was thick, sticking to the roof of his mouth. He grabbed the bottle and jammed the neck into his mouth and forced his head back, the cool liquid touching his tongue. But he couldn't swallow. He'd jammed too many pills in at once. The whisky ran down his chin onto his naked chest. He threw up onto the floor, the half-chewed pills mixing in with his bile. He gazed at the small pool with disgust. He forced himself to think of Sophie. 'Try again, for God sake try again!' he thought. But his resolve was weakening, the whole thing was becoming a nightmare. He hadn't even the guts to finish his miserable life. He let out a long agonised cry and fled from the kitchen, collapsing on the bottom of the stairs, humiliated that he had failed and devastated that he lacked the balls to join Sophie.

Chapter Four.

THREE months had passed since his attempted suicide and his lack of courage had haunted him every day since. To make matters worse his father hadn't died and his relationship with Sarah had been strained to say the least, but she hadn't thrown him out, which he grudgingly admitted was generous. He would have liked to have had a house of his own but the measly allowance his father gave him was only just enough to pay for his forays into the night. He could have worked of course, but he'd given up on that idea some time ago. So he would go on sponging and stealing off his sister and keep hoping his father would die and leave him something in his Will however small.

His self-esteem was at zero. He saw himself as discarded flotsam, a blot on society. He had no purpose in life other than to beat up prostitutes. Of course there was a solution. He could go back to Rosehall and do a sort of trade off with his father. But fuck that! He'd never make peace with the bastard and besides he had to admit he was too far down the slope of perversion to ever be able to clamber up.

He sat back in the taxi, the sweat under his armpits staining his shirt. The fever was stirring. It had been an exciting move taking taxis. It added another unknown quantity to his sexual anticipation. He shifted restlessly in his seat. How many girls was it now? At least a dozen that he could remember leaving beaten with semen splashed over their bodies. He shivered, thinking of the thrill it gave him. But his violence came at a price. He'd had to go further and further afield to find his kicks for fear of being recognised by one of his victims. Tonight he'd picked out Southall on the map he kept in his bedroom. He had given up the streets, preferring to do his picking up in pubs. It was safer and the girls a little bit more vulnerable. It gave him an added thrill to think he was abusing a more intelligent type of girl. The fever spread to his groin. He could never exchange this excitement for a life at Rosehall, working for a father he would always hate.

"Where in Southall Guv?" came the gruff voice of the taxi driver. "Where in this God forsaken place do you want me to drop you?"

He took a second to gather his thoughts, then asked, "Where are we?"

"Norwood Road," came back the reply.

He had no idea where Norwood road was, but it didn't matter. He was sure there would be a pub somewhere not too far away. "Okay, this will do."

He stepped out onto the pavement, paid and looked up into the drab sky. It was a wet May evening. Like the driver said, the area looked a tip. Perhaps he'd been wrong to stop here but he'd been to Clapham, Wandsworth, even as far as Wimbledon.

All very different but in the end all giving him what he wanted. Why should Norwood Road Southall be any different? He shrugged, hunched his shoulders and started his search for a bar. As he walked quickly along the wet pavement he thought of the dangers his strange life might hold for him. He could die in some sleazy room, knifed by his victim. He could kill and spend the rest of his life in prison. But that was half the thrill, the unknown factor. It stimulated him sexually and besides if he died or went to prison who the hell would miss him?

He saw the pub. It was a large Victorian building with chipped brickwork and a tarpaulin hanging loosely from part of the roof. It looked a dump but worth a try. He could always move on. He hurried towards it his heart palpitating violently.

The Wellington was almost deserted at seven on a Monday evening. Several dedicated early drinkers were propping up the long bar, with half drunk pints clasped in their hands. Cigarette smoke swirled around the low ceiling and a threadbare pool table dominated the centre of the room. Several tables and chairs filled the remaining space all of which bore the scars of over use and careless treatment. Some of the tables were still stacked with empty glasses and full ashtrays, the relics of a busy lunchtime and too few staff. The dark red paper that covered the walls was peeling off in places and the white paint on any woodwork was stained almost yellow by the nicotine from thousands of cigarettes puffed over the years. The Wellington offered no luxuries. It was that sort of place.

James's nostrils curled in disgust as he walked across to the bar. It was his sort of place.

"And what will you be drinking tonight smart boy?" asked a pretty girl in a pleasant Irish brogue but tinged with sarcasm, as her eyes took in his grey striped suit, thin red and white striped New & Lingwood shirt and pale blue tie. It set him apart from the rest of her motley customers and she wondered what had brought this rather pretty boy into the pub. She saw him bridle at her question, smiled and said. "No offence, but you are not from these parts are you?"

The green eyes attracted him although he felt insulted. He prided himself on his dress and was not used to it being criticised. He swallowed his anger, wondering if this could be the girl for him later. She was certainly bold and he liked that. "No thank God I'm not and with regard to your first question it will be a double bells with no ice, just water."

She tossed her head in irritation and asked, "Do your sort never say please? Let me be telling you now, no one gets served here with out saying 'please.' Do you hear that pretty boy?"

Inside he was fuming at being called 'pretty boy,' but he bit his tongue, because her brazen antagonism sent a shiver of excitement down his spine. He liked his girls to be a bit feisty. It made more of a challenge and this one was too cocky by half and needed to be taught a lesson. He made an instant decision. She would be his target for the night. He would bait her. Aggravate her Irish temper and see where that led him. He rested an arm on the bar and looked round the room. "What, say please in a dump like this and to a rude young girl like you? You're lucky I'm in here. Now go on get me that whisky, I don't like to be kept waiting."

Her look said it all and she mumbled just loud enough for him to hear, "Oh we have a right little Hitler here."

"Hey!"

But she'd already turned away and begun to fill a glass with two measures of Bells, returning a few minutes later to slam a glass and a jug of water down in front of him.

"Now that's no way to treat your customers," he chided. "Why don't you get me a packet of salt and vinegar crisps with a little more grace than you've shown up to now."

She was boiling with anger inside. She wanted to say, 'Fuck you. I don't need arseholes like you in here.' But she saw the look in his eyes and recognised the danger of having a confrontation. She'd seen the look before in her father's eyes and knew were that had normally led. The last thing she wanted was trouble and to draw attention to herself. She would have to take the abuse, not with a smile, but at least with as much good grace as she could muster. She gave James an icy stare and pointed to one of the empty tables. "You sit down over there and I will bring you a packet." Then she couldn't help adding, "I don't want people like you standing at the bar."

He smiled to himself as he turned away. She was boiling and it was so stimulating. He imagined he could feel her anger. He liked that. This one was certainly different and could be the best so far. But he sensed she would be no easy pushover. He would get her, he was sure of that, but he would have to use all his cunning.

As he sat down he felt the sexual urge power through his body. He thought of her green eyes wide with fear, her auburn hair wet from sweat and the blood running down her face. Before the night was out he would have humiliated her and she would never be the same again. He watched her come across the room. He took in her slim waist and shapely legs. Perhaps she was a little skinny but she would look good naked. As she lent over to put the crisp packet on the table he grabbed her arm. "You're a whore young lady, I can see that. Your arrogance is your come-on isn't it? I like that. I like that very much. Let's talk later."

She tore her arm out of his grasp and sucked in her breath. "Why you arrogant fucking bastard," she hissed quietly. "Do you believe that I could fancy a pretty boy like you? I have news for you, I am just an honest Irish girl trying to make a living, and I don't need creeps like you trying to make out I'm a whore."

His piercing blue eyes stared at her crucifix round her neck. "An Irish Catholic as well by the looks of it," he sneered. My father would know how to deal with you. If he'd had his way I'm sure he would have rid this Northern Ireland of the lot of you and sent you packing back to your bogs where you could practice your miracles and talk to your beloved Pope"

She gazed at him in disbelief. "I don't believe I'm hearing this. How can you say such things. Don't you...." She stopped. She was about to say too much. "You're a shit, did you know that?" she said weakly.

"Yes, I know that. A Protestant shit to you. But I'd like to have you naked beside me and then I would show you what I would do to a Catholic whore. Don't decide now, just think about it. I bet your wages here are crap and I pay well."

Without a doubt she'd have hit him then but luckily for her a customer at the bar called to her. "I won't forget what you have just said," she whispered as she turned away. Shit, he had got up her nose and he was taunting her just like the Protestant boys had done outside the school in Belfast. They had juggled with bricks, made lewd suggestions hoping she would retaliate. She had ignored them just like she knew she must ignore him now. She'd nearly slipped up. She remembered the last words that they had spoken to her. 'Do not do anything Mary O'Neill to draw attention to yourself. Blend into the scene. You are no use to us as a hell raiser.'

But as she served another pint of beer and felt his eyes following her every movement she would have dearly liked to have been able to gorge out his eyes.

It gave him a sense of control as he sat quietly watching her, knowing she was uneasy under his stare. A smile spread across his face. This was getting better and better. He saw her take money from a customer and glance across at his table. He had got under her skin; that was good. Past experience told him it meant she was curious. She had no one else to serve. It was time. He pushed his chair back noisily and moved towards the bar.

"You here again?" she said resignedly as he waved his glass at her.

"Two hundred quid, that's what I'll give you if you take me back to wherever you live later tonight. Two hundred quid! You can't turn that down."

"Money can't buy me Protestant!" She spat, as she grabbed his glass. "Jesus how I hate Protestant creeps like you. Why is it that you all seem to get off on bating Catholics? Why are we so different? Why do you think you are so superior? Or is it perhaps that you cannot match our faith. Does that frighten you perhaps pretty boy?"

"Don't call me pretty boy again," he said angrily and wagged a finger at her. "You certainly don't frighten me and nor am I in awe of your faith. If I believe in God it is because I want to, not because I have been put under pressure by a corrupt Church. And anyway I am no ordinary Protestant. Before his heart attack my father was this Government's Northern Ireland Secretary. He was born in Belfast and comes from a long line of Unionists. He likes to make out he's different and cares for your lot. But I don't think so. How could any man put up with all the humiliation Dublin and the IRA have heaped on him and this Government? No, he hates you for sure. Just like he hates me."

Her hand was visibly shaking as she put the re-filled glass back on the bar top. All her instincts told her she should just shrug and turn away and ignore this young man whose mouth had obviously been loosened by the double whiskies she'd been serving him. And yet her curiosity had been aroused. She asked, "Is your father Sir Richard Hanmore?"

James took a long sip of his drink before answering. "Indeed the bastard is my father!"

"Oh Jesus, oh Jesus!" she thought. "He could be lying but if not this is really something. What do I do?" She only had a few seconds. Seconds that seemed like hours as she swayed from foot to foot struggling to make a decision. She watched him staring at her. She stared back with hatred eating at her heart. He was real danger. 'But, oh God,' she thought irreverently, 'have you sent Him to me?" He was twirling his glass in his hand, beginning to get impatient. The seconds had run out. She leant across the bar and uttered the words that would change her life forever. "I hate your sort and would like to tell you a few home truths. So contrary to what I first said I will talk to you after I finish my shift. But there will be no messing let me warn you now Protestant, just talk. I will put you right on one or two things and then throw you out. That's the deal. If you don't agree then piss off back to daddy. Do you hear me now?"

His eyes lit up and he ran his tongue over his lips. "You will change your mind."

God, his arrogance! "Never. So what do you say?"

"Okay, I'll wait for you. Now fill up my glass and I won't bother you until you are ready to leave."

It had been so easy, so fucking easy. He couldn't believe it. He had thought she'd be a lot harder to pull. He shook with excitement as she returned his glass. This was going to be the best evening yet!

As he walked back to his table she shivered. She was not sure whether it was from fear at what she'd just recklessly done or excitement at the thought of what she might find out. Mary drew a pint of beer for a customer, gave him the wrong change and apologised. Her mind was not on the job. Hanmore (she realised she didn't know his Christian name), had awakened so many memories. When she was ten, throwing bricks at the British soldiers as they patrolled past her parents' house in the Limestone Road. It had been a religious ghetto carved out in blood after the troubles had begun. She had never known a time when Protestants and Catholics had lived in harmony. She thought of the steel barriers that had divided the two communities and remembered the bewilderment on the young soldiers' faces. She knew her age had unsettled them. They had never been briefed that children would attack them.

She risked a glance across at his table. All that she hated was sitting there. The British air of arrogance and superiority. And if he was to be believed he was the son of the man high on the hate list of the Irish Republican movement. Holy Jesus what was he doing here? Why on earth had he walked into the pub? Was there a sinister reason, which might be a danger to her? And why did he say he hated his father when he seemed to despise Catholics? She had to find out. She knew she was taking a huge risk that they would not approve of, but she felt she had no option. She knew she'd rushed into the decision and that he saw it as a 'come on.' But Jesus he was in for a shock! She knew he might turn violent. His eyes spelt danger. She shrugged. Whatever, there was little doubt she'd be a lot wiser by the end of the night. Or she could be dead; a broken, bleeding corpse. She smiled and crossed herself. If ever she had needed God's help she needed it now.

She took another look at him sitting at his table. He was sipping his drink and staring in her direction. The man was sinister, and what was she? Just a headstrong fucking fool.

It was five hours since he'd walked into the Wellington. Now he sat on the threadbare sofa of her rented flat fifteen minutes away from the pub. He was sipping his third cup of black coffee and trying to focus on the girl sitting beside him and silently cursing that he'd drunk so many Bells.

Mary knew how many Bells he'd drunk and it worried her. He hadn't spoken a word since entering her flat. He'd gazed round the dreary interior and then slumped onto the sofa. He hadn't even said 'thank you' as she had fed him cups of black coffee. But at least he'd shown no desire to have sex with her although she suspected it was the drink that was stopping him. As its influence wore off she could be in for a difficult time. One thing was certain they couldn't just sit and look at each other for the rest of the night. She decided it was best to give him the chance to leave. She'd been a fool to ask him back anyway. She touched his hand. "Look, you are obviously tired and a little drunk so why don't you just get up off that sofa and go home. It might be the best for both of us."

He rubbed his eyes and tried to focus on her. He couldn't understand what was happening to him. Normally alcohol made him more aggressive, but now he felt listless and much to his annoyance a little in awe of the woman sitting beside him. He still wanted her and had no desire to leave, but he was floundering in his own indecision. He forced himself to reach out for one of her breasts.

His reward was a hard slap on the face, which made him gasp. "Now let's get one thing clear Protestant," she said, controlling her anger with difficulty. "We had an agreement. So either you keep to that and we talk or you leave now. Because there is no way you are going to get a fuck. If you try to force yourself on me I will defend myself and you better believe I am pretty good at that! So what's it to be?"

Her lack of fear added to his indecision. Shit, this was not working out the way he'd planned. She was too fucking sure of herself. He felt his penis shrinking into his pubic hairs and with it the last vestige of his bravado evaporated. He felt all his old inhibitions returning. This was beginning to have the makings of a disastrous evening, but he didn't want to go back to Putney. With his eyes lowered he whispered, "What ever you say, but I would like to stay here."

She noted the tone of his voice had changed, sensed his arrogance was draining away and hurried on while she knew she held the initiative. "Very well, you are welcome. So let's introduce ourselves properly. My name is Mary O'Neill. Twenty-one years old, born in Belfast and a good Catholic. You have a Christian name as well no doubt and I know already you are a fucking Protestant."

He forced himself to meet her eyes. "I'm James." He relapsed again into silence. Her eyes were so brilliant, so controlling. He shuddered and looked away. There was something about her that was not like any of the other girls he'd assaulted. Somehow she'd turned the tables and he felt threatened. He struggled to stand up determined to try and assert himself, but the room spun in front of his eyes and he collapsed back onto the sofa with a moan. "Yes, I am James Hanmore," he said weakly. "Though I would give anything to have another name."

She smiled. He would be no threat. The danger had gone. She looked down on his shaking body and felt nothing but contempt. He obviously got off on threatening women. Well she'd called his bluff and punctured his bubble. His eyes no longer radiated danger and his whole demeanour had changed. In fact she thought she saw the sign of a tear in his eyes. Fuck that! He was still a bastard. She asked again, "So you really are Sir Richard Hanmore's son? No messing now."

He sank deeper into the sofa as he saw the hatred in her eyes. "Yes, I'm afraid I am."

Jesus, this didn't make sense. Why had he seemed so anti Catholic if he hated his father? Because he was pig ignorant? That was possible. After all the whole of the British media was biased and no doubt his father's views wouldn't have helped. But the question she really wanted answered was what was he doing in her pub? Was he what he seemed, an arrogant over sexed weirdo looking for thrills, or something far more dangerous? She looked at his ashen face, his round frightened eyes and simply could not see him as a threat. But perhaps he was clever. After all he was a Hanmore and despite her loathing of his father she had always had a sneaking admiration for the man. So if he was a threat? Well, she'd been trained to kill.

It was time to test him.

"I have read your father's lying speeches, even watched him on television spouting on about the Irish problem and how he wanted to see peace between the two communities. What crap. He was just like the rest of his Government—a fucking hypocrite. I prayed he'd die when he had his heart attack. I have wanted to kill him with my own hands for years. Then suddenly for some reason I can't quite fathom you walk into the Wellington tonight, all arrogant and seemingly wanting a pick up. To my mind it does not add up. I think you have some explaining to do."

"I just wanted sex."

"Do you expect me to believe that?"

"I swear it's true."

She eyed the drawer where she kept the Walther. "I could kill you Protestant boy. I could drill a hole in your stomach and watch the blood seep out of your body while you cried out in agony, just as my mother did when your side gralloched her. I would be pleased

because I would have killed a Protestant and gone
some way to avenging her death. So convince me
why I shouldn't do just that."

He gazed at her in bewilderment. What was the
bitch going on about? What had her mother's death
got to do with him wanting sex? Why should she want
to kill him? She didn't know he was planning to beat
her up. Shit, perhaps he'd overdone the religious
bit. Whatever, she frightened him and words fell out
of his mouth. "I wander around sometimes at night
looking for girls. When I find one I beat them up
and masturbate over them. It is the only way I can
reach an orgasm. I am no use to anyone. I don't know
what you are thinking but I swear that is the only
reason why I came into your pub. I am an outcast in
this shitty world we live in. I am an embarrassment to
my father who hates my guts. My mother tolerates
me. My sister, well she kind of guards over me, but I
don't think she really likes me. The only pleasure I
get out of life is my occasional nightly activity, and I
know that's pretty weird. I blame my bastard father
for all my troubles. He's always put me second to his
political career. He did it to my sister as well but he
never set such a high standard for her. I never looked
like attaining the standards he set for me so he quickly
gave up on me. My mother just followed him. She
loved me I'm sure, probably still does, but father's
word is her bible. Now I have come to hate his wealth,
his politics and the society he lives in. To put it simply, he has ruined my life." He looked fearfully at
Mary wondering if she really might kill him.

She had no intention of easing his anxiety. She
reckoned while he still thought he was under threat
he would talk and talk and she wanted to know a lot

more. For the embryo of an idea was forming at the back of her mind and it was dynamite.

Her voice was cold when she replied. "It all sounds fucking sad, but you're not out of danger yet so tell me more. Like why did you choose the Wellington? Did you know I worked there?"

He interrupted her. "Why should I know you? What do you mean? I don't understand. I have told you I came upon the Wellington by chance that's all."

She took a deep breath. Could she believe him? Her instinct told her this weak, pathetic young man was not capable of deception on such a scale. Jesus no! "Okay, forget it, just tell me a bit more about your father."

"What's so special about him?" he asked suspiciously.

Careful girl, she thought. 'Don't seem too keen or he might clam up.' She replied, "Oh nothing really, but you seemed to want to talk about him."

The whisky and the disappointment of the evening had made him feel sorry for himself. He would probably have talked to anyone and although she frightened him she was obviously prepared to listen. He needed no further encouragement

She sat and listened, feeding him cigarettes and mugs of black coffee whenever he asked. At times he cried. At times he became bitter. At times he spoke with self-disgust. But underlying every sentence he spoke was the hatred for his father and the excitement began to churn in Mary's stomach. Finally, with sweat soaking his body he fell silent and Mary suspected she'd struck gold. They would say kill him, a Hanmore cannot be trusted, but she had other ideas. She was as sure as she could be that he was no threat and probably could be manipulated if she gained his confidence. He was an unstable misfit awash with bitterness, crying out for help and probably a reason to live. Well, she felt she might be able to give him that, but first she would have to overcome her revulsion for a man who stood for everything she despised. Fear would not be the way. She shivered as she gazed at his face swollen by crying. Oh shit, sleep with a pervert and a Hanmore to boot? Jesus, she hoped they would acknowledge her sacrifice.

Glancing at her watch she saw it was nearly two am. The carpet was littered with fag ends and the room stank of their sweat and stale tobacco fumes. She ran her hand through her matted hair and closed her eyes. She was exhausted, but there was no time to relax. She had a drunken weirdo in her flat and the next few hours would be crucial. She noticed his eyes were half closed and reckoned he posed little threat at the moment. She held out a hand. "Come on you look played out and you have said enough tonight. I won't throw you out, nor kill you. I must be fucking mad but there it is. You can stay tonight." She pointed at the bed on the far side of the room. "You can sleep there and I'll take the sofa. Then we will see what the morning brings. Okay?"

As he'd walked back with her from the pub he'd imagined smashing his fist into her face and watching the blood run from her cracked lips. He had surreptitiously glanced at her breasts and imagined his fingernails scouring red marks across the naked flesh. He had thought of her cry of disgust as he pumped his semen over her face and he'd shivered in the damp air. But he hadn't done a thing. He'd lost it completely. He'd been pathetic, allowed himself to be frightened and now she was trying to sweet talk him. Well shit that! He lunged at her with a cry of frustration, but for the second time that evening she was too quick for him and she caught him with a stinging blow across the face. Her contempt was too much for his fragile state of mind and instead of retaliating his head dropped onto her shoulder and he started to sob. She held him tight, rocking him back and forth in her arms and every now and then running her hands through his hair. As time past and he showed no signs of drawing away cramp in her legs increasingly became a problem, but she was fearful of breaking the spell for she wanted this man to be hers. Hers to do with as she liked. Hers to listen and to learn every word she would tell him. Hers to believe her role in life was the one he should follow without question. Then when she'd won his heart and mind and changed the way he thought she planned to put him to use. After that she would kill him.

For two hours she held him like a drowning man until at last she felt him relax and realised he was asleep. Then carefully easing him away from her body she managed to lie him down on the sofa without waking him. She decided she would use the bed for some badly needed sleep. There were going to be vital decisions to make and she needed a clear head. She dragged herself towards the bed, not bothering to undress for fear of waking him. She collapsed onto the soiled duvet and closed her eyes, but sleep would not come. Every way she chose to lie a thought invaded her brain. She cursed under her breath and started to count sheep as her mother had told her to do when she'd been a child. It hadn't worked then and it didn't work now. Eventually she gave up the unequal struggle and thought of the extraordinary evening.

If she'd been bored before James's arrival in the pub she most certainly wasn't now. In some ways he reminded her of her father. A lecher, continually undressing woman in his mind and a constant erection in his trousers. But that was where the likeness ended. Her father had been a small emaciated figure with thinning black hair Brylcreamed down onto his scalp, making him look rather like a drowned rat. In fact he'd been a dangerous and dedicated member of the IRA and had never held a job down in his whole life. He'd spent most of his time plotting violence, and once the Troubles had started he'd revelled in killing those he loosely referred to as 'the enemy.' He had kept his freedom by animal cunning and instilling fear into anyone who might have been tempted to tip off the RUC or the Security Forces of his murderous life.

She pulled the single sheet over her head as the first light of day filtered through the single window and thought a little more about the man who had been her father. She had never known how many people he had killed but as she'd grown older and more embittered it excited her to think that he was killing, as he put it, 'fucking Brits and Protestant bastards.'

Her mother had tried, Jesus how she'd tried, to persuade her that God was on their side and things should be left to Him. But to a young girl on the verge of puberty and filled with religious patriotism her father's way was far more exciting. She remembered the time her father had stood shouting at her mother in their small front room, "What's normal around here woman? How do you expect our daughter not to be influenced by what is going on out there. Do you think it's normal to have roadblocks, steel barricades and soldiers in bullet proof vests roaming our streets day and night? Wake up to the realities of life Jenny. We live in an occupied country, ordered about by our British invaders and their Unionists lackeys. To put it simply, we are prisoners in our own country."

She had listened and in spite of loving her mother, admiring her courage and her unswerving devotion to God, she had believed her father's way was the only way out of the prison. She ground her teeth. The prison walls had not yet been breached and the cost of trying had destroyed what family she'd ever had. How could she ever forget the evening when the door burst open and two masked gunmen had come into their house and shot her father three times in the head in front of herself and her mother. It had been his forty second birthday. Then three months later her mother had been gunned down from a passing motorcycle while she and Mary had been shopping in Belfast City Centre. After leaving The Mater Hospital an orphan she vowed she would never shed a tear again until she had exacted her revenge. She had gone home only to find their house burnt to the ground, the neighbours' doors firmly shut. She remembered walking down the street shouting her hatred to an empty street.

She was sweating now, the memories as clear as ever. She'd been seventeen, bloody only seventeen, and her life had been in ruins. If it hadn't been for Seamus Flanagan she'd probably have topped herself. Jesus, how she still hurt, how she hated. But it would not be long now. The pervert on the sofa would do her bidding. He would be her weapon of revenge.

James didn't go back to Putney and as the days past he became more and more under Mary's spell. At first she struggled to hide her disgust but as time past the enmity she felt towards him grew less and she was aware of a strange sort of uneasy alliance developing between the two of them. If he questioned her about her life she was evasive but always careful to give him a few little crumbs which kept him satisfied. At first she'd wondered why he hadn't been more curious, but soon realised that his desire to stay over-rode any desire to dig deeper. But if she told him little she bled him of information, until after three weeks she felt she had enough to make her next move. A move that was a dangerous gamble, but one she thought was worthwhile.

At the beginning of the fourth week she plucked up enough courage to put pen to paper.

She wrote,

> *I know your first inclination will be to chastise me for my indiscipline, but I have befriended a young man who could prove to be very useful to us. Before you raise your eyebrows in that superior fashion of yours let me say that 'befriended' is probably the wrong word, but as you know I'm not very strong on words so that will have to do. I have an idea, yes an idea which is so exciting and although I say it myself so audacious—there you didn't think I knew such words did you?—that I must share it with you urgently. Oh yes I know I'm not supposed to contact you but this is something so different that I am prepared to risk your wrath. This young*

man is dynamite and knowing how your mind works my idea may well appeal to you. I therefore throw myself on your mercy and beg to see you. If then I cannot persuade you, I will no doubt die. As you see I have no illusions over what the result of my actions might be. So I await to hear from you through the usual channels.

Chapter Five.

A squall had whipped up as they left Stranraer. Under scudding clouds the ferry ploughed her way towards the island. Mary stood on the deck her face defiantly looking towards her destination. She didn't seek the comfort of the other passengers, the warmth of the bar or the cafeteria. She wanted to be alone. The squall helped her. She had been unnoticed, no stares no words of welcome. It was a time to gather her thoughts and to work out her strategy before she met the man who now held her life in his large hands.

Seamus Flanagan, erstwhile buddy of her father's and no less dangerous had come to her rescue when her parents had been killed. She thought of the large ebullient man of around forty whose engaging smile and twinkling brown eyes belied his violent streak. He could have been mistaken for almost anyone except the ruthless killer he was. He had taken part in the London bombings in the 1970s and was one of IRA's most wanted assassins. He'd been one of her father's closest friends and had seen her blossoming into a tough street wise girl with no love for 'the English pigs.' as he'd called them. He'd given her shelter in his whitewashed cottage a few miles from Lisburn where he'd lived with his elderly widowed mother and started the process of training her to become a future operative for the IRA. He had been a good teacher and she a willing learner.

She had learnt fast. Soon she was proficient at firing a 9mm Walther p38 or a M1 Carbine and how to make a semtex bomb. She remembered his large hands so deceptively gentle as he handled the explosive. She smiled. In spite of the loss of her parents and all her possessions it had been a good time. Seamus had made her life exciting and it wasn't long before she knew exactly the direction her life would take her. She could still feel the excitement that had coursed through her body the day that Seamus had told her there was a part for her to play within the IRA. Never had she imagined she would be chosen. Now here she was going home to face an organisation she both loved and feared, to put in front of them an idea that might lead to her summary execution. She must be mad. She blinked as the sea spray hit her face and for some reason it brought back memories of her father's face exploding in front of her, his blood soaking into the threadbare carpet. She knew why she was taking such a risk.

She shivered. Jesus, Seamus and his pals had better listen. She'd waited so long. Now surely she had an idea that would give her the chance to exact revenge.

Larne was wet and dreary. Low cloud hung over the harbour. A typical Irish spring day. She drove off the ferry, her mood matching the weather. She had no illusions about her meeting with Seamus and she was very nervous. She had broken all the rules. She'd raised her head above the parapet, done her own bit of recruiting and might even have endangered other operatives living secret lives on the mainland. She was sure that was not the case, but would Seamus and the IRA high command agree? She smiled rue-fully. They would certainly take some persuading once they knew the identity of the man she'd left in her flat and the IRA had no sympathy for those who put their operations at risk.

As she drove along the M2 towards Lisburn she rehearsed over and over again her defence for her actions that she'd put together on the ferry. She knew she held a good hand if she could only per-suade Seamus that Hanmore was like putty in her hands. That was going to be difficult! She imagined him saying, 'In three short weeks you think you have persuaded a man, whose father we all hate and whose family were staunch Unionists, into being a Republi-can sympathiser and ready to do anything you ask of him? Come little girl what do you take me for?' Yes it would be difficult, and wait until he heard what she had in mind! Jesus, he'd hit the roof! But he didn't know James. If he did he would understand her con-fidence. She would try to explain to Seamus that James was a man awash in self pity, a sexual weirdo. A man who hated his father and would do anything to get back at him, yes anything. He was a weak man crying out to be dominated and above all else a man who wanted to be noticed. He was ready for the tak-ing, she was convinced of that, so the thought of fail-

ure must not even be considered. If she got their
blessing the result would be so exciting. So simple
and yet so devastating! . She had no doubt her gamble
was worth all the risks. Risks? Jesus she'd taken a few
of those, not least sleeping with James the night before she'd left the mainland. Here was another event
in her life she'd never forget. Sleeping with a Protestant and a Hanmore! Jesus! She must never let
Seamus know! But she'd had to do it. She'd felt the
tension growing and watched the dangerous glint in
his eyes night after night as she'd guided him to the
bed and then made a hasty retreat towards the sofa.
It could not have gone on. She'd have lost him.
She'd prepared herself for him to be violent, but to
her surprise he'd been gentle, almost apologetic.
He'd been like a child and it had been rather moving. She cursed aloud. She'd have rather he'd been
violent. She must not allow herself to feel emotion.
He was only with her because she was going to use
him.

But was that quite the truth? She thought for a
moment. Could she have held him naked in her
arms as he had cried out at his inability to get an
erection? Could she have been so gentle that eventually he'd managed to enter her if she had not felt
something towards him? After all she could have just
watched him masturbate. Jesus, she was thinking the
unthinkable! Yet she'd allowed Hanmore sperm to
penetrate her body! She gripped the steering wheel
and shook her head. No, no girl, it was business only,
she thought. But there was no doubt she'd changed
her mind about him, though that didn't mean she
was going soft on him. She'd have to sort that out
bloody quick once she was back at the flat. It wouldn't

do for him to get any ideas! She gave a resigned little chuckle. That was of course if she returned!

She ran a finger across her sore lips where James had bitten her and thought she'd have to be careful after a few glasses of Seamus's Bushmills. He must not know that she had even the smallest feelings for Hanmore and certainly not that she'd slept with him. Her hatred had to be to the fore. She had to convince him that James was only a means to an end.

She drove too fast through the mist determined to get to Seamus before she had anymore disturbing thoughts. When at last she saw the white cottage appear in the gloom she gave an audible sigh of relief and pulled into the side of the road. She needed a few moments of silent reflection before she faced him. She lit a cigarette and inhaled the nicotine down into her lungs. She looked out into the blackness around her and prayed silently to God. She waited for the nicotine to calm her nerves before gunning the engine and driving the short distance to the cottage. Every yard seeming like an eternity in time.

The soft misty rain was still falling as she drew to a halt and stepped out of the car. It was soft rain that tickled her neck as it ran off her hair. It was the rain she loved. Irish rain. It was good to be back. She'd missed her island.

She saw him then, standing by the door of the cottage large and smiling, hands on hips. In the gloom of the rain he looked slightly menacing and she couldn't help thinking that if she'd listened to her mother and trodden the road of her God she might well not now be putting her life at risk. But it was only a fleeting thought.

"By Jesus it's my little girl," Seamus called. "Come on in before you get that lovely wee body of yours all wet." He held out his arms and in spite of her misgivings she found herself running into them and breathing in the familiar smell of gun oil and sweat. "It's good to see you Seamus," she whispered in his ear and to her surprise she meant it.

He chuckled and ruffled her hair as he'd done hundreds of times and she purred with delight. She'd been so worried at the thought of how he'd react that she'd almost forgotten how much she'd loved him. "By all that's holy girl anyone would think you'd missed me." He said in his slightly musical voice as he led her into the cottage and shut the door behind them. He held her at arms length and looked her up and down. He scowled when he saw her lips. "Trouble in the pub eh?" She was quick to confirm he was right but she saw the question in his eyes and knew he did not wholly believe her. Much to her relief he did not pursue the subject preferring to make light of it. "Ah well if you will work in a pub full of those fucking Brits what can you expect. I suppose you've been fighting off their advances as well. A pretty girl like you is just what those drunken bastards would like to have for a night."

She gave an uneasy laugh. "Oh Seamus don't you be worrying about things like that now. I can look after myself you know."

Before he could reply or look too closely into her eyes she moved away from him and gazed round the big room which served as kitchen, dining room and sitting area. As always it was immaculate. On the walls were hung dozens of hunting prints. 'A wonderful sport to be partaking of if only I had the time.' Seamus had told her once. She had often thought he'd have made a good huntsman controlling his hounds with his strong voice and his desire to kill.

Hunting British soldiers perhaps was not so different. She shook her head and moved over to where his mother sat huddled in a wooden rocking chair by the fire that burnt every day of the year. Mary smiled at her in spite of knowing that the sightless eyes would not see her. She bent down and kissed a dry rough cheek. The old woman gave no sign of recognition. Mary marvelled at her fortitude. She knew she was well into her eighties and for all the years she'd known her she'd seemed close to death. The old woman claimed it was her faith that kept her alive. Seamus said it was her cussedness.

"She is close to dying now," Seamus said from behind her, a note of sadness in his voice. "She spends nearly all her time sleeping and hardly knows who I am poor darling. I hope she dies soon. There can be no point in her living and if she becomes more incontinent I will have to send her to a home and I don't think she could take that even in her state of mind. Mind you if wasn't for Sheena Roberts from down the road I would have had to put her in one a long time ago and that would have wrecked my cover. No one thinks a man who seems to spend all the time he has looking after his old mother could possible be up to anything." He smiled at Mary. A smile she knew well. It was evil and she shivered at the thought of what was to come.

"You are a hard bastard Seamus Flanagan," she said angrily. "You have always had the luck of the devil. More than you can say for my poor parents."

"You make your own luck little girl. You are careful what you say. Careful what you drink when you are with people. Careful who you choose as friends. Your father was outspoken when the Bushmills flowed through his veins and chose some of his friends unwisely. He paid the penalty. I hope you haven't caught the same bug."

It was a statement rather than a question and saved Mary from answering but she was quick to catch the threat in his voice. He was suspicious and she knew it would not be long before the questions began. She had to keep her nerve, remember everything she had rehearsed on the ferry. She had nothing to hide, nothing to be ashamed of. Hanmore meant nothing to her. Shit, she needed a cup of tea!

"I'll put the kettle on," she said quickly as she moved towards the stove and reached for the familiar battered old kettle. "Still the same I see," she said as she held it out to him. "It must be nearly as old as your mother." She tried to laugh but it stuck in her throat.

"Very nearly." Seamus said lowering his bulk into a chair by the stove. "We've both just had a cup but you go ahead. It might calm the unease I detect and anyway I think we have a long night ahead of us."

Shit, was she that transparent? She'd have to be careful when the inquisition started.

Seamus stared at her back as she bent over the stove. He was not happy. He was fond of the child, would have made a pass at her if she'd been older when she'd first come to the house. He didn't want to have to kill her but his orders had been specific. 'Extinguish her life if she's jeopardised anything. Don't bother coming to us, just do it.' There would be no question of him shirking his responsibility. He served only one master and as fond of Mary as he was he would not hesitate to kill her if he thought she had in any way endangered the Organisation or any of its operatives. He knew Mary would understand this and as he watched her pouring the water into the teapot with shaking hands he felt a slight pang of anxiety. Something was not quite right and he felt there was a fifty fifty chance that by the end of the night Mary O'Neill would be joining her parents.

She turned with a mug of tea in her hand. The room was warm and she was sweating. She thought,' Jesus girl get a hold of yourself.' But as she looked into his eyes her confidence was at a low ebb. Oh shit, shit, she thought, as she put the shaking mug to her lips.

He coughed and glanced at his watch. "No more small talk little girl. Time to get down to business. Let's move away from here to the table."

Mary followed him over to the pine table where she had eaten so many meals. She sat down facing him and leant her elbows on the tabletop. Now that the moment had arrived she felt calmer and when she looked across at Seamus she held his stare. Determined to show she had no concerns she asked, "Do you remember those walks we used to take beside Loch Neagh when I first came to live with you? How you told me the water made you relax? How you ruffled my hair and told me that sometimes you regretted your life of violence? I can hear you even now telling me that it was the only way and that God was on your side. I believed you then and it may come as a surprise to you to know that nothing has changed. I need you to remember that this evening and have confidence in my loyalty. So please give me a chance to tell you what I have in mind without interruption."

He pushed back his chair and reached for a half empty bottle of Bushmills on the table. He put the neck to his lips and took a long swig before answering. "Very well little girl the floor is yours. But what you say better be good, fucking good I be telling you."

There wasn't a flicker of a smile on his face as he
took another drink. He gargled the liquid in his
throat before swallowing. "The general opinion is that
you have been at best foolish at the worst a person
who can no longer be trusted. So remember your
future depends on how convincing you are. Now let's
hear about this playmate of yours and your ideas."

She wanted to ask him how he could possibly
doubt her, but she knew it was pointless. She just
had to tell her story and hope for the best. She began. "My playmate as you call him is none other than
the son of that bastard Sir Richard Hanmore." She
allowed herself to smile as she heard his sharp intake of breath. "Yes' I thought that might interest
you. Seamus, and what's more my plan is damned
good. I have the son James, in the palm of my hand.
He will do anything for me. Far from putting my
mission in jeopardy or endangering anyone else's life
he has provided us with something that will not be
forgotten in a hurry. Do you think I'd have come
back and risked my life if I wasn't confident that I
have in my head a plan that would boost moral
amongst us Republicans and probably silence talk of
peace for many years. Listen well to me Seamus. I
am loyal to the IRA. I have not gone soft on the need
to kill. I am as good a soldier as you. Oh don't raise
your hands like that. I know you will have been ordered to kill me if you think I've done wrong. So do
you want to hear more or pull the trigger now?"

He gave her a weak smile. "No, no I'll hear you
out but Jesus girl, a fucking Hanmore! You don't do
things by half do you?"

She laughed then. "You should know me by now.
Yes, a Hanmore and that's what makes it so perfect.
I suspect we hated Richard Hanmore more than

anyone else in the Government. We know he was an astute politician and with his background he was good at undermining our influence in certain important quarters. You know he was a thorn in our flesh, believing that the IRA could be rendered impotent by reasoned and gentle persuasion of the masses, both Catholic and Protestant. He knew he would never get us to disarm so he set out to portray us as butchers who killed indiscriminately and so isolate us from the people who banked rolled us and were our life blood. Let's face it you have told me of at least three targets the IRA aborted on because they were frightened of losing vital financial support from America. One of those targets was Hanmore himself! Now it may come as a surprise to you to know that I believe he might have succeeded in his plan if he'd not had that heart attack. He was a fucking clever man. Now, I accept he may be a spent force, but can we take that for granted? I'm sure the High Command will not think so and neither do I. The British Prime Minister would be a fool not to consult him on the Irish Issue. So how fucking lucky that his son wanders into my pub and I had the guts to do something about it. Now I have the perfect answer to the problem."

Seamus leant across the table and grabbed her arm. "You do little girl?"

For the first time that evening her voice was full of confidence as she replied, "Believe me I have. Oh Jesus, Seamus I have!"

"So let's hear your plan."

Her voice shook with excitement as she replied. "I get James to assassinate his father."

Seamus leapt to his feet, the chair crashing backwards onto the floor. "You just tell him to go and kill his daddy! Come, come do you expect me to believe that!"

Mary stared up at him. "You are a fool if you don't believe me. He will do it, no mistake. As I said earlier he will do anything for me. Just give me a chance. I won't let anyone down. I have after all gambled my life on it."

"Sweet Jesus, indeed you have! Let me be telling you a few home truths before we discuss this idea of yours. You were trained to be a sleeper on the mainland. You were put in place so as to be ready for a strike when the word came. A lot of money and hard work was put into getting you into the right place. You were told to blend into the community and keep your head down. But what do you do? Break every rule in the book and perhaps put a lot of our future plans in jeopardy. For all you know a target might already have been chosen for you, which the High Command might have thought more important than your fucking Sir Richard bloody Hanmore. Did you think about that when you sweet talked this unstable man back to your house? Did you? DID YOU?" He slammed his fist down on the table. "Talk yourself out of that you bloody little fool," he growled.

Anger welled up inside Mary. Could he not see how sensational the death of Hanmore would be? And by the hand of his own son. Of course it was worth all the risks she'd taken. Shit, had Seamus become a moron since she'd last seen him? Couldn't he see that the death of Hanmore would be a huge propaganda coup and have enormous repercussions? In a voice shaking with frustration she replied. "Alright I am in breach of discipline, but I know in my heart I did the right thing. Don't you tell me Seamus Flanagan that Richard Hanmore is not an important target. How many times did the IRA try to kill him? Once, twice? No. I believe it was three times. So I have no doubt that High Command still want him dead and here is the perfect opportunity. So what if I have spoiled the chance of another strike on the mainland for a wee while? There will be another chance; another operative to carry it out and Hanmore will be dead! Jesus, Seamus, it's fucking brilliant!"

He had to admit she was very convincing and brave, but he would expect that from an O'Neill. Her father might have been reckless but he had never questioned Dermot's bravery. Nevertheless the rules of the dangerous game the IRA played were very simple. Do as we tell you or face the consequences. There had been others beside Mary who had found out what that meant. Maybe he was impressed but would the High Command feel the same? He chose his reply carefully. "Okay, let's for arguments sake only say I go to Belfast and get the go ahead. How can I be sure you can really persuade this man, who by your own admission is unstable, to kill his father?"

"You can't be sure, but I am. You haven't seen the hatred as I have. It is fucking terrifying. Let me say one more thing. Ever since my parents were killed I have waited for a chance to get my revenge and prove to the IRA that I am a true Republican. To see Hanmore die would go some way to easing the pain that constantly eats at my belly. I would never put my life at risk by coming to you unless I was as certain as I possibly can be. All I ask now is for you to acknowledge that what I have done is in the best interests of the Organisation and to see the merit of my plan.

You know me for Christ sake Seamus, so take a little gamble and support me."

Seamus smiled. "I'm alive because I have never gambled, but you put your case well, no doubt about that. But let me ask you one more thing. Has it ever occurred to you that he might be working for the Security Forces? What worries me is why would a Hanmore be in the pub?"

Mary nodded. "I admit I was very suspicious at first. But I've had three long nerve wracked weeks to evaluate him. For starters he came to pick up a girl to beat up. He's wept every night telling me that and I believe him. Secondly he hasn't got the guts. Thirdly he hasn't made any attempt to be on his own so I'm sure he's not in contact with anyone. Finally it all comes back to what I have just said. His hatred consumes him. He has told me he would like to see his father dead and although I'm getting fucking tired of saying this, I believe him."

Seamus grunted and reached for the Bushmills, but his eyes never moved off Mary's face. "I don't like it, I tell you. I think the whole thing is too iffy, but I do know you as you said and I'm thinking I should at least give you a chance to save that pretty little body of yours. I can't say I will speak with a lot of confidence when I go to Headquarters but I think you deserve a chance. I would have liked to take you with me but that has been forbidden. One thing that might be in your favour is this talk about peace talks. I for one haven't killed for all these years just to allow politicians to sit down and try to make peace. The gun and the bomb are the only way we are going to get what we want. We will win. Now I know there are men who think the same as me and just perhaps the death of someone like Hanmore might kill off these fucking rumours about peace talks and ceasefires before they ever begin. So for the first time in my life and much against my better judgement I will, as you say, take a gamble."

Mary jumped up from the table and kissed him. "Jesus Seamus I thought I'd had it!"

He laughed then, his old laugh that she knew so well. "I like the idea Mary O'Neill and it has the mark of your scheming father. It would just be the way his mind would work. I like the thought of the bullets ripping into Hanmore's chest. Even better that he will die at the hands of his son. Yes, if it works it's good. But I leave here giving you no promises. If I fail, well you already know what will happen." He rubbed his chin thoughtfully. "I shouldn't be saying this, but you could just disappear into the night and run back to the mainland. I could say you didn't come over. I would be believed."

"No! No! I stay and take the consequences. What's the matter Seamus? Getting nervous at the thought of killing me?"

His eyes ran over her face, down over her body and she shivered. "I would break your neck just like that"—he clicked his fingers. "You better believe it little girl."

She did and it made her feel sick. Her mother had warned her about Seamus and she'd chosen to ignore it. Looking at him now she understood what her mother had meant. She nodded at him and looked away saying quietly, "Oh I believe you Seamus, you ruthless bastard."

He'd finally gone, muttering under his breath. She'd felt relief as she'd watched him shut the door.

She'd seen him in a new light and she wasn't sure she liked what she'd seen. He'd never been threatening towards her before. Oh yes she'd listened night after night to his verbal attacks on the British troops, and the RUC and how he wished to see them all dead. But he had never lost his temper with her. It had been different tonight. His anger, though tempered, had been directed at her. She'd landed him with a problem that he could have done without and it had upset him. Well fuck him. She'd brought to him a plan she was proud of. If she died it was only because they had become inflexible.

She made his mother a fresh pot of tea and held the mug patiently to her lips while she sipped greedily. A lot of the liquid spilt on the old lady's shawl and Mary was surprised how clean she smelt. But then Seamus would never allow her to become foul smelling in his house. When the mug was empty Mary wiped the shawl and covered her emaciated body with a rug which lay neatly folded by the chair. Then she moved to the sink to wash the mug and rinse her own face.

Exhaustion folded her in its embrace. She'd not slept properly for nearly forty eight hours and her argument with Seamus had drained the last morsel of energy from her body. A headache threatened and as she dried the mug her hands shook. She was at the end of her tether. 'I'm frightened fit to piss,' she thought and knew she would not sleep until he returned in what, an hour? More likely two or perhaps not until dawn. Whatever, it would seem a very long time. She dragged her aching body to the sofa, stretched out and prepared herself for an uneasy wait.

It was two in the morning and her eyelids were heavy. The kitchen had become stiflingly hot and every now and then the old woman passed wind. She couldn't sleep.

It was three in the morning and her nerves were at fever pitch. Jesus where was the bastard?

It was just gone four when the door opened and he almost fell into the room. She watched from the sofa as he staggered across the room. Jesus, the bastard was drunk! She lay still as he moved unsteadily towards her, watching the smile on his face. Was he about to kill her or had he brought good news? She could bare the tension no longer and sat bolt upright. "Well? Shit you've taken your time! For Christ sake tell me what happened!"

His eyes were bloodshot as he slumped down beside her on the sofa. He stank of Bushmills and she heard him belch. The drunken bastard! He gave her a lecherous smile. Christ how could he be thinking such lecherous thoughts when her life hung in the balance? "Oh for Christ sake Seamus don't even think of it! Just tell me what happened!" she shouted.

He withdrew his hand from his groin and said, "Your idea has met with approval. It was a close run thing I be telling you, but in the end the thought of Hanmore being killed by his son was too good an opportunity to miss. However there is a condition." She stiffened and held her breath. What the fuck was coming? "As I suspected a target had been chosen for you and within the next few days you would have received your instructions. Of course you have buggered that up, but they see it as a plus now, so you are lucky. Before you loose young Hanmore onto his father we want to test his commitment to 'The

Cause,' so he will now carry out the assassination instead of you. He will either run or he will be trapped. Either way we will know where we stand."

She smiled. It was very cunning. It was the way she would have dealt with it. She hardly dared ask, "And when he has carried out both tasks as I know he will what is his future with the Organisation?"

Seamus's voice was cold as he replied. "Zero. You will then kill him. He will die a hero of the Republican movement."

Her throat was dry as she asked, "And me?"

"You too will be a hero, but a live one."

"And in the unlikely event of James refusing, I die as well?"

"Of course."

"By your hand?"

"Do you want me to answer that?"

She stared at his leering face. By God the bastard would do it without even a small stab of conscience. But what else could she expect? He had worked for a ruthless Organisation for years and he wasn't about to change now just because he'd taken her in and treated her like a daughter. She heard the voice of her mother saying, 'If you go down your father's route you will be along side ruthless killers and no good will come of it. You may have 'the Hatred' in your heart Mary but you tell me this, could you murder me in cold blood? The likes of your father and Seamus wouldn't hesitate.' Well fuck the man, he wasn't going to frighten her.

She forced herself to smile. "I can smell death all over you Seamus Flanagan. By God you are a sadistic bastard. But you won't get the pleasure of putting your hands around my throat because I won't fucking fail. So remember that." She tossed her head defiantly and turned away, no longer wanting to be in his company and headed up the stairs to the small bedroom she knew so well.

There was an unpleasant feeling in her stomach as she sank exhausted onto the bed, which she could only attribute to the fact that the man who had been her hero had sown a few seeds of doubt in her mind. If they germinated she could find herself in a fucking muddle, for where would that leave her beliefs? Oh shit she thought, The war, the ultimate victory is my life. I've been bred to fight the Brits. I have been taught how to kill and believed my actions were legitimate. Could I have been wrong all these years? She remembered Seamus once saying to her that a conscience was something she could not afford. Jesus! she thought. Is that what I'm fucking getting!

Chapter Six

THE thunderstorm crashed down on London. The lightening lit up the morning sky as the first of the commuters fought their way through the traffic congestion to their offices. The streets were running water and the air was oppressive, crushing the breath out of those trying to reach their place of work. It was a day when not much work would be done.

He stood in the bedroom watching the storm raging over London. Large drops of rain hammered at the window. Although nearly nine in the morning the heavy cloud hanging over the city made it seem like dusk. Every few minutes flashes of lightening made him close his eyes and hunch his shoulders as he imagined the electric charge cutting through his body. James had been terrified of lightening ever since the age of eight when he and Sarah had been caught in a violent storm while out playing in the woods at Rosehall. As another flash illuminated the morning sky, followed by a crack of thunder close by, he shuddered and hurried towards the bed. He'd cover his head with a pillow as he'd done many times before and ride out the storm. How he wished Mary was with him. She'd soothe his shattered nerves, but it wouldn't be long now. She'd rung the evening before to say she would be back in the morning. Thank God he wasn't going to have to spend another night on his own in the dismal surroundings of the flat. It was beginning to feel like a prison.

He'd obeyed her instructions to the letter, staying away from the Wellington (who thought he and Mary were suffering from food poisoning), and only leaving the flat to buy papers and cigarettes. Mary had left him enough food, but God he was getting fed up with eating out of tins. He had surprised himself by not turning to the bottle, but she was returning just in time. The rumble of thunder grew more distant and the panic died in him, allowing him to enjoy the smell of her cheap scent on the sheets and to think about the last three weeks, which he acknowledged had irrevocably changed his life.

The surprise to him was that a woman was responsible. After Sophie's death he'd given up all hope of meeting anyone who could replace her. He knew the beating up of women and his sexual perversion stemmed from his loss. Mary seemed to offer him an alternative even though he didn't quite understand what was happening. Why had she been so successful in controlling his violent streak? Was it because he saw a little of Sophie in her character, or because she seemed to hate his father as much as he did? Perhaps it was a bit of both. Certainly she'd shown him more compassion than he thought he deserved and he'd proved himself to be a man at last. He smiled as he thought of her naked body, so hard, so urgent and yet filling him with confidence. He would never have believed a woman would do that. It was a miracle and whatever he did he mustn't risk putting this new friendship in jeopardy. He stretched out under the sheet and felt a jab of excitement at the thought of her mapping out his new life. Because she'd given him back the will to live he was prepared to do anything for her even desert Sarah.

He thought of her sick with worry. Was it fair that he'd just disappeared into the blue? In fact by now she probably thought he'd met a gruesome death at the hands of some prostitute or pimp. Several times since Mary had left he'd toyed with the idea of calling her, but Mary had told him that if he wanted a new life the first thing he would have to do was sever all connections with members of his family. He couldn't have cared less about his parents but Sarah was different. He felt a bastard. Well what was new? His father had been telling him that for years. So Sarah had to be sacrificed. He was not prepared to throw away the chance of a new life. It was as simple as that. He pushed back the sheet and gazed up at the ceiling where a small black spider was hanging from a cobweb. He wondered if it had been as frightened as he'd been by the storm. Perhaps spiders didn't know fear. He lay still listening for another crack of thunder but all he heard was the silence. The storm was over. He blew out his cheeks with relief and rolled off the bed and looked across at the window. He could see the last of the raindrops running down the glass and once again hear the familiar sound of the moving traffic. Everything was back to normal. He shuffled over to the sink, piled high with dirty crockery. He hadn't washed a thing since she'd left. He picked up a mug and switched on the kettle. He was sick of fucking tea. What he needed was a good slug of whisky. Perhaps tonight they would get drunk together and end up in bed. Absently he cleaned the inside of the mug with his fingers. He'd got used to the filth they lived in. At first it had made him almost physically sick and he'd tried to persuade her to be a bit cleaner. Mary had refused to listen to his pleas saying, "If you want to fucking clean the place or wash the sodding crockery you go ahead, but don't you be expecting any help from me. This place was a tip when I came here and if I have anything to do with it, so it will be when I leave."

He hadn't bothered and slowly he'd come to accept the dirt. In fact he had to admit he rather liked the chaos, preferring it to the comfortable surroundings he'd left behind. He no longer had a bath every day and had only washed his hair twice since meeting Mary. He'd only had the clothes he stood up in so he'd gone with her to buy a few vital necessities. "So that you will blend more into the neighbourhood," Mary had said staring at his suit with amusement. It now lay crumpled on the floor probably never to be worn again. His nostrils widened as he thought of Mary's body smell. Apart from having to look presentable at work she was no cleaner than him and he'd become almost addicted to her musty smell when she stripped off. She was five foot three and carried no extra weight. Her breasts were small and firm, her nipples dark. Her legs were all muscle and she had a thick mat of dark pubic hair. She was certainly not the most beautiful woman in the world but to him she was perfect. What she thought of him he wasn't sure but he suspected it was nearer contempt than love, but he didn't care. He'd been despised all his life. He likened her to a blood transfusion, filling him with new strength. He had no doubt he'd die if the transfusions were no longer available. He thought of their sweat soaked bodies the night before she left for Ireland. Never in his wildest dreams had he expected to experience such pleasure. She'd been so gentle at first, so understanding. But once she'd felt his erection grow she'd become urgent, pulling him inside her and driving him to the final climax. It had been quick, probably too quick for her, but for him it had been a miracle. It was an experience he'd never forget.

Although the storm had passed over London by the time Mary turned off the engine of the Renault 5 outside the flat, the rain still poured out of the leaden sky. It was not the warm gentle rain that she'd left behind in Ireland, but a hard, almost hostile rain. It did nothing to raise her moral.

Still unnerved by the feelings that had taken root in the cottage in Lisburn she was reluctant to leave the car and face the man inside until she'd had time to evaluate her dangerous situation. Although she'd accepted she'd taken a gamble before she'd left for Ireland somehow her meeting with Seamus had brought home to her the terrifying risk she'd taken. Her life hung in the balance—no doubt about it. If she'd ever thought that was not the case she had the answer now. It would be foolish to admit she wasn't frightened, but she could deal with that. After all she'd spent most of her life living on the edge of fear. What really worried her was the nagging doubt that perhaps she'd find it hard to kill James. A few

weeks ago she wouldn't have batted an eyelid, but
something inside her told her things were different
now. Shit, shit,shit. Perhaps it had been a mistake
sleeping with him, but she'd wanted to feel she had
control over him and she'd used her body to great
effect. She looked across the unkept garden divid-
ing her from the man inside. Part of her hoped he'd
fled back to his world where there was a little sanity
left, not stayed to experience her world of violence
and death. It would mean she'd die, but it would
end the turmoil in her brain that he'd unwittingly
stirred up. In fact as she pulled urgently on a cigarette she felt she almost wanted to die. What had
life to offer her? The answer was probably very little.
She was steeped in hatred and would almost certainly find herself in prison one day or die by the
hand of some fucking Unionist shit or British soldier. Jesus! What was happening to her! You're getting yourself into a mess girl, she thought.

She gave herself a rueful smile in the car mirror
and opened the door. Nothing would be gained by
sitting in the fucking car. Her legs felt weak as they
took her weight and she had to muster every ounce
of willpower to drive herself up the path to the front
door, where she stood looking at the black paint peeling off the wood. 'The place is a dump.' she thought
irrationally as she fumbled in her handbag for the
key. Oh shit where was the fucking thing! She shook
her bag violently and the contents spilled onto the
long grass. 'Fool,' she thought as she bent down to
search for the keys.

"Having trouble Mary?" His crisp upper class accent was unmistakable.

Oh God, she thought, he's still fucking here! She
looked up and saw his unshaven face smiling down

at her and she felt a surge of relief that he hadn't run. Without thinking she stood up and kissed him. 'A big mistake,' her brain told her. But she still couldn't stop herself saying, "Oh thank God you haven't gone."

He sucked his lips where she'd left the traces of her lipstick and asked, "of course I'm still here. Does that present a problem or something?"

She looked into his eyes and saw his concern. By Christ she'd got to him. Oh shit she'd have to watch it. She couldn't allow him to get too infatuated. It would just make her job more difficult. She said slowly. "No, there is no problem now. I've just realised I'm not ready to die."

The Wellington was as always packed on a Friday night. Cigarette smoke hung in the air as the seething mass jostled to reach the bar and shout their orders to the overworked staff. Many of the men were from the Irish Republic employed on the building sites throughout London. The Wellington was their meeting place on a Friday night and their pleasant lilting accents were recognisable even above the hubbub.

Mary worked hard behind the bar, the sweat pouring down her body. Every now and then she would glance across at James to see how he was coping with the good natured shouts of those trying to get served. He'd been working with her for two weeks now and she had to admit she admired the way he'd taken to this new life. But the longer she had to wait for the messenger the more difficult life became in the flat. She gazed out into the crowded room and wondered if the man would ever come. The tension was beginning to get to her.

Then as she pulled another pint of beer for one of the regulars she became aware of a small ginger headed man standing behind him and staring at her intently. 'Oh Jesus,' she thought, 'My prayers have been answered.' She held his gaze as she gave the regular his change and couldn't help thinking that the man's eyes were as cold as Seamus's. He moved into the space left by the customer and leant his elbows on the bar top, a thin smile spreading across his face. "Well by heaven you're busy in here tonight and by the sounds of it I might be in Dublin. I be taking it you be Mary O'Neill?" There wasn't a hint of friendliness in his voice.

"That I am Sir, and what can I be doing for you?"

"I will be wanting a Bushmills first my girl and then a little talk to you over there by the window. I know the night be busy, but I have little time to waste so be quick about it will you." He reached out and touched her hand as he gave her a fiver and said quietly, "A certain Seamus Flanagan sends his regards."

She did her best to smile as she took the note and replied in as quiet a voice, "So we have a friend in common. I don't know whether we should count ourselves lucky or not. You go over to that alcove and I'll bring you the drink and your change in a minute."

She looked frantically round for James. The last thing she wanted was his curiosity to be aroused, but she needn't have worried. He was too busy with the crowd at the bar. She worked quickly, pouring the whisky and putting it on a tray with the change. The sooner the meeting was over the sooner she'd be back behind the bar and know what fate awaited her and James.

"Thank you my little darling," the man said as she put the tray on the table and sat down beside him. "Now you be listening to me carefully, for I don't like dwelling too long in places. It is unhealthy and by the looks of this place you've got your work cut out tonight. I will repeat nothing, so don't let your mind wander." He leant towards her and she could smell the Bushmills on his breath as he whispered into her ear. He spoke for only two minutes before sitting back and smiling at her. "You got that my darling?"

Indeed she had and it made her shiver. She looked at him and nodded. "Yes your instructions are quite clear."

"That will be it then. So now I will be leaving you and darling," he threw her a withering smile, "Don't you be giving us any trouble girl. We will be watching."

Before she could say anything he was up and disappearing into the crowd. Just as well as she would probably have thrown his empty glass at his ginger head. She was fuming with rage as she hurried back to the bar. "For Christ sake,' she thought, 'who did he think he was talking to? Can't they understand I'm loyal.' She gave a wry little smile before looking anxiously for James and was relieved to see he was still over run with orders. For sure he'd not noticed her brief absence and that at least would make things easier. She moved across to him. "You okay?"

"Fine, but bloody hot. Shit this has been my worst night so far. You managing?"

She just nodded and moved back to her side of the bar. His question had shown far too much con-

cern for her liking. She didn't need some weirdo
Brit going soft on her.

It was an hour before dawn. A time when the
spirit can be at its lowest and Mary felt dreadful. She
hadn't slept since returning to the flat just after midnight. They had drunk mugs of coffee in an attempt
to ease their dehydration and James had eventually
staggered to the bed and fallen into a deep sleep.
She had not joined him. She didn't want to touch
him, or worse go through the motions of making love.
How could she when his death warrant had just been
signed and how could she expect to sleep when she
was going to have to face him with that fact as soon as
he woke?

How would he react? It probably depended on
how much he'd already guessed. Would he go along
with her or would her death sentence be confirmed
before the day was out? Could she still ignore the
gremlin that was chiselling away at her brain? She
would find the answer to the first question very soon.
She knew the answer to the second question already.
It had to be addressed. She shot a glance towards
the bed and saw his body moving rhythmically with
his breathing. Underneath his arrogant and
perverted character she felt there was a gentler side;
a side which she suspected had never been given a
chance. She guessed he'd once wanted to be a
decent law abiding citizen, faithfully following in his
father's footsteps. Well there wasn't much chance of
that now! She smiled ruefully at his inert body. In
fact he was about to become a killer and she was in
danger of going soft! Holy shit! She forced herself to
think of her mother's cries as her father's head

disintegrated in front of her. She remembered the smell of shit as she'd tried to scoop her mother's intestines off the Belfast street and she saw her home burning and the shut doors. Oh you stupid bitch, she thought. Who the fucking hell do you think you are kidding? Fat chance of you going soft when there is so much hate in my heart? She was a killer intent on revenge, always had been and always would be. Words like 'love,' 'caring, 'a conscience' were simply not part of her vocabulary. So forget any thoughts of becoming miss nice fucking lady, she thought, and get on with the job you were trained for. She slapped her hands against her thighs. There, the crisis was over. All this 'going soft business' forgotten. Now it was time to wake the bastard and tell him why she'd brought him home. But as she walked across to the bed she still felt that little gremlin nudging away at her heart.

In her frustration she shook him harder than she meant to and he woke with a start. "What the fuck's going on!"

She touched his arm. "Sorry James I didn't mean to wake you like that, but I have something very important to tell you and I don't think it can wait. Are you prepared to listen?"

He rubbed his eyes and smiled. "Are you going to tell me you love me?"

Mary pushed him back onto the bed. "No you silly fool. This is far more important, so stop fooling around and listen well." She could see the disappointment in his eyes. Shit the bugger was serious! "You ready?"

He said nothing, just nodded.

She began. "I was born in Belfast. I had a father who wanted to kill every Brit on the Island and a mother who thought God would put everything right. Jesus, I don't know who was the maddest, but I chose my father's route because I watched both my parents butchered by the Unionist bastards. I went to live with a man called Seamus Flanagan, an IRA commander and he taught me to shoot and make bombs. He also filled me with even more hatred if that was possible. I was chosen a few months ago to become a sleeper on the mainland. Now normally I would be a member of a cell, but the IRA High Command saw the hatred in my heart and chose me to operate on my own. So there I fucking was blending into the local background of this area when you fucking walk into the Wellington and tell me your father is Sir Richard Hanmore.

I don't know what you thought was the reason for me asking you back to the flat but the truth is James I wanted to use you. I thought I could put your hatred of your father to good use. I had a plan forming in my mind and I thought it fucking brilliant. That is why I went to Ireland. I have put my life on the line, now in a few moments I will know if I am going to lose it. I persuaded the IRA that my plan was good. I now have to persuade you to work for me."

His eyes were wide with excitement as he thought. Bloody hell, there is more to her than just being an Irish Catholic, but shit I never imagined she was involved with the IRA! I have heard about people like her from my father. Cold blooded murderers he called them in spite of having some sympathy for a United Ireland. He hated the likes of her. Now I'm looking at one, and I've fucked it as well. Oh God if only my father could know. It might actually kill the bastard!

She could sense his hatred and almost feel the tension building inside him. Holy Mary the next bit was going to be easy. She told him what the messenger had told her. He smiled and said, "your life is safe." She breathed in deeply. Yes! She'd been right. He was a pushover. Nevertheless her voice still showed some apprehension as she asked, "You are with me then?"

"Too bloody right I am. Nothing will give me more pleasure. Oh shit Mary, you really have given me something to live for. The IRA need have nothing to fear over my loyalty to their cause. It is just. Thank you for putting me right." He leant forward and kissed her hard on the mouth before she had time to pull away. 'Jesus, the bastard has an erection,' she thought, staring at his crutch. 'He's actually turned on by the thought of what he is going to have to do. I've released the devil inside him and I should be pleased.' She gave another one of her rueful little smiles and shook her head.

It was just after ten in the morning when Sarah sat on the edge of her father's bed reading the letter. The contents stunned her and her voice carried little conviction as she asked, "Do you think he actually means what he has written? Could he not just be trying to frighten you? You and I know it's the sort of thing he might do."

Richard smiled sadly. "I'm afraid I think the letter is genuine and we would be wise to treat it very seriously. James in this sort of mood could be very dangerous."

"Who on earth could have prised open his mind and sown such dreadful thoughts? For heaven sake father we know James wouldn't be capable of behaving like this on his own. At heart he's a coward. He has been brainwashed."

"And saw it as a chance to get at me and your mother," Richard added.

"This is treachery," Sarah cried. "How awful that he could contemplate something so evil and that you his father can think he is capable of such an act. It is really dreadful that your relationship has come to this."

He reached for her hand. "I know, and it hurts me terribly, but much as it pains me to say this, I am not surprised. You see I don't see him in the same light as you do. I'm prepared to admit I have not been the best of fathers but he had his chances just like you. He's fluffed them and now he seems to have turned into an evil young man. But whatever either of us may think it is too late to change anything. James has set his stall, now we must decide what to do."

"And you must accept a lot of the blame," Sarah retorted angrily. "I don't want to upset you anymore than you are already, but you were a lousy father. I believe that if you had been half a decent father nothing like this would have happened. Let me tell you it would have been very easy for me to have gone the same way."

Richard dropped her hand and threw a look of despair at Blanche. "She speaks the truth I'm afraid," Blanche said quietly as she moved from the window and sat on the bed. "So the least you can do is try to put a few things right. It may be too late but I think you should give him a chance to explain. So I suggest we do not involve the police for the moment. I can't believe that any of our lives are in danger. Good God Richard he's our son!"

"Heavens woman don't you think I know that! Don't you think I care? I would give anything for him to walk in here now and tell us it was all a mistake. But that's just not going to happen is it? Come on don't grab at straws."

Blanche could think of nothing to say. In her heart she knew he was right. A silence settled on the room and Richard lay back on the pillows and closed his eyes. He knew he should ring the police. It was all very well Blanche saying James couldn't kill any of them, but until a few weeks ago who would have ever dreamt he'd write such a letter? He had little doubt that James could kill him and however implausible that might seem he knew any threat would be treated with the greatest respect by the Security Services. After all how many times had attempts been made on his life while he'd been in office? Good God Rosehall would be swarming with uniform within a matter of a few hours if he picked up the telephone. But he was tired and depressed and in his present mood didn't really care if James did come and blast him off the earth. Nor did he relish the idea of his grief and guilt becoming the property of other people. Against all his better judgement he said, "I agree with you Blanche, we give the boy a chance." Those words were to come back and haunt him many times.

The ring of the telephone made them jump. Being the nearest to the set Blanche jumped up and grabbed the receiver hoping it might be James. She made no attempt to hide her disappointment as she turned to Sarah. "It's Henry for you."

"Don't mention the letter," Richard said urgently.

Sarah took the receiver from her mother. "Henry darling, what a surprise, I thought you were out un-

til later today. What, James has just rung you!" she
gasped. "What on earth did he want? I see! Why you
and not us? He what? Wants to come and see you
this afternoon and doesn't want any of his family
present? Well that's rubbish! He owes it to us. I will
come immediately. You say no! Oh dear God Henry
why on earth not?" There was a long silence as she
listened to Henry's sympathetic voice. When he'd
finished she said reluctantly, "Okay then. I suppose
you are right, but for God sake be careful. And Henry
darling, thanks for letting us know he's alive and I
will see you tomorrow morning."

She turned to face her parents who were both
looking at her with open mouths. "James has rung
Henry?" they asked in unison.

"Yes. Apparently he wants to talk this afternoon
without any of us being there but Henry has suggested I go down tomorrow morning early and see
James. He will try and keep him at home over night.
Oh yes, and Henry thought we might like to know
James was alive. Without mentioning the letter I
couldn't really tell him we already knew. That was
my first lie ever to him and I don't feel good about it.
I think we should have taken him into our confidence especially now that James is going to see him."

Henry carefully replaced the receiver wondering whether he'd done the right thing by telling
Sarah not to come down until the morning. But
James had been very specific that no member of his
family should be present. He'd felt it best to go along
with him, especially if it led to James telling him what
the hell he'd been up to. He'd taken a gamble even
in asking Sarah to come in the morning, but he felt

he owed her that after all the weeks of worrying if her brother was alive. At least he'd been able to tell her that he was. The odd thing was she hadn't seemed surprised and he wondered why.

Chapter Seven

HENRY Marshall had often wondered why he'd become a friend of James's at Eton and the only rational reason he could give was that his sister was the most desirable girl he'd ever set eyes on. He'd fallen in love with her on a warm June day by the river and had never looked at another girl since.

At first the same could not be said about Sarah and she'd found his adolescent attendance rather boring and restrictive. She'd wanted a few romances before settling down and she wasn't at all sure she could love an overweight young man whose love of eating food came only second to his apparent love for her. But she'd kept in touch, mainly because she couldn't bare the thought of hurting him and she was ashamed to admit because his parents threw wonderful parties for the young at their house six miles west of Gloucester. By the time he'd left Eton she had felt they were good friends and nothing more.

That is probably how it would have remained, but for Henry's desire to become a journalist, rather than work in his father's engineering business. So after a short and boring spell with a local paper he'd managed to get a job as a lowly sports reporter with the Daily Mail. For two years he'd slaved away with no thanks from anyone until a chance meeting with the political editor of the Daily Telegraph at his parents' home. This gave him the career move that was to change his life. A month after moving jobs he'd found himself interviewing Sarah's father at Rosehall. He'd told Sarah later that it had been the most fascinating two hours he'd ever spent with any man. The result was that he became hungry for knowledge about Ireland and at Richard's invitation he'd started spending a fair number of weekends at Rosehall listening to his views and of course spending as much time with Sarah as she would allow.

She had begun to see him in a different light by then, not just another rich idle young man, and before long she found her feelings changing towards him. Six months before James's disappearance she and Henry had become engaged.

By then most of his articles were devoted to attacking the IRA atrocities and putting forward the suggestion that they could never be defeated militarily. 'The way forward,' Richard had told him, 'Is to cut off their supply lines of money and guns and the way to do this is to keep talking to the Americans. I can't speak out in public as I would like, but you can.' Henry had done just that.

Filled with youthful enthusiasm and oblivious to any danger he'd delved into the workings of the IRA. He'd slowly become aware of the complexities of the problem and at first he'd sympathised with the

Republican aim for a United Ireland. Thanks to Richard's influence he'd gained access to the Maize prison and interviewed convicted Republican terrorists and risked his life interviewing some of the victims' families. Then one evening four members of a Protestant family that he'd interviewed a week before were shot down in their home. The youngest to die was six. When he learnt of this atrocity all sympathy for the Nationalist Cause evaporated and the IRA had made a bitter enemy.

From that moment onwards he'd worked tirelessly to explode the myth that they were fighting a war of freedom. He wrote about their cynical approach to violence. He exposed the gun running from America and Libya, the extortion rackets and the drug trafficking. He wrote about the rottenness of a violent Organisation and it had not been long before he'd earned the dubious accolade of being top of the list of several journalists who the IRA would like to silence.

To those who knew him well this angry side was alien to the man. His generosity to fellow journalists at their lunchtime drinking sessions was legendary. Standing only five foot six his large frame could be found propping up the bar around midday on the days he was in London, drinking pints of beer and tucking into several large sandwiches. By his own admission he was a thirteen stone glutton and cheerfully took all the ribbing that came his way. To his colleagues he was an enigma. A man full of compassion, seemingly at peace with the world and yet possessing this burning desire to destroy a dangerous Organisation single handed.

It was three in the afternoon and Henry lay draped over a sun lounger by the side of his parents' pool. He'd placed himself so that he could keep an eye on the drive. He felt surprisingly ill at ease and although he couldn't put a finger on the exact reason he suspected it was a lot to do with his telephone call to Sarah. It puzzled him that she had not seemed more surprised by his news that James was alive. If he hadn't known her better he would have thought she was keeping something from him.

He wondered what the outcome of his meeting with James would be, and where had the devious bugger been all these weeks. He had a lot of questions to answer, not least how he could make his family suffer so much. Henry knew he would have to bite his tongue. Too many stinging rebukes and James would clam up. He hadn't known him for all these years without learning that he hated to be criticised.

He lay back and thought of Sarah. She was constantly on his mind these days. Not only because he felt he might be putting her life at risk by continuing with his attacks on the IRA, but also because she loved her brother and felt that somehow she was a little responsible for his disappearance. It was nonsense of course. The man to blame was her father. Much as he admired his dedication and driving ambition, he had become well aware of his total lack of interest in his children. There was no doubt in Henry's mind that this present crisis could be laid fair and square at Richard's door. He ran a hand across his large stomach and reflected that the three men in Sarah's life were the cause of most of her present unhappiness. Not least myself, he thought, being forced to live like a nomad, moving from flat to flat in London. Never taking the same route to or from the office. Sometimes travelling by car, other times by train, even by air so that no one can be sure of my whereabouts. Not even Sara knows where I am half the time. That is no way to treat the woman I am going to marry.

He knew what he should do, but like Richard before his heart attack, there was a goal in front of him and he didn't want to give up now. Just a little more time, he told himself. Then I'll promise her I'll quit. He remembered her saying to him once in a sad little voice as she'd rested her head on his chest. 'I would never ask you to give up the job you love, but please, please don't forget that to marry you I need you alive.'

Those words haunted him day and night for he knew how badly she needed a man she could trust and love. She'd been robbed of the emotion as a child and he suspected that, coming as he did from such a settled and happy family life he did not quite understand her enough. He looked up at the large neo-Palladium façade of Thornbury Hall and felt the familiar flutter of pleasure in his stomach. It was his home. The warmth that enveloped him every time he came back was special and one day he'd nurture the Estate as his grandfather and father had done. He would bring up his children in the large echoing rooms and play all the childish games his parents had taught him. He sat up and looked towards the lake. How wonderful, he thought, to take them to smell the garlic in the woods in the spring and have picnics with them and Sarah by the lake in the summer. He fingered the unfinished article on his latest attack on the IRA and thought he was a fool to put all that at risk. Perhaps, he thought, I am becoming a bit too much like Sarah's father.

The sound of a car interrupted his thoughts. God, the ungrateful bastard had arrived. He heaved his bulk off the chair and waddled reluctantly to greet his guest.

James looked out of the car as he drew to a halt and watched with disgust as Henry came towards him. Shit, he's a fat slob! he thought, What on earth can Sarah see in him? He was jealous, full of envy and because he was blind to the fact it made a dangerous cocktail. The fat man represented a class he now despised and perhaps even worse he was attacking an organisation he now admired. James shuddered with excitement. Well the fat fucking slob was in for a surprise. He glanced over his shoulder at the black Head Bag and smiled.

Charged with adrenaline he jumped out of the car and stood hands on hips waiting for Henry to come to him. "Good of you to give me the time Henry." He said with a smile and holding out a hand. "Know how busy you are knocking those bastard in Ireland these days. Bloody good thing someone has the guts to tell the truth, but I just had to see you. Very, very important you see."

Henry tried to look pleased to see him as he took his hand. "There is always time to see an old friend," Henry assured him. "Come on up to the pool and have a drink and then we can talk. We will have no interruptions as the parents are out for the day." He wiped his forehead with a bright red handkerchief and added, "Getting quite hot eh?"

James winced at the strength of the handshake and thought. Hot for you no doubt fat slob. He said, "Yes indeed, but cooler than Lóndon." He bit his tongue. Shit he shouldn't have said that. Mary had told him not to let on where he'd been all these weeks. Ah well too fucking late now and anyway the slob probably wouldn't pick it up.

Henry had, but chose to ignore it, just as he did over James's changed appearance. The military style hair cut was gone and so were the immaculate clothes. Henry sniffed at his strong body odour and thought he looked an unwashed mess. It was totally out of character. When they reached the pool he waved towards a chair. "Take a seat James and I will get you a drink. Alcohol or something soft and long?"

Knowing he would need his wits about him James replied reluctantly, "Oh I'd better keep off the alcohol, so a long drink will do thanks."

"Fine, said Henry reaching for a jug on a table by his chair. "I've got a nice cold drink here. Much as I fancy a beer at this time of the day I find it sends me to sleep and I would hate to drop off while you were talking." He laughed lightly and past James a glass. "Right then, now perhaps you can tell me what this is all about and why you didn't want me to ring Sarah."

James took the glass and smiled weakly. He and Mary had rehearsed his story time and again. "Well you see I wanted to talk to a man. A woman just wouldn't understand, certainly not my sister and you know me Henry, never been much good at organising my life. I've become a bit of 'a spur of the moment man' you might say. I just walked out of Sarah's house a few weeks ago and met a girl. I have been shacked up with her ever since. I know I've been a bit of a bastard in not contacting Sarah but I'm sure you know how it is?"

Henry longed to say no he didn't and even if he had that would be no excuse for being such a selfish bastard by not contacting his sister. But he held back again and just nodding his head said, "Of course; but you have been a bit unkind to the poor girl. She's been worried sick."

"I'm sure and it was very wrong of me. Tell you what, I'll go and see her after I leave here tomorrow. Make it up to her; I'm sure she'll understand. You did say I could stay didn't you?"

"Of course."

James felt a great surge of relief. He wasn't sure what he'd have done if Henry had said 'no.' It was something he hadn't thought of. "Good. That will give us plenty of time to talk and perhaps you can advise me on how to placate my angry sister."

Henry chose not to tell James that Sarah was arriving in the morning and merely said, "Being the forgiving girl she is I doubt if you will run into much trouble especially as she will be so relieved to see you in one piece. Anyway we can talk about her later of you wish. For now let's concentrate on this girl. I presume one of the reasons you are here is that you don't think your father would approve and you want me to be your ambassador and go and see him?"

James smiled. "Something like that," he confirmed. "Certainly he would not approve of her, but no, I don't need you to be an ambassador."

Henry shuddered as he saw the hatred written all over his face. "This relationship could be what I've been waiting for all my life," James lied, "and I badly want Sarah's approval although I doubt I will get it. Perhaps mother's as well, but that's even more of an unlikely possibility. As for father I couldn't care less what he thinks. After the way he treated Sophie I would never again expose a girl to his vitriolic tongue. Anyway, as no doubt you know from my sister, he and I have parted company. I will not be inheriting Rosehall. Shit Henry you don't know how lucky you are to have decent parents. Christ mine have ruined my life!"

Henry felt little sympathy for James. He'd certainly had a difficult childhood, but he had contributed a lot to his own downfall ever since; and what was more he had a strong feeling James was lying through his teeth. He couldn't put a finger on it, but he had been avoiding eye contact ever since he'd arrived and Henry had learnt you couldn't trust anyone who had shifty eyes. But it was the wrong moment to challenge him. First he had to humour him, then perhaps the truth might slip out later. James had never been a very good liar. "Okay your parents will disapprove and Sarah will be hard to win round. What's with this girl? Is she that bad?"

James rubbed his chin. Shit, how he longed to wipe the smug look off Henry's face but he knew he must resist temptation and stick to what he and Mary had rehearsed. She had told him to keep as close to the truth as possible. 'Then there is little danger of contradicting yourself when you are asked questions at a later date.' "Well to start with she's an Irish Catholic," James went on. "She's small, intelligent, funny and shares many of my feelings. She too comes from a broken home and longs for a stable relationship. At the moment she works in a pub near Shaftsbury Avenue and she has a flat in Wandsworth." There, he'd shifted the locations as he'd been told. "I know nothing about her, but I like her. In fact I think I could be falling in love."

"Well don't you think it might be a good idea to find out a bit about her first? Like where's her home?"

'Be vague were possible,' Mary had advised him. "Frankly I don't really care, James said casually. "She's not asked me where I come from. We are just two people with secrets locked away in our hearts. I like that and I don't want to change it."

"Well if that's the way you feel so be it. After all it's your life. So, what you are telling me is that you want to live with her whatever happens?"

"Definitely. Fuck the shitty parents and Sarah as well if necessary. I think I deserve some happiness, don't you?"

Henry looked at him with something close to disgust. His callousness was nauseous and where on earth had he been to become so rough tongued? He would like to have known a lot more about this girl who had obviously had such an affect on him but he decided just to say, "I certainly do." It was better to keep his feelings to himself. There was nothing to be gained by antagonising James, but nevertheless he couldn't help adding, "I do wish you happiness but please, whatever you do, don't put Sarah through such hell again. She loves you, you know and I would find it very difficult to support you if you hurt her again."

"I know, and I promise I won't do anything to hurt her again. Is that good enough for you?"

"Of course," Henry replied being careful not to show his scepticism. My intuition tells me he's lying, Henry thought. I'm missing something here and it pisses me off. He lifted his glass to his lips convinced that within the last twenty-four hours two Hanmores had lied to him. Why? What would make Sarah lie to him? There was something going on he didn't like. He felt a growing sense of unease.

James watched Henry's large feet drumming on the canvas of the chair and the sweat pouring off the body that disgusted him so much. He suspected there was considerable doubt in Henry's mind about his story. Well too fucking bad slobo old boy, he thought, it doesn't matter a fuck!

Resigned to the fact that he was going to get no further information at least for the time being. Henry reached for the now tepid jug of fruit juice. "A fill up? Or shall we go into the house and open two bottles of cold beer? It's nearly six now so I think we can indulge ourselves in that small luxury before my parents return and start shouting for supper."

"Okay, a beer would taste fucking good now."

"Good, then let me get your bags from the car first."

James leapt to his feet. "No!" Said urgently, too urgently. A questioning look from Henry. "Sorry. I didn't mean to be rude. It's just that it is very hot and you looked bushed. Really I can manage on my own"

"Very well."

The palms of James's hands were ringing wet as he walked towards the Renault. Shit! He'd over re-acted. He had to keep himself under better control. Henry's job had trained him to smell a rat miles away. 'I can't afford too many mistakes like that,' he thought as he opened the car door and focussed on the Head bag innocently nestling on the back seat beside his other holdall. He froze for a second. This was no prac-tice run in the quiet of the flat, this was for real! Oh shit, how the fuck was he going to get through din-ner?

It was nearly half past seven when he walked into the drawing room. Standing by the fireplace, one elbow resting on the mantelpiece and one hand holding a crystal tumbler full of whisky was the imposing figure of Guy Marshall. Just over six feet tall and weighing almost two stones less than his son, he looked a lot younger than his fifty-eight years. At the other end of the room sat Henry, playing his usual pre dinner game of backgammon with his mother Madge. The two men were dressed in light weight tailor made beige jackets which covered identical blue Turnbull and Asser cotton shirts open at the neck. Henry wore a pair of dark blue trousers and his father wore green. Both pairs were immaculately pressed. Madge was in a light sack type multicoloured frock which could have come from Marks and Spencers but which had cost her a fortune from St Laurent. There was an air of wealth and comfortable companionship in the room.

James was quickly aware that his crumpled T-shirt and faded yellow cords did not fit into the surroundings and nor for that matter did he. The last thing he wanted was to be made to feel inferior by fatso's parents and only the thought of Mary's anger stopped him running from the room. His eyes took in his surroundings. Nothing seemed to have changed since his last visit. The eighteenth century furniture glistened with regular polishing. The magnolia coloured walls were hung with family portraits and a priceless Utrillo hung above the fireplace. If he'd harboured any regrets about walking away from his family he knew this would have been the moment. But all he felt was contempt for the man who was walking towards him with a smile on his face.

"James dear boy, so sorry, didn't see you standing there," said Guy Marshall. "Nice to have you here again. So what's your poison? I'm drinking whisky."

You fucking lying bastard, James thought You're not pleased to see me at all. A thin smile stretched across his face as he took Guy's proffered hand. 'Nice to see you too Guy and yes, a whisky will do fine."

Guy pointed to the drinks table. "Over there. Help yourself."

As James made his way to the table Madge came over and kissed him lightly on the cheek. "Hello James, it's been a long time." She had always disliked him, though when asked why by Henry she had not been able to give him a good reason. It was just something about his attitude that disturbed her 'Unstable,' she'd once called him and from what she'd heard recently she saw no cause to change her mind. All in all she felt it was going to be an awkward evening.

It had been three hours of hell. How he'd got through it without standing up and telling them they were all stuck up shits and he hated them, he would never know. Perhaps it was the knowledge of what was to come. Now at last in the solitude of his bedroom he could concentrate on more important matters than listening to fatso's father telling him about the troubles beleaguering the manufacturing industry and Henry pontificating about his next article in the Telegraph. And all the time he'd sensed Madge giving him disapproving glances. Why the silly old bitch she'd soon have the smirk jammed up her arse! Perspiration broke out on his forehead as he picked up the Head bag and pulled back the zip. His hands were steady as he dipped them into the bag and lovingly lifted the bomb, that Mary had made with such loving care, from its resting place. 'Oh shit, shit!' he thought excitedly, the bastards have no idea what's coming! He would have liked to have told them; seen the fear in their eyes; even heard them beg for mercy.

His hands were still steady as he checked the device. When he'd finished he glanced at his watch and was surprised to see it was not yet quite midnight. He would have to wait another hour just to make sure the house was asleep. Then like a ghost he would move down the stairs and plant the bomb. He knew the precise spot where it would do maximum damage. He gave a low laugh. What a pity he couldn't be around to see the carnage; to watch the house disintegrate before his eyes and to see the shock of those who came to the rescue, but were forced to stand and watch as the heat of the flames drove them back. For a moment he thought of Sarah. She would be devastated, but too bad. Mary had told him there had to be casualties in a war and sometimes inevitably it affected families

Of course no one would suspect him. Sarah and his parents had no idea he had been coming to see Henry. Or would he have told Sarah? He pursed his lips. The fat slob might just have done that, but no matter, he knew his parents. They would never be able to bring themselves to believe that he could kill Henry. He would at the very least have a breathing space and that was all he'd need.

He heard a clock strike midnight somewhere in the house. It was going to be a long hour. He chewed at a fingernail. Mary had told him the waiting would be the worst. 'That's when you begin to wonder if you have the guts to do it,' she'd told him. 'You may even wonder if you are doing the right thing and find yourself asking if you can live with the consequences. If you get through all that you may then start worrying about what could go wrong. I warn

you James your guts will probably turn to shit and
your resolve will probably be tested—it often happens the first time. If this is the case remind yourself
that you are killing an enemy of Ireland and that
nothing can go wrong. I know you can do it.'

He buried his head in the soft downy pillow and
understood what she'd meant. She was right,
conflicting emotions were already churning about
in his brain. He thought of Sarah mourning Henry's
death; she would grieve; she was in love; her life
would be in tatters, but she would recover. He thought
of the innocent caught in the blast; saw Madge's and
Guy's faces as they screamed with pain. He shook
himself violently. Fuck, what was he doing! He
couldn't care fucking less! He was a trained assassin
now, fearless and proud to serve the IRA. Mary had
told him he would be a hero and no longer live in
his father's shadow. Too fucking right he wouldn't!
His name would become part of Irish history. God,
he'd never imagined his life would turn out like this!
He couldn't lie still; a nerve twitched in his right leg.
He heard a clock strike one. Shit, it was time! He ran
to the bathroom clutching his stomach and threw
up in the sink. Jesus Mary had been right! He sat on
the green lavatory seat for several minutes while he
collected his thoughts. "Come on, come on!" he said
quietly to himself. "Don't fuck up now! Give it
another half hour just to be safe then make your
move." He rose slowly from the seat and moved back
into the bedroom. The sight of the bag seemed to
calm him. That was power—real fucking power! God
what a feeling!

He heard the half hour strike somewhere down
the passage and blew out his cheeks as he reached
for the bag. Time to strike, no more time to shit his

trousers and have doubts. He opened his bedroom door and looked out onto the darkened passage. He could see a light was still on downstairs but he'd have to risk it. If he was caught he'd just say he'd decided to go home. To abort, Mary had told him, would not be the end of the world as long as he got away without suspicion. There would be another time.

He walked carefully towards the stairs. The light was in the hall, a small table light obviously left on by a mistake. Nothing to worry about. Everything was quiet. He eased his way down the stairs and at the bottom he stopped and listened. Everything was still quiet. He gripped the bag and his other bag and moved towards the dining room and hiding place he'd chosen. The room was very dark. He felt his way towards the large French windows and placed the bag behind a curtain. He flicked on the timing switch—Mary had taught him to arm the bomb blindfolded—blew the shiny black bag a kiss and slowly and very carefully made his way out of the room.

Henry woke to the sound of a car engine. Hurrying to a window overlooking the drive he saw the figure of James illuminated by the security lights hurrying towards the Renault. 'Damn, the bugger's running,' he thought. 'Now I'll never get the chance to find out the truth.' He looked at his watch and knew he should ring Sarah and tell her not to come, but it was very late and besides he was longing to see her. He smiled as he turned away. Well at least he would now have her to himself. As he crawled back into bed a thought struck him. James had forgotten one of his bags. He shrugged. A small detail and anyway what the hell did it matter. If James had left one behind he'd give it to Sarah to take back to London.

Chapter Eight.

MARY woke with a pounding headache to the sound of the telephone ringing. Half asleep she fumbled for the light switch and almost fell out of bed in her hurry to reach the telephone. It could mean only one thing—James had fucked up. She glanced at her watch, it was one forty five am. Panic gripped her as she picked up the receiver. "Yes?"

"Mary, that you?"

"Who else you fucking bastard? What's happened? Fucked up?"

"Shit no! It's done!"

Anger replaced her panic. "You fool, get off the line! I told you only to ring if you'd encountered trouble. Now get your arse back here pronto!"

"Okay."

He sounded so deflated that she couldn't help adding. "Well done Jamie boy!"

The line went dead. She was shaking. Fuck, the bastard had given her a fright. What's more he had disobeyed her. She'd have to watch him carefully.

She remembered what Seamus had said and smiled. Probably this time no harm had been done, as she was sure her phone wasn't tapped. But it had served as a warning.

She made a cup of tea and shuffled back to bed. There wasn't much else to do until he arrived back. And as she lay staring at the ceiling she realised she wasn't experiencing the surge of adrenaline she'd have expected. It came as a shock. She'd spent months preparing for a moment like this, sweating her arse off in a crap of a bar so that she could be ready to press a button or pull a trigger and she felt what? Shit, empty. Perhaps it was because someone else had done the job? Yes, yes of course that was it. But as she tossed and turned a small voice in her head kept repeating her mother's warning. 'One day you will regret this road of violence you have taken and then my child you will turn to God. I can only pray that he will forgive you.'

It was a few minutes before nine in the morning when Sarah braked to a halt outside Thornbury Hall and smiled with pleasure as she saw the rotund figure of her fiancée standing by the open front door. Already the air was warm and sultry, the prelude to a storm later in the day and Henry was sweating profusely as he enveloped Sarah in his arms. His excitement made her feel good, she liked being loved by him. There were no complications in his love; it was simple and straightforward. She buried her head in his ample chest and breathed in the familiar aroma of Givenchy eau de toilet and sweat. Loving Henry meant getting used to his sweat, even on the coldest day he seemed to sweat. It tantalised her. It was so basically sexual and very much just him.

Reluctantly she pushed herself away from his hardness and whispered in his ear, 'Time for that later darling. Let's get this business with my brother over with first.'

Henry ruffled her hair and gave her a rather apologetic smile. "I'm sorry to have to tell you this but he buggered off early this morning. Just went without saying a word. God knows what the beggar's up to. All I can say is that I was most suspicious about his excuse for disappearing. It involved a girl, which of course came as no surprise, but somehow his story just didn't ring true. I'd hoped to get more out of him after he'd had a few drinks. But he was uneasy all evening as I'm sure you can understand with my parents being in attendance and after dinner he fled to his room without even saying good night."

Sarah gripped his arm and looked at him guiltily. "I'm not surprised he left, because he was lying to you. His disappearance did involve someone, but I don't know if it was a girl or not. In the context of what he's done it matters little."

Henry threw her a questioning look. "How do you know this?"

"I feel terrible about this darling. I should have told you over the telephone, but father had sworn me to secrecy. I was wrong though, very wrong. I have never lied to you before and you should have known."

"I had a feeling you were keeping something from me," said Henry. "Is it serious what you failed to tell me?"

"Very."

Henry touched her lips. "Very well, but don't tell me here. Let's go and have a cup of coffee inside and you can tell me everything then. It's getting too damned hot out here anyway."

They walked hand in hand into the dining room to find Guy and Madge sitting round the table finishing off their breakfast. Guy jumped to his feet and kissed her lightly on the cheek. "Lovely to see you Sarah, so much more pleasant than saying good morning to that difficult brother of yours."

Sarah gave Guy a wane smile and moved to sit down beside Madge. "Well I think he's blown it this time," she said sadly. "He's done something really terrible."

Madge patted her hand gently. "Perhaps you better tell us all about it my dear. Get it off your chest. I'm sure it will make you feel better. Get her cup of coffee will you Henry?"

As Henry moved towards the sideboard he noticed a bulge behind one of the French window curtains. Curious, he pulled back the fabric and stared down at a black Head Bag. He recognised it at once. "Ah," he said in a surprised voice, "why on earth would he leave it here?"

"Leave what dear?" asked Madge,

"James has left a bag behind the curtain here. Seems a funny place." He bent down and picked it up and was surprised by its weight. "Bloody heavy too. Well I suppose I might as well have a look inside. He's not here to tell me off after all." He unzipped the bag. His eyes widened in horror. "Oh my God!"

"What's the matter? What's in it?" Sarah asked, running towards him as soon as she saw the horror on his face.

Henry held up a hand. "Don't come any nearer for God sake!" He was struggling to keep his voice calm. "Just do as I say Sarah. Please just do as I say. I don't think there is time to ask any questions. Don't panic but get out of here, all of you, as quick as you can, and I mean FAST! Go on girl, don't just stand there. RUN!"

Sarah hesitated for only a split second. She had caught the note of urgency in his voice and instinctively knew by his reaction that the bag represented a terrible danger. She had such belief in Henry's capability to look after himself that she hardly gave him a thought, only thinking of his parents' safety. She whirled round and grabbed Madge by the arm. "Come on, you heard him, get the hell out of here both of you!" She dragged Madge towards the door pushing Guy in front of her as she went. As she reached the door she looked round at Henry and saw him struggling to open the glass doors of the French windows.

It was his only way out. If he ran back into the house he'd risk cutting off Sarah and his parents. The double glazing stopped him from hurling the bag through the window. He had to open the doors. To his frustration the palms of his hands were wet with sweat as he fumbled with the catch. How long had he got? He heard the relentless ticking from the bag and swore loudly. They were the last sounds he was ever to hear.

He was blown apart; his flesh and bones scattered to all corners of the room, turning the walls red with his blood. The blast caught the others a few inches short of the door. The force of the blast picked up their bodies as if they were paper dolls and hurled them across the floor crushing the life out of them before they came to rest against a wall. Rankin, the butler, had a second to gaze in horror at their flailing limbs before the huge glass chandelier, hanging above the hall, broke away from the ceiling and crashed down on his skull. Within minutes of the explosion the bodies were incinerated and the tentacles of flames, were roaring up the stairs.

The explosion was heard several miles away. And although one of the estate workers rang the fire brigade as soon as he saw the first flames the Hall was beyond saving by the time the fire fighters arrived. All the men could do was damp down the stable block so that it did not suffer the same fate as the main building and watch as the Hall crumpled before their horrified eyes. By mid day it was a blackened shell with five mutilated corpses lying somewhere in the smouldering ruins.

The BBC One news flash confirmed it. With a shout of excitement James threw his cup of tea across the room and pulled Mary into his arms. "Fuck in hell I did it!" he exclaimed excitedly.

Mary looked at his flushed face and smelt his stale breath wafting over her face and felt like puking. She should have felt the same excitement coursing through her veins. Instead there was just the numbness she was growing used to. But she was well aware that he'd expect her to be full of praise, and why not? After all she'd trained the bastard and sent him to his target. "Well done Jamie, you did it!" She tried, oh God how she tried to make it sound right.

He smiled at her—it was almost a leer. "Well that will serve the bastard right eh Mary?"

"By Jesus indeed it will! Now I must be going to ring the papers so that the British bastards know that no one can fuck with the IRA and get away with it. It's too risky to use this phone. So you stay here and rest up and I'll be back soon." 'Please God don't let him say he'll come too,' she thought. But she needn't have worried. He was far too high on his success to worry what she was doing.

She almost ran out of the flat, so keen was she get away from him. Everything was wrong. The adrenaline should have been flowing. The carnage should have thrilled her, but what did she feel? As she jumped onto a passing bus she was shocked to realise it was something horribly close to guilt. Christ what was happening to her!

She chose a kiosk a mile away from the flat. Dialled the number of the Daily Telegraph and gave the code that would confirm IRA responsibility for the bombing. She finished by saying, "Let that be a lesson to you meddling fucking reporters. The next one who dares to question our right to fight for freedom will be blown sky high just like Marshall." She slammed the receiver down and hurried back onto the street. It wouldn't do to hang around in the location too long but she decided it would be safe to walk back. She needed a little time on her own, away from the blood thirsty gloating that she knew would greet her as soon as she walked back into the flat.

It took her a long time to walk the mile home. It was a mile that she was never to forget, for in the forty five minutes it took her to walk from the kiosk to the door of the flat, her whole reason for living, that she feared had been shifting ever so slowly, suddenly gathered pace. It would not be right to say that she was completely turning her back on the war she had so vehemently supported but she was getting damned fucking close. What puzzled her was why. Ah that is still the mystery Mary O'Neill, she thought miserably. But for sure girl you will be soon

finding out and when you do, by Jesus you are going
to be in a right terrible mess.

Commander Tim Roberts had witnessed some
shocking IRA atrocities in the five years since he'd
been in the anti terrorist squad, but this one was high
on his list of mindless carnage. After each attack he
vowed to resign from the Force and find a quieter
job, but his determination to bring what he called
'the murderous bastards to justice' always stopped
him. This time would be no different in spite of the
now familiar pleas of his parents to come and help
them run their newsagents in Brighton 'and forget
those vile people from across the water.'

It was three in the afternoon as he stood on the
stage of Thornbury Village Hall and gazed down from
his considerable height at the crowd of journalists
eagerly awaiting his report. Rumour had it that a sen-
sation was on the way. There was sadness in his eyes
for all to see as he fumbled with some papers and
cleared his throat. A deathly hush fell over the room.

"Good afternoon ladies and gentlemen." His
voice broke as he continued, "Once more we are
faced with the slaughter of innocent people. All because one man had the guts to print the truth about
a rotten Organisation". He took a deep breath. He
knew they didn't want to hear the usual condemna-
tions, nor did they care about his emotions. They
were bored with things like that—they only wanted
the story. That's what would sell their papers. He
continued. "The facts are these. At a little after nine
this morning an IRA bomb exploded in Thornbury
Manor killing four people whom have been identified. They are Henry Marshall, his parents and the

butler. However we fear there is a fifth as yet uni-
dentified body."

A buzz went round the room. This was what they
wanted to hear. A familiar female voice asked, "Why
do you think this and have you any idea who it might
be?"

He had a very good idea, but he was not certain
enough to give the assembled company news that
would change the whole tragic scenario and hand
the IRA an unexpected propaganda coup. He gave
a sad little nod to the girl from The Telegraph who
had worked along side Marshall for the last year. "Yes
Jane, I have an idea and the reason why we think
there is another body is because there was a car
parked outside the house which did not belong to
the family. As no one has come forward to claim the
car we fear the owner may have perished in the explosion. That is as much as I am prepared to say at
the moment. However let me assure you I will call
you back here as soon as we know anything, whatever the time."

A murmur went round the room. They knew him
well. He could be trusted. They trudged reluctantly
out of the Hall, all making wild guesses amongst
themselves as to who the fifth victim might be.

Tim waited for the hall to empty before moving
across to the stable block and into a packed incident
room. A young constable was waiting to hand him a
message. "For you sir and urgent." Tim's hands were
visibly shaking as he took the piece of paper. The
words jumped out at him, *"Forensic confirm a fifth body.
Identified by the teeth as that of Sarah Hanmore."*

It was at times like these that Tim hated being a
copper. He knew Sarah well. He'd been one of Sir
Richard's security team for a year. If time and cir-

cumstances had allowed he'd have gone to Rosehall and broken the news himself, but he didn't have the time. He would send a trusted colleague from the Yard immediately. In spite of his promise to the journalists he reckoned he could hold back the press conference for a few hours so as to give the family some peace before the news broke.

Once he'd made the call and several other vital arrangements he took time off to sit at a makeshift desk and sip a cup of tea. He looked round the room at the sombre faces of his team and the shocked faces of the local force, who unlike his hardened team had never seen such horrors. He wondered how much longer the carnage would have to carry on before someone came to their senses. He'd seen so many young people die and listened to the sobbing of their families standing over the coffins. He'd felt their pain, their anger and sometimes taken their abuse. He crashed his cup down onto the plastic top of the desk and swore loudly. Surely there had to be a better way. Surely the evil men, probably at this very moment planning their next atrocity, would one day see that the only way to settle their differences was to talk. Arms, bombs, torture. None of these things would ever succeed.

He felt a tap on his shoulder. "Telephone Commander." He took the receiver. It was the Yard. The Hanmores had been informed of their daughter's death. It was almost as if they had been expecting it. Tim was not surprised. They would have known where she was. He looked at his watch. "Okay everyone listen up. Press Conference in two hours. In that time I want everyone, and I mean everyone, in the village and anyone living within hearing distance of the main road interviewed before I give out the name of the fifth person to have been killed. Once this story breaks I fear we may not get accurate information. I want to know if anyone heard or saw a car being driven at speed in the London direction in the early hours of this morning. Right, get to it."

One of his team asked, "Do you think the bomber planted the bomb this morning Commander?"

"It's a pretty good guess Derek. You know the form. Most times the bombers are still in the vicinity when the target is attacked."

It was six in the evening. Tim was back on the stage having delayed the press conference as long as he could. Once again he gazed down on the hundreds of expectant faces, (the crowd had grown considerably since the morning conference) and wished they would all evaporate into thin air. He had no wish to ruin the privacy of mourning and yet his job dictated that he should. And by God the Hanmores privacy was about to be shattered for a long time. Marshall's death was front page stuff, but Sarah Hanmore's death was sensational. The evening and morning papers would be full of nothing else. But that was nothing to the rejoicing of the IRA High Command. How many times had they tried to assassinate Hanmore while he'd been in office and failed? And now, just a piece of bad timing had delivered them a member of the family. It was a triumph they would long remember. He thought of the girl's voice that had claimed responsibility for Marshall's death. If she'd had any idea that Sarah's body had lain amongst the smouldering ruins of Thornbury she would have gloated. God, it had been a stroke of bad luck.

He tapped the table in front of him. "Ladies and gentlemen thank you for coming back. I can now tell you that there definitely was a fifth victim. It was Henry Marshall's girl friend Sarah Hanmore."

Within thirty seconds the Hall was empty.

Richard had been holding Blanche's hand for hours. She had made no attempt to pull away. She knew he needed her strength, for she feared his was not enough on its own to face up to the awful fact of Sarah's death and the terrifying thought that their son might be involved.

Her red rimmed eyes looked at him as she said, "We should have told Henry about that letter Richard. Dear God we could be responsible for our daughter's death, not to mention Henry and his family. Can we live with this! Can we?"

Richard gripped her hand harder and shook it gently. "Now listen Blanche, you must not think like that. We have no proof at all that James had anything to do with this dreadful thing. A letter is very different from actually planting a bomb to kill people."

"But we can't just forget the possibility for heaven sake! We must accept that at least. We must tell the police of our suspicion. It is our duty."

"No, no! We will not say a word. There is no way our son would do a thing like that. No way we could have stopped the tragedy happening. If we say anything to the police it will only point them down the wrong alley. No, no, we say nothing."

Blanche released his hand and looked at him aghast. "I can't agree. We must show the letter to the police. We must face up to our responsibilities whatever the outcome."

He raised his hand as if to hit her. Dropped it limply by his side and began to cry. "God, I never thought I would ever think of doing that!" he cried. "What on earth is happening to us Blanche?"

"What is happening to us Richard is quite clear. We had two children who we should have loved and taken care of. Instead we employed numerous nannies while you were building your career. The result was we neglected them when they most needed us. Sarah was able to cope with her our constant neglect and still loves us. James, sadly has been the opposite and has become bitter and twisted. Now we are paying the price. We have just lost the one who loved us, and the one who survives may well have been implicated in some way in her death. In short our world is falling apart."

Chapter Nine

JAMES lay panting on top of her, his weight pushing her back into the thin mattress. She could feel the unforgiving springs biting into her buttocks and spine. She looked at his face, reddened by his exertions, smiling down triumphantly on her. The silent television blinked behind them.

He'd fucked her as soon as she'd returned. Perhaps 'raped' would have been a better word. He had used brute strength. She could probably have fought him off but she'd figured it was best not to resist. Better to humour him. He'd ripped off her clothes, entered her with a cry of excitement and pumped energetically away. Thankfully it had been over in seconds.

As he went to move away she reached up and clasped his face in her hands. She didn't want him to go and leave her lying there like one of his whores. How different he was to the last time they had lain together. Then they had come together in the ecstasy of what she had foolishly thought was a growing affection for each other. He tried to push her hands away but she held on tight. "Not yet James. Please not yet! For some unexplainable reason she wanted to believe he cared for her. She whispered in his ear, "Don't you be thinking you can treat me like a whore!"

His smile said it all. There wasn't a trace of affection in his eyes. The bastard didn't care. He was too intoxicated by his morning's work. She pushed him away with a cry and rolled off the bed just in time to see the face of Richard Hanmore on the television screen. "What the fuck!" she exclaimed as she rushed to turn up the sound. The news reader was saying, "It has just been announced by the officer in charge of the Marshall murders that a fifth body has been found in the ruins of Thornbury Hall. It has been confirmed as the body of Sarah Hanmore, daughter of the ex Northern Ireland Secretary. We will now go over live to the Press Conference at Thornbury Village Hall."

In one swift movement Mary ripped the television cord from the socket. "Jesus!" She looked round at James. His face was as white as a sheet. "Shit!" he gasped. "Bloody shit! What was she doing there!"

Mary's stomach churned. Brought up as she had been to accept violence as a necessity this was something she had not expected and her first reaction was to rush towards him and take him in her arms. He'd told her they had been very close. "Jesus James I'm sorry, so very sorry. I know how much you loved her and I would never have sent you had I known she'd be there."

"She shouldn't have got in the way should she."

Mary reeled away and stared at him in disbelief. "But you loved her for Christ sake! You have told me that dozens of times."

He shook his head. "I did once, but you told me to cut myself off from my family so the love was dying anyway. Besides it may be good she's dead."

"What do you mean?" she asked in amazement.

"Don't you see Mary? It will probably destroy my father. He loved her you see. Perhaps even with luck it might kill the bastard!"

Mary managed to mumble, "But she was not supposed to be there. She did not deserve to die in such a way."

She watched a smile spread across his face. "That comes rich from you! You have preached nothing but violence to me and now you are shedding a tear over a woman you didn't even know? What's so different about her than the Marshall family? Why are you going soft over her?"

She looked away from him because she didn't know the answer. Was she going soft? Was this just a progression of her earlier thoughts? Jesus, Mary O'Neill, what's happening to you? she thought. You can't afford to go soft in this game and certainly not in front of the man you have trained to be a killer. Sort yourself out girl!

When she had control of herself she turned to face him once again. He was standing hands on hips waiting for her answer. "No James, I be not going soft, but I do feel sadness for the innocent caught up in this war." As soon as she'd said it she realised she'd made a mistake.

"But that's balls! Only a short while ago you were telling me that innocent people must die in a war. So what's changed you so suddenly?"

Lost for words, furious at showing him a weakness, and irrationally blaming him for the hatred that was haemorrhaging out of her, she lost control and threw herself at him with a cry of despair, racking her nails across his face. She wanted to wipe the grin off his face. She wanted to hurt the man she'd turned into a monster.

Taken by surprise James cried out with pain before shouting, "Why you fucking little bitch! Grabbing her hair he pushed her onto the floor and threw himself on top of her, sinking his teeth into her shoulder until he tasted her warm blood. Memories flooded back of his frenzied attacks on prostitutes and he rained blows down on Mary's head.

She thought she was about to die but she didn't cry out or fight back. She had a feeling that her only hope was to be passive. Then she felt his penis harden and thrust between her thighs. It was all she could do not to tear at his flesh. She didn't want him inside her again, but when his warm semen shot into her womb she couldn't help crying out. He took it to be a cry of pleasure and he thrust once more deep inside her before rolling off her and lying spread-eagled on the floor. She cried silently beside him, her body aching from his blows and his semen running down her thighs. At that moment her mother's words rang clearly in her head and she sat up and spat over his naked body. He didn't move. To her astonishment he was out to the world.

She lay for some time listening to his even breathing wondering what to do. Her mind was telling her that the planned killing of Richard Hanmore would for her be a killing too far. It came as a terrible shock to her. For why the fuck should she care about Hanmore? The answer was she didn't.

It just happened to be a killing too far. Jesus how
could she think like this! But as she lay biting at a
nail the answer became quite clear. She was more
like her mother than she'd ever been prepared to
admit and she'd seen two men turned on by killing.
That was wrong. You killed only for a purpose, not
for the glorification of the act. She ground her teeth.
To make matters worse she feared she was pregnant.
Holy Mary you're in a mess girl, she thought ruefully.
It would be the devil's child for sure. She would be
damned before God. Once she wouldn't have cared
but now her emotions were fucked. She was on the
verge of an enormous change of heart and she was
probably carrying James's child. Not that she would
live long enough to give birth if she aborted the
attempt on Hanmore's life. The IRA would have no
sympathy. Well that would solve all her problems!

But as she lay bruised and mentally in torment
she realised she didn't want to die. Why? She wasn't
sure. After all her future was pretty bleak. So what
could she do to survive? She could kill James now—
she'd have no difficulty doing that! She could run
from the flat and if she was lucky his body wouldn't
be found for days. The Wellington didn't know where
they were living. And it would take the IRA some
time before they started worrying about their
operative. Yes, she'd certainly have time to make a
run for it, but where could she run and hope to
survive? The IRA was well known for catching up with
their rebellious operatives. She really was going crazy!
Look girl you hate the British. You hate them
occupying your country! That hasn't changed and
yet . . . She shook her head. Nothing made sense
anymore. She thought of her father. Thought of all
the times she'd sat at Seamus's knee and thrilled to

his stories of killings. Thought of how she'd ignored her mother's advice and dreamt of one day being like her father and Seamus so that she could avenge her parents' deaths. Think girl think. But the more she thought the more she knew she'd changed. She wrung her hands and looked up to the ceiling. "Oh dear God," she said out loud. "What on earth have You done to me?"

She stood up and looked down on James's inert body. Killing him was not the answer, tempting as the idea was. A plan was forming in her mind, much more subtle than a cold blooded killing and it would give her a better chance of survival. She crossed herself and couldn't help a little smile, wondering if her mother was watching.

She dug a foot into James's ribs. He groaned. She shook his shoulder. He looked at her through half closed eyes. "What the fuck?"

She mustn't show any hostility. She needed to regain his confidence. "I'm sorry I attacked you. I was just being stupid. You did well today. As for your sister, well if you don't care why the fuck should I? It's just one less Hanmore on this earth and that must be good."

He looked surprised. "You really mean that? Just now you gave me the opposite impression."

She swallowed hard and forced herself to lie. "I know, I was a bit shaken by the news, honestly believing that you would be devastated and that I would lose you. But I can understand your logic now that you have embraced the cause. You have become like me and that is good. Now together we can finish the job and you will become a hero of the nationalist cause"

He shuddered with excitement and asked, "What more do I have to do to become a hero?"

She'd deliberately never told him the real target. She'd seen no point until he'd been tested. Well he'd certainly been that! Now there seemed little doubt what his answer would be.

"You must assassinate your father."

"Kill Father!"

"Yes. Can you do it?"

"Too bloody right I can! Oh shit, I can't wait!"

She forced a smile, hiding the revulsion that was churning in her stomach. "I thought you would like the idea. My only regret is that I have been denied the chance to pull the trigger. But orders are orders. You are a lucky man."

He kissed her hard on the mouth before saying, "Shit, a hero! A hero of the IRA! I only wish father would be alive to hear it! But then you can't have everything can you?"

Indeed you can't Jamie boy, Mary thought. Dream while you can you bastard for the only hope you have is to die a martyr and if I have my way your chances of that are going to be fucking slim!

Chapter Ten

BLANCHE sat at the dining room table reading the report of the bombing in The Daily Telegraph. She'd read it at breakfast every day for a week. It had become like a drug to her. She knew she should tear it to shreds before it destroyed her. Perhaps just once more and then she'd throw it away. Through tear swollen eyes (she'd hardly stopped crying since Sarah's death), she stared at the front page headlines.

FAMILY AND BUTLER SLAIN IN
GLOUCESTER MANSION

SIR RICHARD HANMORE'S DAUGH-
TER AMONGST THE DEAD

IRA CLAIM RESPONSIBILITY

There were three pages of photographs, reports and obituaries. Every word on each page she knew by heart. Every page was stained with her tears. She cried out and threw the paper angrily to the floor, burying her head in her shaking hands. She wondered if she would ever be able to sleep without waking from the nightmare of smelling Sarah's burning body. It had been so badly mutilated that she and Richard had been unable to identify her. She couldn't help thinking that perhaps if they had told Henry about the letter Sarah might still be alive. It was not a thought she could share with Richard and that made her pain even worse.

She rose stiffly from the table, having half heartedly chewed on a piece of brown toast(she couldn't remember when she'd last eaten a decent meal), and wandered into the garden where she knew Richard would be walking aimlessly, trying to rid himself of his guilt and grief. On the night of the tragedy they had tried to make love, hoping that they might find some solace from their devastation. As their bodies had touched they had pulled away aghast that they had considered taking part in the act that had created their daughter on the day she'd been brutally murdered. They had been so affected by what they considered was such a disloyal act that they had not slept together since. Each night they kissed on the landing and retired to separate rooms, both missing the touch of each others body.

Blanche spotted Richard sitting on a bench under a large Oak tree and gave a little wave, which he returned. He'd changed the last few days, almost regaining his gentleness that she so loved. She knew how much of an effort he was making and as she stood smiling at him she decided it was time for her to pull herself together. She knew they would never forget the horrors or rid themselves of their guilt but they needed each other more than ever. "I'll be over in a minute," she shouted and turned back into the house. Firstly she went into the dining room and picked up the discarded Telegraph and began to tear it into shreds. That task completed she went upstairs to the room where Richard had been sleeping and began to pick up his belongings and take them back into their bedroom. Lastly she returned his pillows to his side of the bed. As she walked out of the room she swore she saw the dragons smiling.

Blanche and Richard sat on one of the two sofas in the Rosehall drawing room listening nervously to Tim Roberts. He was sitting opposite them in an upright chair saying, "We are no nearer finding the bomber I'm sorry to say. But as you well know Sir Richard these things take time but eventually a mistake will be made and we will make an arrest. Not all the young idealists working for the IRA are that good at wiping out their tracks and we do have informers within their ranks." Then leaning forward and looking hard at Richard he asked quietly, "Any word from your son yet?"

"Richard shook his head. "Not a word, but that's no surprise to us. He's been gone a long time now but you can be sure he's read of Sarah's death and I'm sure he will be at. her funeral. Whenever that may be," he added in a sad voice. "Anyway Tim he won't be able to shed any light on the case. He's strange I grant you, but no murderer. From what we hear he will almost certainly have been in bed with some prostitute at the time of the explosion. Sorry we can't help further."

Quick to notice the look of unease that Blanche threw at Richard, he thought, you are hiding something, but chose to ignore it. There would be another time, for James was still very much on his mind.

"We lied to him."

Richard nodded at Blanche. "Yes we did, and for good reason. Like us Tim is uneasy about James not getting in touch with us. He puts more into that than we do at the moment. Okay I grant you his behaviour has been very strange, but I think we have struggled with our guilt quite enough already." And then his voice broke. "Oh God Blanche what did you expect me to do? Tell him our son is a murderer? We have no proof, no proof. I just cannot make myself say the words, 'we think he might be the killer.' He's our son for God sake!"

Blanche thought, I've been through this all before and I don't see any point in going over old ground. There is nothing to be gained. She took Richard's head gently in her hands and said firmly, "I agree. We say nothing. We deal with this in our own way. And besides nothing will bring back our Sarah."

Richard pulled away and smiled at her. "Do you know what I think? I believe that if he killed Sarah his conscience will bring him here eventually. He won't be able to live with her death on his conscience without telling someone. In the end it will be his father he will confess to and of course I will turn him in. But he will come to the funeral, I know he will, and that will prove to me that he is innocent"

Blanche stared at him in amazement. "Oh Richard darling you are being utterly naive. Do you honestly believe that James will come to you of all people? Can't you see that he hates you? Why else would he write such a letter? For a man of your intelligence you are being very stupid. We both know why neither of us wish to voice our suspicions to Tim. It is quite simply because James is our son and only child left alive. We also feel partly responsible for what he has turned out to be. However much we resent his behaviour, however much we despise him, we want to protect him. God knows why! No. no, that is wrong. Of course we know why—or at least I do. Parents don't want to believe that one of their children is a killer! But that said, we have our suspicions, and if you think James will come to you admitting his guilt than I think you are kidding yourself. Sadly I'm afraid I believe that if he comes at all it will be with mischief on his mind. Think about it. If he can kill his sister in cold blood......"

Richard held up his hands. "Oh God don't say that! Please, please can we leave it for now? It is pointless torturing ourselves further. But I promise I will speak to Tim if James doesn't turn up for the funeral. That will be the test." Then throwing a look of desperation at Blanche he gasped, "Oh God I hope he turns up!" and began to cry. Long choking sobs, well overdue. She pulled him close and began to gently stroke his greying hair. She suspected he'd already made up his mind about James and was too frightened to voice his opinion. She understood how he felt. It was not easy to accept that your son was capable of killing his own flesh and blood. She said quietly, "I know how you feel and I share your distress and guilt. I will do as you wish. We will see this through together and hopefully be stronger at the end. But if James doesn't come to the funeral I will hold you to your promise."

He watched her unwrap the sawn off 12 bore shotgun from its oily rag. It was to be his weapon. He smelt the oil and shivered. He couldn't wait. "You know how to use one of these no doubt?" Mary asked.

He nodded.

"Good. Normally it would be too large a weapon, difficult to hide, but you will have no problem in getting into the house. Your father will be only too pleased to see you and not looking for a shotgun hidden under your coat. For sure he will be longing for you to say you had nothing to do with your sister's death."

"It will be a piece of cake," James said with a smile. I'm sure there will be no security around the house because my father got rid of that as soon as he'd retired from government, and even if my letter has made him suspicious he will not have said a word to the police. He is too proud to admit to anyone that his son might be a killer and by the time he realises I have not come to mourn the death of Sarah it will be too late. Shit, I can't wait to see his face. To see the fear in his eyes when he knows he is going to die. I want him on his knees begging me to forgive him for all the years of hell he has put me through." He reached out and stroked the barrel of the gun. "God, I can't wait to pull the trigger!"

Mary shivered.

A whispered "proceed" into Mary's ear at the Wellington was the beginning.

That same night just in case the Renault had been spotted by someone at Thornbury it was spirited away to be replaced by a blue Ford Fiesta. The next day all bomb making equipment and guns, except for the shotgun and Mary's Walther PPK, were removed from the flat and Mary and James scrubbed the flat clean, wiping away any evidence that might link it to an IRA active unit. Everything was now ready for the hit.

Mary knew there could be no turning back. She felt strangely lost, unable to understand why she wasn't thrilled that her plan was about to be put into action. For most of her life she had waited for the chance to strike a blow for a free Ireland, but instead of excitement all she felt was a sort of numb feeling inside her stomach. As she did so often these days she thought of her mother saying to her, 'Mark my word girl whatever your father may want you to believe let me be telling you that things seldom turn out the way you want them to.' Mary shrugged her shoulders, forcing her mother out of her mind. There was no more time for thinking—her decision had been made. She tucked the PPK into the top of her trousers and looked in disgust at James still naked and asleep on the bed. Jesus, thank God it was the last time!

It was a glorious mild autumn morning and the swallows were lining up on the telephone wires outside the flat making plans to migrate to warmer climes. The air was fresh, the heat of the summer having past. It was a day for most people to treasure, but not for Mary. For her it would be a day of violence, a prelude to an uncertain future. The contrast was not lost on her as she pulled back from the window and moved to wake James. She shuddered as she touched him. It surprised her how much she hated him. Once she'd thought she might even grow to love him, but now she blamed him for all her troubles. He'd had no right, no fucking right at all to change her. And he didn't even know what he'd done! She touched her stomach, not yet extended, but nurturing a foetus she didn't want. Jesus! How could she have been so stupid!

James stirred. She spat on his stomach and turned away. Her life was a mess. Her mother would probably say she deserved it.

At about the time that Mary's saliva was running down James's stomach, Tim Robert's was easing his large frame out of his squad car. The benign façade of Rosehall gazed down at the frenzied activity. It was three hours to the funeral. Tim reflected that the Hanmores had certainly had a long wait to bury the remains of their daughter. It could not have been easy for them.

It had been a very depressing week. Three days earlier he'd been in Manchester burying Rankin, the butler and the next day he'd been at the graveside of the Marshalls. That had given him only a little over twenty four hours to fine tune the security arrangements for Sarah's funeral, which were turning into something akin to a nightmare, as Richard, despite Tim's urging, had refused to have a small private funeral. "We have no family," he'd said by way of an explanation, "and anyway I'm damned if I'm going to bury my daughter in secret because of the IRA."

Tim quite understood, but thought Richard was being fool hardy, especially as what he'd feared most had happened. The Prime Minister and nearly the whole bloody cabinet were coming, not to mention the Leader of the Opposition, The Duke of Kent and a large contingent of MPs from all parties. The lessons to be learnt from the Brighton bombing were never underestimate the capability of the IRA to strike at will, and try not to encourage large gatherings of VIPs at events that might catch the IRA's eyes. Sarah's funeral definitely came into that bracket, but Tim had no intention of allowing them a free entry ticket. So security had to be as water tight as possible. Every road within a radius of ten miles of Rosehall Church was being watched. Side roads, much to the annoyance of many locals, were to be closed for three hours from eleven in the morning. The grounds of Rosehall were swarming with special branch officers and armed marksmen were strategically placed on house roofs overlooking the Church. Even Sarah's open grave was guarded. But still Tim felt he hadn't done enough.

He couldn't put a finger on it, but he had a gut feeling something was not right. He'd had the same feeling once before and had ignored it. He'd nearly died. He spoke urgently into his mobile phone. "I want the fields nearest the house thoroughly searched. I don't care if this has already been done, it must be done again. Request another helicopter to join the one already hovering above the village and make sure that six armed officers stay in the house while we are in the Church." He pushed the phone into his pocket and started to walk towards the house feeling he'd done all he could to protect the Hanmores and their guests. He knew he was

good, but he never underestimated such a dangerous enemy.

The Church was full. Those that were unable to
get a seat stood outside where loudspeakers had been
set up to relay the service. As the Hanmores took
their seats Tim slipped into the pew behind them.
He suspected the chances of an IRA strike were
pretty small inside the Church but he was taking no
chances. He glanced across at the Duke sitting between his two bodyguards and then he looked at the
Prime Minister and members of his cabinet. He had
twelve plain clothes policemen scattered round the
Church and six armed officers hidden in the Church
grounds. He was as secure as he could be. But he
was still nervous, not least because there was no sign
of James Hanmore. That young man worries me, he
thought. But of course there could be a rational explanation. After all I put a stop on all press announce-
ments about the funeral. How could the young man
know?' He gave a rueful smile. He'd handed Richard the perfect answer when he was questioned as
to his son's absence.
    The coffin was carried into the Church by four
members of the Rosehall staff at two minutes past
midday. Tim watched Richard's shoulders droop and
Blanche's hand shoot out to steady him as the coffin
past their pew. Thank God for Lady Hanmore, he
thought, remembering his conversation of earlier in
the morning when Richard had told him he had
nothing more to live for. 'Better to have an assassin's
bullet through my brain or die today from another
heart attack than live a few more years of hell', he'd
said quietly to Tim. His reply had not perhaps been

the most tactful coming from an ex bodyguard but he'd felt it needed saying. 'You have Lady Hanmore to live for surely?' Richard had stared at him for several seconds before replying, 'You are quite right commander. Thank you for reminding me.'

"We meet here today to thank God for the short life of Sarah Hanmore." The vicar's voice cut into Tim's thoughts. How he hated anything to do with death. Perhaps it was time to quit the Force, marry and have kids. The violence of the last few years was beginning to take its toll and it would not be too late to start a new career.

The vicar's voice was a little unsteady as he read the opening prayers and Tim realised he was affected just as much by the poignancy of the moment as the congregation. Tim swore he could see the relief on the man's face as he sat down and the Prime Minister slowly climbed into the pulpit vigorously polishing his glasses. He nodded at Richard and began to read the poem by Bishop Brent that always brought tears to Tim's eyes.

'What is dying?

I am standing on the seashore. A ship sails and spreads her white sails to the morning breeze and starts for the ocean.'

Tim watched Blanche fumbling for a handkerchief in her bag.

'She is an object of beauty and I stand watching her until at last she fades on the horizon, and someone at my side says, 'she is gone.'

Gone where?

Gone from my sight, that is all;

She is just as large in the masts, hull and spars as she was when I saw her, and just as able to bear her load of living freight to its destination. The diminished size and total loss of sight is in me, not in her, and just at the mo-

ment when someone at my side says, 'She is gone,'
there are others who are watching her coming, and
other voices take up a glad shout 'There she comes,'
  And that is dying.

As the Prime Minister walked slowly, head bowed, back to his pew the only sound to be heard in the Church was Blanche crying.

Mary drove.

She turned off the M3 at junction 9 as her watch read two seventeen. She glanced at James sitting hunched up beside her. She'd watched him drink too much the night before and hadn't bothered to try and stop him. What did she care if he fucked up. She poked at his shoulder. "Which way now?"

He shook his head and winced. "Christ my head feels as if it's going to fall off."

"Too fucking bad lover boy! Now which way?"

"Fucking slave driver," he moaned and pointed at the sign post. "Follow A31, says Petersfield and Alton. Christ I need a drink!"

"Well you're not having one! You need a clear head and steady hands, so you had better sober up fast."

"I'm sober enough to kill the bastard, don't you fucking worry!" He drew his knees up under his chin and closed his eyes. What was it with this woman? Where had the affection gone? Why was she so antagonistic towards him? It pissed him off.

He was quietly fuming over her behaviour when she prodded his arm. "Lots of police cars about" There was a hint of nervousness in her voice. "Are there normally as many in this part of Hampshire?"

Angrily he hissed, "Fucking hell I don't know, and does it really matter?"

He was sulking. Shit, perhaps she shouldn't have told him off. Better try and get him back on her side. "I'm sorry if I have seemed a bit off just lately but this operation is so important to me. Please try and understand. I'll be okay once it's all over. In the meantime we need to work together, not fight. So please try to get your mind back onto the task at hand." She bit her lip as two more patrol cars past her. "That makes seven cars and three motor bikes since we turned off the motorway. I don't like this. If you ask me something is going on. Probably nothing to do with us, but all these police scare the shit out of me. Is there anywhere we can stop before we reach your village? Perhaps we can find out what if anything is going on."

"Alresford." Then thinking he should be a bit more helpful he added, "about five miles from here."

"Okay, we will stop there and I will make a few enquiries. There is probably a rational explanation, like a fucking Royal being in the vicinity, but I want to be sure it is nothing more, for let me tell you James so many coppers make me feel nervous."

James grunted. Frankly he thought she was being fucking stupid, but he'd humour her if that was what she wanted. His father wasn't going to suddenly disappear.

Alresford was packed with people, making Mary even more nervous. "Shit!" she said quietly as she turned down Broad Street, one of the busiest roads in the little town. She looked around for a parking space and swore loudly. "Now what do we do?"

"Double park by that hardware shop." James said, pointed at a building a few yards away. "It will only take a second to find out if anything is going on. I'll jump out, and you can move if you have to. I'll find you."

"That is not a good idea! For Christ sake you might run into someone you know!" Mary drew to a halt. "There is only one answer. It has to be me." Before he could start to argue she opened her door. "Okay I'm off. If anyone tries to move you on just stall."

With a sulky shrug of his shoulders he mumbled, "Okay."

It took her three minutes. She ran back to the car—noted an angry driver unable to get out of his parking space—raised her hand in apology and jumped back into the car. She drove off quickly before beating her hands on the steering wheel. "Shit, oh fucking shit! Guess what? It was only your sister's funeral at midday today! Your sister's funeral!" she repeated aghast, "What a day for us to choose! We must get out of here fast!

James stared at her in disbelief. "Sarah's funeral! Are you sure? Why didn't we know? Surely it would have been on the television?"

Mary shook her head. "I can't be sure but I bet it was for security reasons. The shop assistant told me the Prime Minister and a Royal had been expected. It would have been procedure to have said nothing knowing that your sister had died in an IRA attack, not to mention the fact that the police might fear another attack on your father. Now their suspicions will have been well and truly alerted by your absence at the funeral. You should have fucking been there! After your letter I suspect someone is growing just a wee bit worried about you James Hanmore. I think we have no choice but to abort the operation. Your parents' house will be swarming with police."

She glanced across at him. He was just smiling.
"What the fuck are you smiling about?"
"I'm thinking it's a good day to kill my father."
"What!"
"Yes, a bloody good day. No one will expect a hit on him now and my parents will think I haven't turned up because of the media blackout. It's nothing to worry about. And I know father. He will want to get rid of any security as quickly as possible once the guests have gone. He will want the house to himself and mother. Believe me I'm right on this one. So let's go to Winchester and wait a bit there. I'm starving anyway. Give more time for everything at Rosehall to settle down. Then we return later and I chop the bastard. He will be off guard and what's more pleased to see me. It will be simple and it will work."

She decided not to argue. He could be right and besides what did it matter.

It was four in the afternoon. For the first time that day Tim felt he could relax. The VIPs had gone shortly after three and most of the other guests half an hour later. Now only close friends remained and they were about to bid their farewells.

The cost of policing the funeral could be counted in hundreds of thousands of pounds and Tim marvelled at the capability of the IRA to spread panic amongst those responsible for the security of the nation. It was their unpredictability that was so potent.

At five he decided it was safe to stand the security operation down. The skies above Rosehall at last became quiet. The streets and roads emptied of police cars and motor cycles and the big house closed its doors to the uniformed and plain clothed policemen who had tramped round its rooms since early morning. Richard and Blanche shook Tim's hand gratefully and stood at the front door as he walked towards his car. He would have liked to have stayed or at least left a small police presence in the house especially bearing in mind his growing suspicions about James Hanmore. But as expected Richard had used the excuse Tim had handed him. Blanche had looked angry but said nothing. So he accepted that questions would have to wait, but not for too long. He had always felt that Richard was keeping something from him. He felt frustrated, sure that he was missing something. Now the funeral was over it was time to put some pressure on the Hanmores.

They were sitting in Macdonalds behind the High street in Winchester. James was noisily drinking his fourth Coca Cola and chewing on his third hamburger.

How can he be so calm? Mary thought. She had no appetite. The events of the day were still troubling her. She would still have liked to abort. But on the way to Winchester when she'd brought the subject up again he'd sworn at her and refused to discuss it. She glanced at James with disgust as he ordered his fourth hamburger. Shit, he was behaving like the seasoned operative while she was agonising over her mistakes. Well fuck, she thought, it's his fucking life! But she was a professional and it was difficult to turn her back on her years of training with Seamus. He had constantly impressed on her that there was nothing wrong in aborting an operation if things didn't look right. 'Remember girl.' he'd say, 'on most occasions there will be another time.' Now here she was ignoring that advice. She decided to give James one last chance.

"Are you sure you don't want to abort? There will be another time you know."

He hardly bothered to stop chewing. "Yes, yes, we go ahead," he grunted.

Mary shrugged. She wasn't prepared to push him any more. He could get difficult and that was the last thing she wanted at the moment. She glanced at her watch. She made a decision—a sort of compromise. There were a few hours yet to darkness so time to recce the situation. She would insist on that. She knew he'd use foul language, even get violent but she wasn't prepared to walk into a trap. "Okay. But I want to have a look round before it gets dark. If we see any signs of the police we get out fucking quick! No argument."

He wiped his mouth with his sleeve and half closed his eyes. He's going to be trouble, Mary thought. But to her surprise he nodded. "Okay I'll go along with that. But I'll decide if it's safe for me to go in. After all it's me whose taking the biggest risk."

She couldn't argue with that. "Very well I agree. So let's say we move from here in fifteen minutes?"

James nodded and went on chewing. Mary sat silently watching him with something close to bewilderment. What had turned the introverted, unsure pervert into this seemingly confident young monster who enjoyed the act of killing? Was it his hatred for his father or her persuasive tongue? She decided it was probably a little bit of both. After all she had fed him with her hatred, and being a weak pathetic individual perhaps it was not surprising he'd been so easy to change. And she would have been proud of her work if she hadn't surprisingly had a change of heart herself. She looked away from him and allowed herself a smile. Christ, how on earth had that happened? She still hated the Brits. Still wanted them out of her country. Would have willingly died for her ideals, which had not changed. But...and here was the problem. Was she still burning for revenge? A shock wave coursed through her as she realised the answer to this was 'no'. She rubbed her chin thoughtfully. Shit! Was it the blood of her mother in her veins that was changing her? Yes, probably a little. But as she stared at James she knew that she could no longer ignore the one fact that had been haunting her for weeks. James and Seamus were the culprits. Seamus's total disregard for her life had shocked her. James's pleasure at the death of his sister had filled her with disgust. It should have been so simple to accept, but for her it was a change of heart she had never wanted or ever dreamt would come about. So was there an alternative to the killings and all the violence to achieve her goal? Her mind went back to all the times she had watched Hanmore and other politicians on the television spouting what her father called 'fucking rubbish' about negotiations. Could she now be thinking the unthinkable? Stepping into the same camp as all those Brit politicians and their like? "Oh fuck!" she said out loud.

James leered at her. "Something wrong? Getting nervous?"

Mary bridled. "Of course not!" Then quickly she said, "Now time to move"

James jumped up and moved close to Mary's ear. "Ready to go!" he whispered. "Ready to kill the bastard. Then mother will wither away from sadness. What an ending for two sad old people eh Mary?" She turned away, not bothering to answer.

The hour hand of her watch was touching six as Mary drove the Ford through a gateway into a field about a mile from Rosehall. It was the vantage point chosen by James and as she got out of the car she understood why. The fields in front of her slopped gently down towards the house. They would be able to lie on a bank hidden from the road and any curious eyes from the house and observe all the movements in front of them. "This is perfect," said James. "And we won't get stuck here either. The ground is as hard as concrete except after heavy rain."

Mary smiled and nodded. She was already sweeping the ground in front of her with a pair of binoculars. Her eye was caught by a pair of roe deer grazing by the side of a small wood to the left of the house, the evening sunlight playing on their backs. A little reluctantly she moved the glasses away and picked up a herd of cows lowing contentedly as they buried their heads in the last of the autumn grass. She couldn't stop herself comparing the peaceful scene to the violence about to erupt in the house below them.

They lay without speaking until the light went. Nothing had happened to concern them and Mary was forced to accept that the grounds of the house were quiet. Certainly there were no cars in the drive but it worried her that she couldn't see inside the house. If she'd been Hanmore she would certainly have had security hidden somewhere at the end of such a day but she could no longer delay. James wanted to go and it was his life on the line more than hers.

Mary shivered as the first drops of dew settled in the field. She was growing cold. "Time to move I think," she whispered to James as she stood up and stretched her stiff body.

"Okay by me. Told you there wouldn't be anything to worry about."

Mary touched him on the shoulder. "You were right, but far better to be sure."

James grabbed her hand. She noticed he was shaking. "Well this is it! This is it Mary! God, I can't wait! The bastard is about to die!" He let out a sort of howl and danced towards the car.

It was nine in the evening when the telephone rang. Richard and Blanche were sitting wearily in the drawing room staring at a blank television screen. Neither of them could find the energy to get up and turn it on. As Blanche pushed herself off the sofa Richard waved a hand. "Leave it. Probably only some bloody reporter."

Standing in the public phone booth James's fingers beat an impatient tattoo on the dirty glass. "Come on, come on answer it," he said urgently. "Fuck it's the ansaphone. Surely they must be there!"

It had never occurred to him or Mary that his parents might have decided to spend the night somewhere else rather than in the sad surroundings of Rosehall.

"Try again," said Mary, cursing silently that she had not thought this a possibility. "If they are there curiosity will probably get the better of them a second time."

He re-dialled. "Come on answer!" He thumped a fist against Mary's shoulder. "Come on you bastard answer the fucking thing!" Suddenly—hand quickly over receiver. "Got him!" Smiled. Then said, "Father, it's me James." He grimaced at Mary as Richard started to shout at him.

"I know, I know, and I'm desperately sorry. Should have thought and been in touch earlier. But of course I'm devastated by the news. Behaved badly I know— very sorry—can I come and explain? Yes, now seems as good a time as any. Yes, I'm quite close. Of course you're tired but I think we need to talk. Okay thanks. I will be with you within the hour. Give my love to mother."

He slammed the phone down before his father could change his mind and gave Mary a triumphant look. "I'm going in! The old fool was furious with me but he can't wait to see me!"

Richard's face was drawn as he put the receiver down. Blanche, who had watched him go white, asked fearfully, "That was James wasn't it?"

Richard took a few seconds to recover his composure before answering, "Yes, and he's coming here tonight! I didn't want to put him off, but he didn't give me the choice anyway. My God Blanche, we could never say our son was predictable!"

"You can say that again! agreed Blanche. "Where on earth has he been all this time? He didn't say anything I suppose?"

Richard shook his head. "Not a word. Just said he would explain everything to me later. He sounded flustered. Perhaps he's feeling guilty at not getting to the funeral."

Blanche gave a weak smile. "I would like to think it was only that, but I very much doubt it." "But you did the right thing. I know we are tired and have had a terribly sad day but you have to see him. However if I were you I would ring Tim Roberts just to be on the safe side."

Richard shook his head vigorously. "No! I have nothing to fear from the boy and if by any chance your suspicions are confirmed I can ring Tim then."

Blanche said quietly. "Oh Richard please. Do you honestly believe he'd give you the chance?"

Richard ran a hand angrily through his hair. "Well that won't be put to the test. I know he's innocent."

Blanche looked at him in disbelief. "How can you be so sure! You should take every precaution just in case. For heaven sake Richard darling, don't lose sight of the fact that he wrote in that dreadful letter that he wished you dead."

There was an obstinate tone to Richard's voice when he replied, "That means nothing. That was just his anger showing. He comes here as my son, innocent until we have more proof and that's the end of it. However given the way you feel I think it would be better if you weren't here when he arrives. I don't want you standing by my side giving out all the wrong signals. I need to be alone with him. You go over to Jane and Horace Batchelors for a while. You know they will have you at a moment's notice. Now I know it is a waste of time to order you so I will beg you to do as I ask."

"What if I refuse such an unnecessary request? After all I could go to another room. There is no need for me to be by your side as you put it."

Richard didn't look at her as he replied. "Please don't say 'no'. I know what I'm doing."

"Yes, getting rid of me because you are worried what James might do."

"Oh come now."

Blanche's eyes flashed angrily. "Don't treat me like a child Richard. I know you are not as confident as you make out."

He smiled weakly, and as he always did when losing an argument with her he reached out for her. She couldn't bring herself to move into his arms. She was boiling with frustration. So she just touched his cheek and said, "You are an obstinate and foolish man Richard Hanmore, but I will go because I could not stand to have a row with you tonight of all nights. But remember Jose and Maria are in the house and I will be on the end of the telephone."

Richard was not slow to guess her frustration and made no attempt to embrace her, much as he longed to take her in his arms and assure her he'd be alright. Instead he said, "When this is over and James is back with us I will somehow try to show you how much I still love you."

Close to tears Blanche said, "I don't need you to do that. Just don't take me for a fool. I know why you are sending me away, and I love you for it, even though I think you are playing a dangerous game. So take care and remember I will not be far away. I will pray for you my darling."

Chapter Eleven

THE grandfather clock in the hall was striking ten as Blanche drove away from Rosehall. Richard watched the rear lights of her car disappear up the drive with a feeling of relief mixed with foreboding. It would be wrong to say he was frightened, but he feared Blanche's concerns might be pretty close to the mark. He had to admit there was plenty to make him suspicious whatever he'd told Blanche and Tim. The mix of James's disappearance, the letter, followed by the horrors of Thornbury and then his failure to turn up at his sister's funeral could not be lightly ignored. A tear tickled his cheek. He was devastated that he could harbour such suspicions about his son. He stood on the drive numb with despair. Even the familiar sound of the cows chewing the cud on the other side of the fence could not work its usual magic on him. It had been a dreadful day and he was well aware there might be worse to come.

He turned back into the house expecting its warmth to embrace him. Instead it felt cold, almost threatening. James was putting a curse on all he loved. Damn him! He bit his lip. That was not fair. The boy must be given a chance. With all his heart he wanted his nightmare to end, but somewhere deep within the recesses of his mind a small voice was saying, 'false hopes are a fool's downfall.'

Mary and James watched the Rover come through the Gates of Rosehall. It was a few minutes past ten and they were parked opposite the gates. "Mother making a run for it," whispered James as Blanche's face was caught by one of the security lights above the gates. "Shows father must be worried. Sending her away in case I turn nasty I expect. Always has treated her like some china doll. Pity he couldn't have found time to give a bit of that love to me." The last sentence was laced with bitterness.

Mary chose to ignore it and said quietly. "If what you say is correct, he will be on his guard, even armed. You will have to be very careful. If you fail I doubt if you will get a second chance. I still think you would be wise to wait another day. Let everything settle down a bit."

"Never! I'm not turning back now so fucking well don't suggest it again."

She shrugged. "Okay, it's your funeral. So let's be running through the plan one more time. Once you have left the car you are on your own. How you deal with your father is up to you. I will wait here for an hour at the most. That should be giving you plenty of time. If however I sense something has gone wrong, don't bank on me waiting to see if you are alive or dead. I will be out of here shit fast. If you are alive and free try and get yourself to Stranraer and catch the ferry to Larne. We might meet up there, but if not to be sure the Organisation will be there to meet you."

James gave a low contemptuous laugh. "You are a doubting cow Mary O'Neill. I won't fail and I won't be in danger. I will be back here within the hour you have so generously given me." He reached over onto the back seat and pushed aside the coats that covered the shotgun. As he gripped it in his hand his heart missed a beat. "And now the fucking cartridges please," he asked.

She held out six. He took two. "That will be enough."

She glanced at the phosphorescent face of her watch. "Okay, have it your way. Now off you be going. She forced herself to lean across and kiss his cheek. "Good luck Jamie, you may be needing it."

He pulled her to him and kissed her firmly on the mouth forcing his tongue between her teeth. The smell of stale tomato ketchup and onions nearly made her throw up.

Once out of the car he started to jog down the drive. He was keen to get the job over. He was surprised at the nervous flutter of his heart. He'd thought quite a lot about shooting his father lately, wondering how the old man would react when he saw the gun pointed at his chest. It never had occurred to him to think that he might not be able to pull the trigger. But as he jogged down the familiar drive to the house where he'd spent all his childhood a few memories came back to him and the first hint of indecision touched him. He stopped, almost stunned that he could have any doubt as to what he was about to do. He shook his head, forcing himself to remember all the times his father had humiliated him. The pain of being ignored when all he'd wanted was to be part of the family and feel loved. "Bastard, bastard" he kept repeating, until he'd whipped himself up into an angry frenzy. He smiled in the darkness, his resolve returned. There would be no more moments of doubt. He started to jog again until the house came into view. He saw a figure standing by the front door. A second later he recognised his father. Thank God for the security lights or he might have run straight into him and he wasn't ready to face him yet.

Breathing heavily he stood his ground until Richard went inside and the lights went out. Then he moved to the back of the house. He had never known the back door to be locked. Nothing had changed. Silly, silly, he thought as he walked quietly into the darkened kitchen. He moved confidently down the passage that led to the back stairs. He didn't need to switch on a light to find his bedroom; he could have found his way blindfold. Nor did he want to risk alerting Jose and Maria, although they were normally in bed by ten unless his parents were entertaining. He had no idea why he wanted to see his bedroom but the desire was too strong to ignore. He turned the handle and walked inside, resisting the temptation to turn on the light. He put the gun down on the bed and moved to the window overlooking the drive. How many times had he heard the noise of his father's car on the gravel drive at the beginning of a weekend and seen his mother rush out to greet him, their embrace fuelling his jealousy? He had never felt he was wanted on such occasions and as far as he could remember his father had never once embraced him on his return. Come to think of it the bastard had never kissed him either. Why? He had never stopped asking himself that question.

But there had been happy times, like when he and Sarah used to sit on his bed listening to their favourite pop groups, pigging out on mars bars and discussing what they would do with their lives when they grew up. He gave a twisted grin. Well, they had been miles off course on that one! Fuck! What a shitty life his had turned out to be, and he'd done Sarah a favour by saving her from a life with that shit Henry Marshall. He ground his teeth angrily. It could have been all so different. But now Mary had given him a reason for living and the chance to get rid of the man he blamed for ruining his life and who he'd become to imagine had forced him to kill his sister. The bastard was about to get what he deserved! He grabbed the gun, pulled out the two shells from his trouser pocket and pushed them into the breech and hurried out of the room. He was ready now. Ready to strike a blow for a free Ireland and end the life of a miserable old man.

Richard sat waiting at his desk in the library, a glass of his favourite malt in his hand. He wondered what the next hour or two might bring. A terrible confrontation with James or the reunion he so desperately wanted? From the moment he'd married Blanche they had decided they wanted children. It wasn't until it was too late that he realised he wanted power more and they were nothing but an interference in his drive for the top of his Party. Blanche would say that he was not being fair to himself and that she had to shoulder a lot of the blame, but in his heart he knew she was only being the loyal wife. Had his indifference been worth while? The answer had to be 'no' even though he had nearly reached the top and even thought that one day he might stand for the leadership. But oh God the dream had been shattered and now he was paying the price of his ambition. Stress had caused his heart attack and he'd lost any hope of being the leader of his Party. Worse he'd lost his children. One dead and perhaps one a murderer. He took a long pull at his whisky. Did he really deserve such harsh punishment? Whatever way he looked at it, it was a terribly cruel indictment of his life. He had never believed God could work miracles but for the first time in his life he was tempted to pray for one.

Mary watched James disappear into the dark. She sat back in her seat and closed her eyes. She needed a few minutes to gather her wits. Who would have ever thought it would come to this, the moment when her life would change for good. The time for agonising was over. Any lingering doubts had to be caste out of her mind. She removed the PPK from its holster under her arm and once more checked that it was loaded. Wiping the sweat from her brow she opened the car door and stepped out into the refreshing night air. As she took her first steps down the drive she felt as if she was enacting out a bad dream. "Oh shit," she whispered, "What the hell am I about to do!"

Blanche stood awkwardly in the Batchelors' kitchen, a weak smile on her face as Jane Batchelor mixed her a strong drink. "This is what you need

Blanche dear," she said sympathetically as she handed over a strong gin and tonic. "And don't apologise for coming over so late, I quite understand that you wanted to get out of the house for a few moments. You have had a terrible day and I think you have been so brave."

What Blanche liked about Jane Batchelor was that she never seemed surprised by anything and tonight she was no different. There was no, "well I'm surprised you have left Richard on his own." There was just the usual friendly smile and a shrug of the shoulders. There would be no questions. Blanche felt relief flow through her body. She hadn't wanted to lie to such a loyal friend but the truth was too horrendous to tell. She took a long pull at her drink. She would finish it and then be on her way home. She wanted to see James. She'd been surprised how much she'd missed him in spite of her dark thoughts. Besides her place was beside her husband and Richard could be as angry as he liked. She wasn't going to wait for his telephone call. She gave a weak smile. "This drink will certainly help. My God how much gin did you put in it? I feel better already and a little guilty at leaving Richard on his own. I'll be on my way as soon as I've finished this and leave you and Horace in peace."

Jane gave her a reassuring smile and said, "You do just as you want Blanche. Come back later if you want to, even bring Richard over if you both want to get out of the house. The door is open any time."

Blanche drained the last of the liquid from the glass and kissed her friend lightly on the cheek. "You are a good friend, and I will take you at your word," she promised.

Holding the shotgun under his arm James walked boldly down the main staircase. It seemed all the lights were on in the main part of the house and he guessed his father would in the library. God, how he hated that room. How many times had he faced his father's anger and disgust across the huge mahogany desk? Well this time it was going to be different. He'd be calling the shots this time. This time his father would be the one shaking with fear and he'd enjoy every minute of it. In fact he'd draw out the time to the execution just so he could see the fear and smell his old man's sweat. It was going to be a few very sweet minutes. He walked across the hall to the large doors leading to the library. He didn't bother to knock, just turned the handle and walked in. It was twenty five minutes past ten...........

Through the open french windows Mary watched James waving the shotgun at his father. She heard his laugh as Richard jumped up from his chair. Shit! Was he about to fire? She was coiling herself up like a spring ready to jump when she heard James speak. He was baiting the old man. She decided there was time for her to get her breath back from her rush down the drive and to control the almost unbearable desire to vomit. For this was treason. No fucking mucking about! This was treason. Could she really be doing this? Oh shit! She saw Richard start to move round the desk! She heard James's warning shout and tensed her muscles. No more time for such thoughts! She guessed she only had seconds left. She saw James raise the shotgun to his shoulder and launched herself through the window. Throwing

herself on the floor she rolled and fired as she came
to rest. She heard James's cry as the bullet hit him
low in the back. Saw the look of surprise on his twisted
face as he turned and recognised her. "Mary!" She
fired again. This time her arm was steadier and the
bullet took him between the eyes, turning his face
into a bloody mass of bone and flesh. As he sank to
the floor she pumped two more shots into his body.
Seamus had once said, "Don't stop shooting little girl
until the enemy have stopped twitching."
Mesmerised she watched James's body jump several
feet across the floor before lying still, his blood
pouring out of his body and staining the blue carpet.
Pain gripped her stomach and she gulped down the
bile that threatened to erupt from her mouth. She
shook her head in dazed amazement at what she'd
just done. She'd slaughtered the father of her child
and saved the life of the man she'd vowed to kill.

But in spite of her inner turmoil she was awake
to the dangers that could face her and she was quick
to point the PPK at the man splattered with blood
holding on to the side of the desk. He didn't look as
if he'd be a danger to anyone but she couldn't take
any risks. "Don't fucking move a muscle or you will
be a dead man as well!" she shouted. Why not kill
him anyway? She would have carried out the IRA's
orders and be a hero. Her finger tightened on the
trigger. "Jesus, I should fucking kill you," she said
quietly. "I have watched you on television and wished
you dead so many fucking times. Yet here I am, standing over the body of your supposed assassin, with a
gun in my hand and I can't fucking pull the trigger!"

"Who are you!" Richard managed to croak.

"Never you be minding about that Richard fucking Hanmore. Just be thanking God that he was on your side tonight." Then they both heard the crunch of tyres on the gravel and Mary threw him a dangerous look. "Not the police I hope?" she hissed, as she moved close enough to Richard to push the PPK into his stomach.

"Not unless my wife has called them,"

"Well by Jesus your life hangs by a thread."

Richard felt a cold hand touch his heart and he held his breath. Would Blanche have called the police? Quite probably., and her good intentions might well kill him. For the second time that night he knew he was within an ace of dying. He felt the pressure of the gun on his stomach and he did his best not to move.

Mary heard the footsteps. Only one person's and they were unmistakably female. She allowed herself to smile and took the gun away from Richard's stomach. He blew out his cheeks in relief. "Your wife I suspect has come back to rescue you, so I must be going now. Tell her your son killed your daughter and that is the reason why you live and he lies dead at your feet."

She saw the door behind Richard begin to open and she turned and ran. When she reached the car she sat breathless in the driving seat her body shaking out of control. There was no way she could drive even though she knew she could be in grave danger. Soon she would hear the sirens and minutes later the anti terrorist squad would be surrounding her. She held the PPK ready in a shaking hand. She might have had a change of heart over some things but to surrender! No! By Jesus she'd take a few of the bastards to hell with her. She waited. Her breathing steadied and her hands stopped shaking and still no sign of the police. Could Hanmore really let her get away? She started the car and moved onto the road wondering if her luck could last. There was no blue light flashing, nor a siren whaling in the distance. Where were the bastards? Further up the road waiting? She cradled the PPK in her lap. She passed through Alresford, and joined the A34 to Newbury. Still no road blocks, still no sirens. After half an hour she let out a whoop of joy. The unbelievable had happened; for some reason Hanmore couldn't have called the police. Perhaps he and his wife were in shock. Then she remembered something that James had once told her "Father will never accept that I have joined the IRA. The bastard is so proud that I doubt if he'd ever tell the police even if he was sure I'd killed my sister."

Well, it looked as if he'd been right about something! She started to hum, started to feel pleased with herself. She'd rid the world of a monster. The first fucking good thing you have ever done in your miserable life Mary O'Neill, she thought. She jammed her foot down on the accelerator. If she drove through the night she'd be in Stranrear by morning. Then she would take the ferry to Larne and face an unknown future, almost certainly a dangerous one. But she'd take her chance with the likes of Seamus. She wanted to have her baby on her island, and if she was to die (pray God not before her child was born), she wanted to die at home. She'd been away from the warm rain too long.

One of the many reasons that Richard had married Blanche was because of her calm nature. It had proved many times the perfect foil to his proneness to lose his temper. Now, as she stood by the door of the library, her eyes darting between the body of her son and her blood stained husband, she was close to losing that calmness that had stood her in such good stead over the years. She had to draw on all her reserves not to rush into the room screaming. She swallowed hard, fought back the tears and fighting to keep her voice steady she asked, "Oh my God Richard what on earth has happened?"

Struck speechless by a combination of relief and shock Richard just pointed a shaking finger at James's body. Blanche did not push him, she could see he was shaking badly. She touched his arm lightly, took a deep breath, summoned all the courage she possessed and walked over to James's body. She knelt beside him and stared at the mutilated face. It was quite obvious to her he was dead. She thought, this is the person I carried inside me for nine months. This is the boy I loved. Oh God, this is the boy I have let down all his life and now it is too late. She swung round to look at Richard, tears finally streaming down her face. Desperately she said, "We have failed him!" Her voice rose. "Did you hear? We have failed him and now he's dead—DEAD!! Oh God, oh God what are we going to do!"

Richard staggered slowly back behind his desk and fell into his chair. "Don't ask me that right now please. He came to kill me Blanche. The boy actually held a gun at me and told me he was going to enjoy seeing me die. Our son was going to enjoy killing me! Oh Blanche what on earth have I done to him to deserve that?" He choked back the tears and held out his arms. "For God sake come here."

Blanche pushed herself up from the floor and ran into his arms, their tears mixing with the blood on Richard's clothes. "What we have both done is failed him," she repeated. "He needed us and what were we doing? Carving out your career. Tonight will live in our memories until we die. Now tell me what happened."

In an unsteady voice Richard told her, shaking his head in bewilderment every time he mentioned James. Blanche realised that he was unable to cope with the knowledge that James had wanted to kill him.

"If the girl spoke the truth about him killing Sarah and Henry then we have got to accept he had grown into an evil young man."

"I find this difficult to say, but I must agree."

"Oh God!" Blanche cried, "It gives me no pleasure to have been right." And she then asked, "And the girl, the girl where does she fit in and do you know who she was?"

"I have no idea who she was, but as I have just told you she killed him because he murdered Sarah. Why that upset her we may never know, but it certainly saved my life tonight. She said, 'Thank God He was on your side tonight', and I won't argue with that!"

Blanche glanced at James and shuddered. "She must have been involved with the IRA otherwise how would she have known he was coming to kill you? I think this proves a lot of things about our son. He didn't write that letter under duress—he didn't care about killing his own sister—and he came to kill you tonight. It all adds up to the sad fact that he'd been got at very successfully by the IRA. In his emotional state he'd have been easy meat. We may never know the answers, least of all what really drove this girl to shoot James. The fact is our son and daughter are both dead, killed in violent circumstances." Her voice broke. "Oh Richard surely we didn't deserve to be punished so harshly!"

"I don't think so," he said quietly. "No, I really don't think so." He stood up and reached for the telephone. "Now I think it is time to ring Tim Roberts and after that I suppose I should contact the local police. When the commander arrives I think we have a bit of explaining to do. We have kept vital information from him." He gave a sad little laugh. "But I don't suppose he will care too much now. After all the killer is dead so end of case." He blew his noise violently, stared for a second at his son's body and dialled the number. "Do you know," he said to Blanche as he waited for the phone to be answered, "I don't think even in my worst nightmares I could ever have dreamt of something so utterly terrible as what has happened here tonight."

It was the telephone call Tim Roberts had been certain would come one day, but the content was certainly not what he'd expected. Although not totally surprised by James's guilt he was shocked by the violence of his death. Life, he thought, was not being very kind to the Hanmores at the moment and he wondered how much more they could stand.

It took him an hour to reach Rosehall where he was greeted by the local sergeant and a CID inspector. . "Evening commander," the sergeant said glancing at his watch. "Poor Sir Richard and Lady Hanmore are in a dreadful state. Had quite a job getting them out of the library I can tell you. They seemed mesmerised by the body. Anyway after a little gentle persuasion I got them into the drawing room. One of my constables who knows them well is with them."

Tim nodded. "And I presume the body is still in the library?"

The inspector answered. "Hasn't been moved commander. I felt it wouldn't take you big boys long to get here."

Tim couldn't help but smile at the note of disapproval in the man's voice. He'd grown used to the jealousies that raged with different departments. "Thank you inspector, good of you to leave things alone until I got here. I know how difficult these things are sometimes." He touched the inspector on the arm understandingly. "But before I take a look I think I'd better go and talk to the Hanmores."

The inspector visibly relaxed. "I think that would be a wise move commander. Sir Richard was babbling all sorts of things that made no sense to me but might well to you."

I'm sure they will, thought Tim as he walked towards the drawing room where he was met by a distinctly ill at ease constable. "Am I glad to see you sir," he whispered. "Sir Richard especially is in a terrible state."

Tim put a hand on the young man's shoulder. "Well I'm sure you've done your best. Now I suggest you go and join your sergeant. I can manage here." Gently pushing him out of the door he closed it behind him and took a deep breath before turning to face the couple. Blanche and Richard were sitting on a sofa by one of the large windows, desolation written all over their faces. Tim moved across to them, feeling almost embarrassed that he'd invaded their grief and said quietly, "Sir Richard and Lady Hanmore

I am so desperately sorry this has happened on what has been such an awful day for you anyway."

Blanche looked up at him with red rimmed eyes. "Thank you commander, and oh God how right you are. After we had buried Sarah I didn't think the day could get worse." She reached out to Richard before continuing. "We have something to tell you which we should have mentioned some time ago. You could say we kept valuable information from you, but that will be for you to judge." She picked James's letter up from the sofa and handed it to him.

Tim took it reluctantly, quickly read it and handed it back to Blanche. "I don't think this would have made much difference to be honest. Of course you should have told me but I don't think we'd have thought of protecting Henry Marshall and we know it was just bad luck that Sarah arrived that morning. I should burn the letter and try to forget it. I have my killer. I think that's all I need to say." He saw the relief on both their faces. Of course the very least he should have done was reprimand them, but they had suffered enough by his book and whatever action he took now would not bring five people back to life.

He saw the tears in Richard's eyes before his head dropped onto Blanche's lap. He hadn't spoken a word, but Tim knew he couldn't leave the room until he'd had Richard's full account of the shooting. His almost hysterical explanation down the telephone had left many questions unanswered. He gave Blanche an apologetic smile and asked, "I'm sorry Sir Richard to intrude on you at this moment in time but you must tell me exactly what happened in the library."

Richard lifted his head off Blanche's lap and sat back on the sofa. "Yes, you are quite right commander, of course you must know. It was really quite terrible." Then in an unsteady voice, which at times was almost inaudible, he told Tim the full story. By the time he'd finished he'd managed to regain some of his composure and said quietly, "I don't suppose you will ever find the young woman, and to tell you the truth I will be glad. She saved my life commander. I trusted James and he used that trust to try and kill me. I can't believe I'm saying this, but whoever the woman was and whatever her motives, she has put an end to a miserable and evil life. The terrible thing is that Blanche and I are to blame."

Mary stepped off the ferry at Larne knowing she was a free woman. There had been no sirens, no hand on her shoulder on the ferry and there were no RUC standing on the dockside waiting to arrest her. She found it hard to believe her luck had held, but she still had a very uncertain future. To say she was frightened would be going too far but the excitement of coming home was tempered a bit by the knowledge that at the very least she was going to face some very awkward questions. She had a lot of explaining to do and Seamus caste a long shadow. As she walked out onto the street she decided that if he knew she was back she and her unborn child would probably be dead before dusk.

She saw the car approaching fast and steeled herself for the pain of the bullets, but instead it skidded to a halt by her side and a young man shouted out of the window. "Get in Mary O'Neill, the Army Council want to see you."

It was the sort of command you did not ignore and at least it wasn't Seamus after her. Mary jumped in without even thinking of running. As she sat through the journey looking at the driver's thick neck she knew there would be no point in lying. James's death had been splashed all over the papers. She had rehearsed many times what she was going to say. She could only hope that her story would be accepted and that they would acknowledge she had done the best thing in the circumstances. After all, the outcome, though not what had been planned, would have a devastating effect on Hanmore. She closed her eyes and prayed to God.

She stood in front of the Commander and Chief and the remainder of the Army Council, the palms of her hands wringing wet. She had been greeted coldly and now she was being asked to explain herself. Fighting to keep he voice steady—for she knew it could be fatal to make a mistake—she replied, "It was all set up beautifully. James Hanmore showed nothing but pleasure in the deaths of his sister and Henry Marshall and he couldn't wait to get to his father. But as you know things worked out very differently on the night. He left the car with the gun and at that moment I had no reason to think that things were going to go badly. He seemed so pumped up at the thought of killing his father. Luckily I followed him to the house and watched through the open french windows as he confronted Hanmore. Then things started to go wrong. By Jesus they did! Suddenly he was begging his father to forgive him. He was crying, almost hysterical. I couldn't believe my eyes! He'd fucking lost his bottle! I realised he wasn't going to kill him. I had a split second to decide what to do. I shot him. Well you know that already. I just hope you think I did the right thing. I killed James Hanmore as you had already ordered, and Richard Hanmore will suffer until he dies. You can't lose your children in such violent circumstances and not be affected, can you?" I put it to you that that is the perfect scenario. Maybe it was a split second decision but it is one I am not scared to face you with."

That was it, she had nothing more to say. The room went quiet and she stared boldly in front of her awaiting the verdict

Chapter Twelve

WINCHESTER station was heaving with restless humanity. The London bound train was running its usual twenty or more minutes late. Richard feared he would never make Downing Street on time. He swore silently under his breath. He remembered how fussy the PM had been about time and it would be a bad start if he was too late. It was two years since he'd travelled on a train to London and he'd forgotten how frustrating it was, this unpredictable journey to the capital city. It was also close to two years since that dreadful autumn night that James had held a gun at his chest. He shuddered involuntarily as he thought of the dreadful scene, that even after such a long interval was as clear as if a photograph had been implanted in his brain. He and Blanche had become reconciled to the fact that they would never fully recover from the deaths of their two children. They had never had time for their children, now they missed them dreadfully. The irony of the situation was nor lost on them. To make it worse guilt still haunted them and it was not unusual for them both to wake up on the same night screaming from a nightmare. But in their shared misery they had grown even closer than they had been before and Richard knew that without her constant support he would now undoubtedly be dead.

The loudspeaker's announcement that the train was arriving interrupted his thoughts. He stared up the line waiting somewhat apprehensively for the metal beast that was to take him to London and perhaps a chance to rebuild his shattered life. For the first time since his daughter's death he felt he might have a future. The invitation from Downing Street had come out of the blue and been deliberately vague, but he knew it had been given careful thought before it had been issued. Northern Ireland had been mentioned but not much else. Nevertheless he was to say the least surprised that the PM wanted a word with him on such a subject given that it had become public knowledge that his son had been lured into the clutches of the IRA.

Blanche had not hidden her surprise or her concern, but she'd encouraged him to go. "Just see what the PM has in mind darling. After all you can always refuse." He'd drawn her close and kissed her, knowing that any mention of Northern Ireland filled her with foreboding. He understood her feelings and was grateful for her unselfish support. He'd tried to persuade her to come with him. They had hardly been apart for the last two years, but she'd shaken her head and said it was time for them to grow up. The wording had made him smile. Nevertheless he was already missing her by his side as he boarded the train feeling threatened by the other passengers jockeying for seats. He forced himself to stay calm, fighting the desire to get off the train. After what seemed an eternity, but was in fact only three minutes, he found a vacant seat. Even then, sitting behind his paper he felt strangely vulnerable. He found it impossible to read but equally impossible to lower the paper and look at his fellow travellers. Shut away at Rosehall and mourning his children had taken its toll on his confidence more than he had expected. He knew eventually that it would be regained but the feeling of vulnerability persisted. When just over an hour later the train pulled into Waterloo he waited until the carriage was empty before leaving his seat. As he stepped onto the platform and saw the face of Tim Roberts waiting for him on the platform he was suddenly struck by the thought that his life might well be about to change.

Tim greeted him warmly. They hadn't seen each other for several months and they had grown quite close during Tim's spell as bodyguard. Nor could he forget that he was deeply in Tim's debt. "There's a government car waiting for us Sir Richard and the PM is expecting you to be a little late, so don't worry. I want you to be rational about this please. Take your time in deciding what to do."

Richard took no offence. He was used to Tim's plain speaking. He gave him a long steady look as they walked through the barrier. "You mean you don't approve of me being here?"

Tim smiled slightly. "I didn't say that, but let's face it you don't need to get involved in politics again and certainly not the murky bits. Frankly I think the PM is expecting a lot from you. And another thing that worries me is that he is keeping this meeting from his cabinet and perhaps worse from the Unionists."

Richard grimaced. "Well instead of talking in riddles why don't you tell me what the PM has in mind as you are obviously privy to his plans. It might help."

They were coming out of the station as Tim shook his head "I don't think so. I am too biased. I might put you off before you have heard what the PM has to say. That is the time I think you should make up your mind." They got into the back of the car and settled back into their seats, neither finding it necessary to speak to each other until they drew up outside Number 10. Then Tim looked across at Richard and said gently, "Best of luck, You may need it Sir Richard."

They were met at the door by a smiling PM. "Good to see you again Richard, and looking so well. Follow me gentlemen, I have something important I want to talk to you about." He led them into his private office and pointed at two chairs facing his desk. When they were all seated he put on his glasses, gave a nervous little cough that Richard remembered well, and looked across his desk at the two men. "I'm not quite sure how to begin this Richard but let me say that whatever is said here today must remain a secret between us three and of course the Northern Ireland Secretary, who sadly can't be here but is privy to all that has preceded this meeting."

Richard couldn't help thinking that Government departments seemed to be leaking like sieves these days and if what the PM was about to say proved news worthy it would probably be headlines within a day. But he kept his thoughts to himself.

"A source close to us,"-The PM smiled knowingly at Richard,—"has approached us about the IRA command wanting to talk about peace. I mean real peace, not just a ceasefire arranged for the convenience of the IRA. What a prize if we could get it. My stock along with the Governments would rise almost overnight." The PM gave a slightly embarrassed smile. "And we all know how badly that is needed. Now I am sure we can remember the increase of violence that erupted after your attempt Richard at trying to broker a peace with the IRA a few years ago. So this time, if their approach is genuine and our source has given me his word that it is, I want the whole matter kept secret just in case we fail again and more violence erupts. Which is why I invited you here Richard. You were without a doubt the best Secretary of State any Government has had. You had patience, skill, and an uncanny knack of being able to read the IRA's mind. Added to that your understanding of Ireland helped tremendously. You had to retire far too soon and I would now like to ask you to put that canny mind of yours to work for me just one more time. You are so perfect for the job of negotiator. You are out of politics, have been out of the public eye for nearly two years and after the death of your two children you are the last person the damn media would suspect was going to Belfast to talk to the IRA."

By now Richard was on the edge of his chair. "You expect me to talk to the IRA about peace after what they have done to me?" he asked aghast. "Oh come Prime Minister, that is really expecting a lot of my loyalty to you and the Party."

"Maybe, but think of what an enormous contribution you would be making to securing safety in the Province for all the people. Surely having suffered you understand that."

"Oh that is intolerable!" Richard said angrily.

The PM shrugged and took off his glasses. "Oh come Richard don't tell me you have forgotten how ruthless politics can be? I have seen you twisting reluctant arms of fellow MPs several times. So please don't be so indignant. However if you are turning me down because of the past traumas in your family I will have to understand, but can you turn your back on the chance to secure a peace you fought so hard to get for years as my Secretary of State? I am giving you a chance to become a force in politics once again. Not for long maybe but just think how the country would remember you."

Richard looked across at Tim. "I wish you had told me about this diabolical plot at the station. I would have caught the next train back to Winchester."

Tim gave an apologetic smile. "I thought it important for you to hear the proposal yourself."

"Perhaps you're right." Richard stroked his chin. To his surprise he couldn't get the words 'I won't do it' out of his mouth. Angry as he was, and knowing very well he should walk straight out of Downing Street there was a little voice nagging at his brain. He said, "Prime Minister I will not bandy my words. I think what you have done is despicable but you have always been a cunning man and no doubt judged that I might be tempted. But please don't pretend that you are doing this for the nation only. You need a miracle to win the next election and you think this could be it. You are prepared to gamble just as I did, but I put it to you that my reasons were more moral than yours are today." Richard saw the PM's face redden. He'd touched a raw nerve. Good. He was taking advantage of a loyal ex-colleague and friend. "However that said this old fool here would like to see peace in the Province and do almost anything to get it. So give me half an hour with the commander here and then I will give you my answer."

The PM slammed his fists down on his desk and stood up. "Take as long as you like Richard. Use this office please and don't think too badly of me. I think you need something like this to get you back into life. You can't vegetate for ever you know. Give my PPS a shout when you are ready. If I'm in the House you may have to wait a few minutes."

"My God that man has some cheek Tim," exclaimed Richard a few minutes after the PM had shut the door behind him. "But he has a point, I do need something other than Rosehall in my life. And you know how passionately I wanted peace in Ulster. Even though I know the man is playing politics I am sorely tempted to accept. It would be a challenge and could be the culmination of all I have dreamt of since I was a teenager. What do you think? Be honest with me."

Tim cleared his throat. He was stunned, believing that Richard would turn the PM down without a thought. "I really don't know what to say. I was so certain you would refuse. But you want me to be honest so here goes. The Prime Minister has not told you everything—in fact I would say he has been a bit light on the details. Firstly Dublin know of this proposed meeting, for as you well know the Anglo Irish agreement states that we must liase with them over any sensitive matters. I don't like that at all. Secondly this meeting has been brokered by Sinn Fein and you know my views on that already. Worse however is the security situation. One of the IRA conditions is that the negotiator comes alone. There is to be no security anywhere near the meeting place. Oh yes and one other small item the PM conveniently forgot to tell you is that the IRA have been told you might be the negotiator! Now to my mind no security would be risky for anyone representing the Government, but you! After all not too long ago you were top of the IRA's assassination list. So there you have it. One thing I will say is that if you decide to go I will make sure you have security pretty damn near you all the time even if that means ignoring orders."

Richard blew out his cheeks. "Wow, the PM certainly has been a bit forgetful! Tell me one more thing. Do I have a colleague with me?"

"No. You are expected to go on your own."

"I see. And tell me Tim when would I go and where?"

"The date is being negotiated, but I would guess within a few weeks. As for location all we know at the moment is that it will be in the North. Knowing the IRA I very much doubt if you will be told until a few hours before. So I would urge you not to go. The whole operation is risky too say the least especially as we are dealing with a bunch of cold blooded killers."

Richard smiled. "My guardian angel has spoken eh? I'm very grateful for your concern Tim and I have listened to what you have to say. Now I will tell you why I am going against your advice. The PM was right. I would give almost anything to see peace in my lifetime. Also I would love to be the man who brokered it. I would be very proud and it would be a fitting end to my career, which as the PM said was cut short far too soon. Finally I am going to accept because of my children. They died because of this dreadful war. I owe it to them to try and bring about a peace. If I die in the attempt—and I am well aware of the risks—too bad. I think Blanche would understand." Richard slapped his thighs and made for the door. "Right then Tim let's find the PPS and break the good news."

Tim sat in the back of the car returning them to Waterloo, totally bemused by the swiftness of events. He had been so sure that Richard would refuse the PM that he had been totally unprepared for what had happened. He found it hard to believe that a man of Richard's intelligence could have been so rash, without at least giving himself time to think things over. Especially as he could be putting his life on the line. Was it his ego, his desire for public acclaim or just sheer desperation? He caste a furtive look at Richard sitting by his side. He looked quite at ease, in fact he had a lot more colour in his cheeks. There didn't seem to be any sign of desperation, and that said it all. There was no point in dwelling on the man's foolishness if his mind was made up. It was more important to figure out how he was going to be protected. But as they crossed the Thames he couldn't help saying, quietly, but loud enough for the man sitting beside him to hear, "You silly bugger, I thought you had more sense."

Richard just turned and looked at him and smiled, saying, "This is my chance Tim, maybe my last to reach that dream." He knew what Tim must be thinking and perhaps if he thought too hard he might think he was a silly bugger as well! He knew he was risking the wrath of Blanche and ignoring the advice of a man who had once been prepared to die to protect him and no doubt might have to be prepared to die again. He acknowledged he was not being fair, but he needed to be wanted by a wider audience than Blanche. He needed the thrill of fighting for what he believed in. He needed, he needed—and if it killed him? Oh God poor darling Blanche. He closed his eyes for a second as the enormity of what he'd just done hit him. But seconds later when he opened his eyes he could feel the adrenaline of the challenge pumping through him and knew he could never pull out.

She had not died.

To her surprise and relief they had gone along with what she'd done, even if it had been a bit reluctantly. She'd had a telling off, but the fact that Hanmore would suffer, perhaps even die a slow death, weeping for his children was good enough for them. And James Hanmore was dead. For two days she had been unable to stop shaking, so convinced had she become that she was going to die. But she was not out of the woods yet; Seamus Flanagan could still pose a problem. She'd learnt that his mother had died and that his rejection of any talks with the British Government had set him against the leadership. The rumour was he'd gone over to the INLA. At first she'd feared he'd seek her out and do as he'd threatened, especially when he found out she was pregnant. He would have little doubt that the father was James Hanmore. She'd voiced her concern after a few days and been told she'd be protected. 'The IRA will look after you' she'd been assured.

The baby had been born in the Mater Hospital five months after her return to Ireland. She had been to hospital only twice in her life, once for a death and once for a birth, and regretted both. The irony of the situation had not escaped her. The birth had been reasonably painless. The same could not be said of her mind. The first time she'd held her bastard son she'd nearly screamed with the pain. Part of her had wanted to crush the life out of the small creature that had sucked at her left breast, the other half had wanted to shout with joy at the creation of something so exquisite. She had christened him James (it still made her smile when she thought of her stupidity), and even though she found she could love him, she still looked upon him as the devil's child. Now as she sat in the car with the boy cradled in her arms, being driven away from a disused shed on the outskirts of Castleblayney in County Monaghan she was trying to come to terms with yet another twist to her extraordinary life.

She had just witnessed the Army Council cynically endorse Sinn Fein's suggestion that the IRA open secret talks with the British Government on the possibility of starting official negotiations on a peace settlement. It had not been a unanimous vote. There were some who still believed in a military solution, but the wiser heads had prevailed, putting forward the argument that if peace and a United Ireland were placed on the agenda then they would be fools not to at least go through the motions of talking. Especially as they knew there was growing resistance to the violence in many quarters, not least from some of their biggest financial backers in the USA. Also there was renewed pressure from the Dublin Government on Sinn Fein. So the answer was simple, test the resolve of the British Government, and while they were talking they could re-arm and train more operatives (they had lost quite a few in the last year.) Then when they were ready and the British Government had said 'no' to a United Ireland they could walk out of the talks with the Organisation repaired and ready to kill again if necessary. There had been some harsh words spoken. Some very angry men sat glowering at their more dove like comrades as the vote was taken. But the moderate faction had held their nerve and won the vote, agreeing to send a delegation of three to meet the British representative in County Antrim at a date yet to be arranged.

To her amazement she had been chosen to be one of the three. She wasn't sure (given the cynicism that had prevailed in the shed), that she wanted to be part of the talks. But she was wise enough to know she could not refuse. Nor if she was honest with herself did she want to. This was the culmination of her change of heart. It gave her a real chance to play a part in obtaining a peaceful settlement. She was well aware that a few months ago she'd have spat at anyone suggesting a peace but not now. She thought briefly of Seamus. Jesus what would he think? Hopefully she'd never find out! Their dreams for the future were now so far apart. If she'd ever had any doubt about his intentions she had none now. He would view her as a traitor and would kill her. For some reason that she couldn't quite understand, it made her feel very sad.

As they crossed the border Mary stared at the armed soldiers checking the car. A year ago she would have felt the hatred stirring in her bowels as they went about their task with cold efficiency, but now—she shrugged. So much in her life had changed. Now she saw the armed foot patrols, the damaged buildings, the army land rovers and the graffitti on the walls, as a sign that Seamus's way had failed. It had to change, another way had to be found. She must do everything in her power to see that her child's generation lived in peace.

She fumbled for a handkerchief in her pocket as she felt the pain of a first tear. What fucking hope had she got when men like Seamus were running wild with hate buried deep in their hearts? She wondered how the man driving the car would react if she told him she was totally committed to peace, not just cynically playing with the word. Hostile was the only word she could think of. But she had no intention of compromising herself, at least not until the talks. Only then would she show her hand. It might mean a bullet in the head in some run down building on the border. For there would be many within the movement who would, like Seamus, want to finish her off. She shivered, remembering Seamus's evil smile. It might even be him who would pull the trigger. Once she wouldn't have cared; but now she had a son, and yes she had to admit it, a dream. So who would win? She had no doubt many dangers lay ahead and that there would be many more pointless deaths before the word 'peace' became acceptable. And what if peace was unacceptable? Then without a doubt there would be no life worth living for her child. Her island would continue to be a battleground. So the stakes were high and she was gambling with death. But so what? It was the story of her fucking life.

At about the same time as Mary was passing through the army check point Richard received the telephone call he'd been expecting for the last ten days. The PM was brief and to the point. The meeting was on. He was to fly out to Belfast the next day with

Commander Roberts, who would brief him on the plane. There were no guidelines. "Just do your best Richard," The PM said. "Test the water so to speak. You can walk away any time you like and will have my full support. However if you see a chink of light don't hesitate to go for it. I know you won't be able to come back with a deal, that is not the intention of this first meeting, but you might be able to fashion something that we can work on more openly. By that I mean enlist Dublin's support and hopefully all the political parties, not to mention the American President. He is a vital cog in the wheel for he might be able to win over the more hawkish in the Irish American community. So all I can say is good luck. You have a tricky task but if anyone can do it I know it will be you." There was not a word about the danger, not a word about security, nor a word about the location of the meeting. Even more disappointingly not a word of thanks. As Richard put down the telephone the thought passed through his head that this was the last chance he'd have to say 'no' but as at Number Ten he said nothing. He looked across his desk at Blanche nervously stroking her chin. "The PM," he said a little guiltily. "I leave tomorrow with Tim. Is that OK with you?" Why the hell did he ask such a stupid question? He already knew what she would like to say!

Blanche did her best to smile. She knew what he wanted and it was pointless letting him down, even though her grave reservations made her stomach churn. All she could think of was that she'd lost two children and didn't want to lose her husband. In a slightly unsteady voice she replied, "It would do no good if I said I thought you were mad, but I will say I think you are taking a big risk. The vagueness of the whole operation worries me and the lack of security sends a cold shiver down my spine. Nevertheless darling, I repeat you have my support, for I know how important this is to you, and this may come as a surprise to you; but a part of me thinks it is important for me as well. For like you, if you pull this off, I will feel our children have not completely died in vain."

He came round the desk and took her hands in his. "Thank you for that. I know it's not easy, especially with, the element of danger involved. But I am optimistic that the PM will not let me down (he was lying here), and with Tim by my side I know I will be as well protected as possible. He is not about to let me go into the lion's den without some pretty sophisticated surveillance. Tim knows Northern Ireland better than most anti terrorist officers and has had a network of informers in place for years. No. I don't think we need worry too much about this security bit."

Blanche gave a resigned shrug of her shoulders. What was the point in saying she didn't believe that for one minute. "Well I must accept your word but I would be happier if I thought you had a battalion of armed soldiers with you!" Her laugh stuck in her throat.

He sensed the panic within her. She had suffered so much. He ran a hand through her soft hair and felt he had to justify his actions more. "I'm sorry. But I must do this. I accept there are risks and I know it is a gamble. But we would not have come this far unless Sinn Fein were not under enormous pressure to make the IRA tow the line and at least have a meeting. Dublin, and the USA cannot be ignored forever. This is the first chance since my last disastrous attempt foundered. Okay, you can be cynical about the Government's motives, but it really is so important for the country and as I have already said it is to me. And who knows..."he gave a bitter laugh...."The IRA might actually want to talk peace this time. If they do, just think of all the lives that might be saved."

She looked at him with a feeling of love and admiration. She could see the old excitement was back in his eyes—it was a change from sadness. She kissed him lightly on the cheek and said, "I'm sorry. I'm being a silly woman. You didn't marry me to be like this. Just make damn sure you come back to me alive, you hear."

"I will come back alive," he assured her. "And God willing the outcome of my meeting will lead to no one having to suffer the terrible pain we have endured." His eyes flew to the spot where James had died. He could remember the smell of his blood and the flushed face of the young girl as if it was only yesterday. If he could do anything to stop such violence then he was prepared to die and Blanche knew this perfectly well and he admired her for her bravery. Of course she'd mourn, but she'd understand that his life was worth sacrificing if it eventually lead to peace in Ireland. "I will come back alive," he repeated. "I will come back." And then he added hastily, "alive," but a little unconvincingly.

Chapter Thirteen.

SEAMUS had buried his mother in the cemetery of the little church where she had worshipped since a child. Now, even after time should have healed the pain of his loss, he missed her dreadfully. He could still smell her unmistakable body odour and although he was a man not used to shedding a tear, he cried whenever he sat in her old rocking chair. He knew she had been the only person to have ever loved him. Full of stale water, the old kettle from which she had poured so many cups of tea sat on the stove never to be used again. He had bought a second hand electric one the day after her funeral. Her clothes were lain out on her bed upstairs and her shawl, which she'd worn every day since becoming an invalid, was on the back of her chair in the kitchen. Nothing would be moved until he was in his coffin. It was his way of saying 'thank you' to a woman who would have died for him.

His mood was dark. He was lonely and disillusioned, out of favour with the IRA. His very reason for living stripped from him. But how could he serve an Organisation that was talking peace, and if his information was right, was rewarding people who should be dead? For shit sake Mary O'Neill! She was a loser for Christ sake and given birth to a bastard who he was sure was the product of young Hanmore's sperm. Jesus! Now here was this loser all tucked up in bed with The Army Council. It made him want to puck. The world had gone mad! She should have been in a coffin a long time ago. Peace! By all that was holy it was a word that no one should ever dare to speak, and yet here were the IRA bandying the word around while the likes of him were ignored. By Christ how dare they! He'd killed for them for years and risked his life hundreds of times. Was his sacrifice going to waste just because some of the elderly Republicans within the Army Executive were tiring of the war? Well by Jesus not if he had anything to do with it!

The rumour going round was that it was all just a ruse to gain valuable time to re-arm and re-group after a pretty bad year, but that gave him little comfort. It was his opinion that once negotiations were under way the momentum would build up and prove hard to stop. The USA and Dublin would take the initiative and push and push. And with someone like Mary now on the Army Council anything could happen. Jesus! How had the whore managed it! Well the little bitch had better stay away from him. Peace by Jesus—it was a load of shit. Luckily there were still some like him who would do anything to make sure it did not become a reality.

Later that night, stoned on a bottle of Bushmills, he thought about what he had to do. Ireland needed patriots like him and he knew exactly what they would be thinking. It was time for him to offer the INLA his services and there was no time like the present. He was in no fit state to drive but he'd done it all before. He belched, spat on the floor and glanced at his watch. Some of those patriots would still be at the pub plotting their next move. They would be pleased to see him. He'd been approached before and his reputation made even hard men shiver. Cursing loudly he struggled to put on his coat. He gave a drunken smile and reached for his car keys. He'd talk and come home and then wait. He had no doubt the call would come sooner rather than later.

The knock on the door made Seamus jump. Instinctively he reached for his loaded shotgun. It was never far away from him these days. He crept up to one of the windows and looked out. He saw two men. He recognised one from the pub four nights earlier; the other was a stranger to him. He walked to the door and eased it open a crack, making sure they saw the shotgun. He was alive because he trusted no one.

The man from the pub asked, "Can we come in Seamus Flanagan? We need a little talk."

Seamus opened the door just enough for his body to stand in the gap. "You armed?"

The two men nodded.

"Then put down your arms by my feet here or you will not be coming into my house."

Seamus saw the hesitation in their eyes and started to close the door. "No!" one of the men exclaimed, dropping his weapon, to be quickly followed by his companion.

'That's better," Seamus growled as he picked up the pistols and opened the door. "Come in gentlemen. Welcome to the home of a true Irish patriot."

The room was heavy with smoke, and there was an air of excitement round the table. Their voices were slurred and their eyes watered from the cigarette smoke which gently floated above their heads. They had talked for five hours and drunk two bottles of Bushmills. They had spoken in conspiratorial tones, almost as if they feared the cottage had ears. Their minds were fixed on violence.

Seamus smiled as he once more re-filled the glasses from a fresh bottle of whisky. It was a smile that made the stranger shudder. Seamus said, "Thank you gentlemen for making me privy to your plans and for including me in them. It has been a very good evening and I think my track record speaks for itself and I will not let you down. I share your abhorrence of this proposed meeting, which we must ensure never gets off the ground. So I will wait to hear from you. It is time the IRA realised they don't run the whole show any more."

They rose unsteadily from the table. Hard drinking men as they were the brown liquid had taken its toll. As they passed Seamus by the cottage door he held out their guns. "I could kill you both now," he said with some satisfaction. "You are incapacitated with the drink and you gave up your arms. I hope you won't be like this when we go into action."

They laughed nervously and moved towards their car, silently cursing their weakness. Both of them knew Seamus had not been fooling around—if he'd had a change of heart they would now be dead. They had been over eager to recruit him, forgetting that the in their world you should never trust anyone, least of all a man as dangerous as Seamus Flanagan.

"By Jesus we took a risk there," the stranger said to his companion as they drove away. "That man frightened me. Did you see his eyes?"

"I saw them. I have seen them many times when we have been drinking. He is a killer and he enjoys it. God help anyone who doesn't share his views. But he is with us I assure you. He wants to kill every fucking Brit on this island and by the sounds of it he wouldn't be too fussy about killing a few of the IRA as well. You take my word for it, he will do anything we ask."

The stranger crossed himself. "By God I hope you are right."

They were half way into their flight to Aldergrove when Tim finished his briefing. He wasn't sure Richard had been giving him his full attention after the tearful parting from Blanche at Heathrow, but he prayed silently that some of his words had sunk in. "Well that's it Sir Richard. Not very encouraging I'm afraid but rest assured I and several others will be constantly monitoring your movements."

Richard felt like laughing. His security was going to be pretty rudimentary to say the least and decommissioning of IRA arms was paramount before the Government would discuss anything. He might as well not have bothered to board the plane. He was behaving like a fool, risking his life probably only to be sent packing back to the mainland at the first meeting, and yet—the dream was still there. He under-

stood why Tim was so against him going and he knew
he only had to say the word and he would beam his
approval and make contact with London. They would
be home within hours. He closed his eyes and
thought of Blanche—he hadn't stopped thinking
about her since he'd torn himself out of her arms.
She didn't deserve to be married to a fool. He glanced
across at Tim and said with more confidence than
he felt, "Well whatever security there is I will be grateful for and I know you. You won't let me down. You
will conjure up something I'm sure because I'm not
turning back."

Tim gave a weak smile. "I will not try to persuade
you again I promise. However as you are determined
I think I should broaden my briefing and tell you in
some detail what we know is going on. Our intelligence in Ulster tells us that there is friction within
the upper echelons of the IRA over these talks. The
decision to hold them was a close run thing. We are
told the hawks are only holding off because the IRA
need time to re-group. The whole bloody thing stinks
to me but I don't think you are in much danger from
the IRA. Our sources say they are not in the mood to
kill the Government's negotiator as they did last
time."

"I'm glad to hear that," interrupted Richard.

"You're not the only one Sir Richard! But that
does not apply to the INLA. As you well know, from
past experience, they are dangerous and volatile,
especially as they consider any mention of the word
'peace' is tantamount to treason. So you could well
be a target for them. However it is possible they may
just let these exploratory talks go on unhindered,
knowing they can wreck anything more serious at a
later date. That cannot be guaranteed as I'm sure

you are aware. They are an evil Organisation full of discontented madman. Now we have our eyes on one such fellow, a murderous bastard called Seamus Flanagan. Until recently he was one of the IRA's most dangerous assassins. Cunning too, as you can gather by the fact that he is still at large. Well he's had a big fall out with the IRA and defected to the INLA. He is definitely a man not to be trusted. He used to operate with an equally nasty piece of work called Dermot O'Neill, who was shot in his home in front of his wife and daughter by the loyalist para-militaries. Then a few weeks later the widow was gunned down in Belfast City Centre with her daughter by her side. The daughter's name is Mary O'Neill and we have been quite interested in her for some time. We know she found refuge with Flanagan after the death of her parents, and we think she became part of an IRA cell on the mainland. Whatever, she disappeared. But now she's re-appeared in Belfast, and if my informants are correct she is part of the IRA's Army Council. So I wonder what she might have done to rise so high in the command structure? My gut feeling is to say she's been up to no good on the mainland; and do you know what I think?"

Richard nodded. "I believe I do. She could be my young woman."

"Correct. I know it's only a hunch but she fits perfectly. The word is there was a plot to kill you and a woman was involved. I suspect she was to be the assassin. What went wrong we may never know but if she is your young woman she certainly didn't fall foul of the High Command or she would be dead."

Richard gave Tim a questioning look. "But James was in the IRA."

"I know, Tim agreed, "and that is where my guess work falls apart a bit, but I would be prepared to lay a small wager that I'm not far off the scent."

"You may well be right. After all it is not unknown for the IRA to eliminate its own people. Perhaps James slipped up somewhere, like killing his sister."

"I doubt if the IRA would have cared too much about that," replied Tim. "In fact they might well look upon her death as an added bonus. You must realise they would have treated James with great suspicion being who he was. I suspect that the chances of us ever finding out what happened are very small indeed but I would guess that he was a dead man as soon as he joined the IRA. Use him and liquidate him I fear would have been their motto."

"I expect you are right," Richard agreed. "Anyway knowing what happened won't bring back James or Sarah. As for the young woman it doesn't really matter who she is. After all I will never set eyes on her again." He looked away from his companion, not wishing him to see the tears in his eyes—it was still very painful to talk of his children. When he spoke again he asked, "So how long have we got before we land?"

Tim glanced at his watch. "About half an hour I would say."

"So maybe just a little over an hour before I meet the Sinn Fein representative you told me about in your briefing," said Richard quietly.

"Correct. Then I make myself scarce," added Tim. "But don't panic I will be following you."

Richard gave a rueful smile. "I'm banking on that commander; so don't lose me!"

"I will do my best—my very best. However I'm sure you realise it won't be easy. So keep that radio

I've given you somewhere about your body. I know you can't risk it being seen but I think we will both feel more confident if you can keep it with you at all times."

Richard tapped the radio in his breast pocket. "It will be safe in here unless I'm searched."

"Fine." The seat belt sign lit up above them. "Not long now, Tim said. "So I think I had better wish you luck now."

He held out a hand and Richard took it with a tense smile, saying, "Don't you worry too much commander—I will be okay."

I wish I could believe that, Tim thought despondently.

Chapter Fourteen

MARY sat in the small back room of the café in Lurgan Street unable to believe what she'd just heard. The Government's representative was going to be fucking Hanmore! Shit, she'd never thought it would be him! She had imagined it would be someone from the Irish Office, not an ex government minister, and certainly not one who had suffered so much at the hands of the IRA. Jesus, she'd thought she'd never set eyes on him again. She gripped the side of her chair and breathed in deeply. No, she had certainly not expected this! It would be naive to think he wouldn't recognise her. So how would he react? To sit down and talk peace to a woman who had two years earlier shot his son would certainly throw him. Jesus it would! If the tables were reversed she'd feel humiliated; yes that was the word. She glanced across at the whisky reddened face of Liam Keogh, and wondered what he was thinking. Almost certainly he was relishing the thought that it would humiliate Hanmore, even wreck the talks. Well the bastard would get a shock, oh shit he would! For she was not in the mood to let anything get in her way. Liam Keogh might not want peace, but he was in for a shock! She did! OK Hanmore was a problem but in many ways it made things easier. A sick man, she told herself, would not come willingly into the lions' den unless he believed in what he was doing. She'd always admired Hanmore. She'd been able to relate to him although both had had different goals. She still hated him, sometimes had wished she'd killed him as well, but he had balls! She smiled across the room at Keogh. Bet you'd have a fit, she thought, if you knew he was my son's grand father!

When she left the café an hour later to walk the short distance to her flat in Donegall Street, she couldn't help thinking of the triumphant look on Keogh's face as he swigged back another glass of Bushmills and glared at his two companions. He reminded her so much of Seamus and her father. It was 'the mad look' as her mother would have called it. The look that said murder was in his heart. She shivered in the damp night air and quickened her step, longing to get back to her child and feel him close to her breasts. Although he hadn't said it in so many words, she was certain Keogh had already written off the talks. He had made up his mind already, and as Chief of Staff what hope did that give her that her voice would be heard? He would ignore her and spit at Hanmore. But she felt he might be underestimating the man and she would fight her corner. Poor drunken sod, she thought, you might be in for a big surprise!

Patrick Ryan yawned. The plane was late. He scratched his red beard, and lit his thirtieth cigarette of the day. He felt irritable. He hated waiting for anyone. A meticulous planner, he lacked patience. He put the cigarette to his mouth with a nicotine stained hand and inhaled deeply. He coughed. At forty eight he was near his end. His eighty a day addiction was killing him. Three weeks earlier he had been told he had incurable lung cancer. 'Not even worth operating. I'm afraid you may well be dead within the year,' the consultant had told him. Ryan had looked at him in disbelief. Fuck, was there nothing modern medicine could do? The consultant had shaken his head and Ryan had walked out of the hospital feeling sick. Smoking had been his only pleasure since the age of twelve. At first he'd been bitter, feeling that the cards had been stacked against him since he'd been born. What had he done to deserve such a fate? He had never married and was not really interested in women, preferring his own company. Smoking and alcohol had numbed his sexual frustration and given him some sort of life. Worse men than him smoked heavily and survived. But he'd slowly become resigned to his death sentence and become determined to enjoy every last cigarette until the day he died. He should have known the risk he was taking. He had persuaded himself there were worse ways to die.

He had served the IRA since 1967. Gun running. Laundering drug money dishing out the odd knee capping and even killing a man, though that had been more by accident than design. But he had never reached the heights he had dreamt of. Once he'd envisaged himself being Commander in Chief. But after several years he was shrewd enough to realise his star would never be in the ascendancy and he'd moved across to Sinn Fein, where to his disgust he'd been largely ignored. Except for the most menial of jobs like meeting some British piece of shit off an aeroplane. He ground his fag end out on the floor. He accepted he was one of life's losers and would not be missed.

He hitched up his trousers around his beer belly and noticed that the London flight had landed. He heaved a sigh of relief and waddled towards the arrival door. He fumbled for another cigarette—feeling quite nervous now the moment had arrived—and waited for Hanmore. He didn't need the photograph he'd been given. He knew the bastard's face well. Seen him on the television. Read about him in the papers. Secretly quite admired him—he'd been a success, where as he'd been a failure. He was surprised the British Government had sent a man who had suffered so much at the hands of the IRA but perhaps they reckoned his knowledge of Irish politics would be an advantage. He laughed quietly. That was a fucking joke. He could have told Hanmore that he was wasting his time. But then he had never understood the Brits. He would have surrendered Ulster years ago.

Richard was tired and rather nervous as he walked towards the throng of people waiting to greet his flight, his eyes searching the crowd trying to guess which one was meeting him. He'd said goodbye to Tim on the plane and now to all intents and purposes he was on his own. The urge to look over his shoulder was very strong but he resisted the temptation knowing that he might already be under surveillance. He felt his heart beat increase as he thought once more of Blanche. Darling trusting Blanche. He should be at home with her now, not playing the hero. He was too old and too sad for such antics. He smiled and gave a shake of his head. Well she'd always said he never knew when to give up. Obviously he'd never learn.

A voice behind him asked, "Hanmore?" Richard jumped as a hand touched his arm. He turned and saw a small, dishevelled figure by his side, rubbing a cigarette between his fingers. His heart sank. The man's bloodshot eyes radiated contempt. "Yes that's me," he answered, holding out a hand, which Ryan refused to take. He saw no need to be polite. "And you are?" he asked.

"Ryan," mumbled the Irishman, taking Richard's bag and then pointing to one of the exit doors. "You will follow me please." Grumbling under his breath Ryan led Richard through the crowded concourse to the car park. He stopped at an old rusty Toyota. "Get in," he said unlocking the doors.

Realising it would be a waste of time saying anything Richard did as he was told, wrinkling his nose in disgust at the smell of stale cigarettes and the overflowing ashtray. He hoped this wasn't an omen for what lay ahead—a sleazy man to greet him and a filthy car could possibly be a message. As he settled in his seat Richard prayed that Ryan would not turn out to be the talkative type. He needn't have worried. At the best of times Ryan was a man of few words, used to spending his time on his own in a bar chain smoking cigarettes. After hours of waiting in a crowded and noisy airport lounge for a Brit, he was positively non-committal. It suited the moods of the two men well.

Richard watched the familiar landmarks slide past and reflected that it was just a little over three years since his last visit. Not much seemed to have changed. There were still the road blocks, the depressing sight of armed soldiers on nearly every street corner, and the debris of a war that no one seemed to be winning. What hope had he got? Even with the window shut he imagined he could smell the fear, sense the hatred and distrust lurking in the streets. He cursed under his breath. Who did he think he was kidding? He was too damned early. There needed to be more progress in the cross border talks, more pressure from the USA. A little more patience shown by his Prime Minister. Tim's words were ringing in his ears. 'Sir Richard you are allowing yourself to be dragged into a no-win situation.' Perhaps he was right. What on earth was he, an ex Minister of the Crown, doing risking, not only his own his life, but those of others? He could be making a terrible mistake. He glanced across at Ryan, the inevitable cigarette hanging from his lips and wondered what would happen if he told him to drive back to the airport. But he quickly discarded any such request for he was too far down the road to realistically pull out now. He consoled himself with the thought that Tim was probably be no more than a few cars behind—and with him around what harm could he possibly come to? He sighed and looked across at the little Irishman. It was time to focus on the job at hand. He asked, "Not far to go then?"

"Another fifteen minutes," Ryan growled. "Providing we don't get stopped by some bastard patrol.

We are going to the Lansdown. You know it I believe?"

Richard was surprised. "Indeed I do."

"Quite a haunt of yours in your younger days I gather. Pity you didn't leave it at that."

Richard picked up the bitterness in his voice. The man was full of hate. There was no point even trying to have a conversation with him. No doubt if he had something of interest to say he'd eventually get round to saying it. In the meantime he might as well look out of the window and keep his own company.

657 Antrim Road. Richard looked up at the familiar façade of Lansdown Court. There were so many memories. It had been here as a young man, full of idealism and never imagining that one day he would hold a Government post, that he had spent hour upon hour talking to Republicans and Unionists, who at that time were prepared to sit together without pulling a gun. He had learnt about the religious divide and the fears of Ulster people. It was here that he had vowed to do all he could to help bridge the gap. It was here that he had thought how tolerant the majority of the people were. It was here, years on when in Government, that any dreams he had left were shattered one violent night. He had been lucky to come out alive, his fellow negotiator had not been so lucky. He'd gambled he could talk to anyone in the IRA. He'd learnt a swift and terrible lesson. A lesson he should have reminded himself of a few weeks earlier. He gave a wry smile to the doorman as he followed Ryan into the familiar foyer.

Mary opened the door to the knock. Keogh was standing there grinning. "Can I come in Mary O'Neill?"

"You most certainly cannot be doing such a thing Liam Keogh. I know your sort. To be sure you can be telling me whatever it is you want standing here."

Keogh scowled. He didn't fancy getting lip from a fucking whore, especially one he considered lucky to be alive, given her cock up on the mainland. He was also still smarting from having her thrust upon him when he'd objected so strongly. His only satisfaction was the thought of her coming face to face with Hanmore. Ha, by Jesus he could hardly wait for that moment! He growled, "I don't fancy a woman who has given birth out of wedlock and so insulted the Catholic faith. To be sure you are just another whore. So don't you be kidding yourself Mary O'Neill, for Liam Keogh can have any woman he likes."

Mary gave him a contemptuous smile. "You are a bragging Irish bastard to be sure and your words do not hurt me. But you will not be coming into my flat and tainting the air my child breathes. I may have to work with you Liam Keogh but I don't have to like you. Now perhaps you can tell me what it is you want."

Not used to being talked to in such a dismissive tone Keogh was boiling inside. But he had his orders and he was intelligent enough to know that fighting with her would get him nowhere. So swallowing his pride he said quietly, "The package has arrived. I will be picking you up around seven tomorrow evening. The meeting won't last long." Then he couldn't stop himself from adding. "Then Mary O'Neill I will have time to deal with you."

'The meeting won't last long.' Ah, those were the words that gave so much away. But not wishing to rile him further by questioning his declaration, she asked in a more gentle voice, "And where may I ask will we be going?"

Keogh's face broke into an evil smile. "We will be going to the cottage at Gartree Point. That should shake the bastard."

Mary nearly choked. By Jesus it certainly would! Gartree Point! That might really shake Hanmore! She looked at Keogh in amazement. "Is that a good idea? Don't we want to put the man at ease?"

"Fucking hell Mary O'Neill I want the bastard to be so ill at ease that he will run crying all the way back to his fucking Government and tell them we fight on."

Mary swallowed hard. His words confirmed her worst fears. Keogh had no intention of giving any time to Hanmore. Somehow he had persuaded the Army Council that he was the right man to talk peace. Shit! How had the bastard managed that! What was the point of men like him meeting Hanmore? She felt a cold hand touch her heart. She risked being isolated unless Kelly, the other member of the negotiating team was of the same opinion as her. And that was very doubtful knowing how he went in awe of Keogh. The danger signals were flashing, for someone like Keogh would not hesitate to sweep her way. She looked at his smirking face and wanted him gone. She replied tersely, "Okay, see you at seven tomorrow." Then without giving him a chance to say anything else she stepped back and slammed the door in his face. For a moment she stood by the door shaking. God, how she hated the man. When she'd finally managed to control herself she rushed across to where James slept, fearing her dreams for him might prove to be unrealistic. How could he have a future on a peaceful island with men like Seamus and Keogh about? Would they ever allow the North to become a place where two communities could live in peace with each other? Her hand flew to her mouth. And if not—shit! Could James become another Keogh? The thought made her feel sick and she bent down and lifted the small sleeping body to her breasts. "I will do my best for you," she whispered. "By all that is holy, I will be doing my best!" Holy Jesus her life had been simpler when she'd been like Seamus and Keogh. Then she wouldn't have minded what he son turned into—in fact she'd have been disappointed if she hadn't felt he'd want to kill fucking Brits! But she wasn't about to have another change of heart even if meant James becoming an orphan. She knew without a shadow of doubt she could never turn back.

George Russell had served with RUC for twenty five years. He was forty six and unmarried. The day he'd joined he'd sworn to stay single. He would not risk putting the life of a wife and children in danger. It had been a hard choice, but time had proved him right. He had seen too many families of serving officers left in torment. He was biased. He blamed the Catholics. They were destroying his island. But he had to keep quiet these days, although he knew many of his colleagues shared his views. He risked been thrown out of the RUC, and it was his life. What's more he knew he was a bloody good policeman. Over the years he'd built up a sophisticated network of informers amongst the nationalist community, and the feed back had saved many lives. He was recognised as an intelligent and brave officer and his superiors were grateful. But the bloody politicians had begun to interfere more and more and the RUC was under pressure to change. Officers like George were viewed with suspicion from Whitehall and that made him want to puke. He'd given his life to the service of his country and he feared it might all turn out to be a waste of time.

Now he was lunching with Tim Roberts at the Europa Hotel, warning him that his sources were giving out the danger signals about the meeting. "I don't need to tell you that my information is nearly always correct, and that is why I am so worried. Our Government could be sending a man to his death, and because of the security restrictions they have agreed to, your man is dreadfully exposed. Frankly I don't want that on my conscience. The RUC's hands are tied, but not yours. You are Sir Richard's only hope. Somehow you must give him maximum protection and I think a pal of mine in the Scots Guards might be able to help. The army will not be under such restrictions because they will have to continue with their patrols and the Scots patrol around the meeting area.. However one thing not in your favour is the setting of the cottage at Gartree Point. Isolated and out on its own. It will be difficult to get close to without being spotted. But you are an expert on surveillance commander."

"It sounds as if I will have to be bloody invisible as well," Tim said with some feeling.

"Indeed I fear you will, especially if, as seems more than likely, the INLA decide to cause trouble. The IRA may think it bad PR to slaughter him on Irish soil but certainly the INLA will have no such qualms. It beats me why the British Government sent a man with such a reputation. It is almost an open invitation to the INLA to shoot him! Why couldn't they have sent someone less well known?"

"My sentiments exactly," said Tim resignedly. "But our Prime Minister felt he was the best man for the job because no one on the mainland would ever expect Sir Richard to get involved in Irish matters again. And the silly bugger wanted to come! I don't think anybody gave enough thought to the problem you have just raised."

Russell shook his head. "Well I don't think he has a chance in hell of taking home anything of substance, but then to be frank I don't think anyone else would have either. My information is that the IRA is riven with disagreement over this meeting. If you want my personal view the talks are doomed to failure because I sense they are playing their usual game. They want time to re-group. They have been hit hard just recently but that doesn't change the fact that basically they are murderers Tim. The gun is their negotiating weapon. I have outlived many of my colleagues because I hold this view. It is time our Government got wise and accepted that the IRA may well never come to the negotiating table. Nor will they, or any other republican group, disarm. Just as the British Government will never be prepared to talk about a united Ireland. And if a miracle ever did take place then there will be splinter groups who will still murder and maim here and on the mainland."

Tim glanced at the wide honest green eyes of the big man sipping a glass of white wine, and said, "I hope you are proved wrong my friend but in all honesty I fear you may well be right. Between you and me I don't think either side can win with the gun so I see negotiations as the only way forward. I can only hope that sooner or later the IRA will see it the same way. I think they might once their support begins to dry up which I believe it surely will. For God sake we can't go on killing each other forever! But a strong nerve will be required in the meantime by a British Government, for by God if it starts making concessions the IRA will see this as a weakness and start making demands that should never be considered. Like for example releasing terrorists from the Maize Prison."

"Or getting the Government to tamper with the RUC!" Russell exclaimed.

"Oh I can't see that happening," Tim said. My God that really would upset you lot! But just think of what could happen if at sometime talks failed and all those killers were loose on the streets! But we must not be negative; and despite the wrongs of this mission, I feel it is a beginning—just a crack in the ice. So it is vital nothing goes wrong. Now tell me do the INLA know where this meeting is going to take place?"

"Almost certainly they will have been tipped off by someone within the Army Council opposed to this meeting."

Tim's reply highlighted his deep concern. "Then as I see it we have two options. Either I do my best with the resources at my disposal, which I fear will never be enough with the sort of men you have been talking about. Or we make a bloody great noise about security around Sir Richard and the IRA abort the meeting. So what do you say?"

Russell inclined his head. "Is there not a third option?"

"Which is?"

"You ask Sir Richard to pull out?"

Tim couldn't stop himself smiling. "I'm sure you know a lot about Hanmore already, but I am going to bore you just for a few minutes. Firstly you must realise that he is a Hanmore and like his grandfather has always nurtured a dream. Now there is nothing wrong with that. But in a relatively short space of time he has suffered a heart attack, left the Government, and had both his children murdered. He is convinced that he has little to lose and a lot to prove. If anything comes out of this meeting he will persuade himself that the death of his children was worthwhile and that he has at least obtained part of his dream. But in my opinion he is not in an emotionally fit state to take a rational view of anything to do with Ulster or his dream. But you tell that to the man! No, George there is no third option.

"Russell nodded. "I understand; but it is a pity for the meeting place is not a good omen at all."

"So what's with this cottage?"

Russell leant his elbows on the table and asked, "Do you want the whole story?"

"I think I had better hear it."

" Very well, but get me another drink."

Tim waved at a passing waiter and ordered a glass of wine and a bottle of still water for himself. He wanted to stay fully alert.

"Okay, here we go," continued Russell. "Sir Richard's grand father was not always the moderate voice of Unionism for which he became so well known, in fact far from it. In his early days he hated the Catholics. It was only after his return from the trenches in 1918 that he adopted his more moderate views. Something to do with a dying Catholic soldier. The story goes the grand father watched him die, and was so impressed by his faith in God that his whole attitude changed. Now you probably know all that, but the rest will be news to you. Before he saw the light, as you might say, there was a young dairy-man working for the grand father called Martin Leary. He lived in a small cottage at Gartree Point and horrors of horrors the silly boy fell in love with a young Catholic girl from Belfast. In spite of the dis-belief of the two sets of parents the young couple refused to split up. They might have just got away with that, but foolishly they married, and all hell broke loose. Hanmore was furious that one of his staff wanted to marry a Catholic. Then one day when Leary was milking the estate's cows a gang of youths visited the girl in the cottage. When Leary got home that evening he found her tied naked to a tree, and their meagre possessions smouldering outside the cottage. The next day Hanmore sacked the boy and threw the young couple off the estate. They were outcasts—ignored by both communities. I'm sure you are old enough to understand that?"

Tim nodded.

"Well they would surely have starved or worse, if it hadn't been for old Hanmore's American wife. She took pity on them and bought them passage to the USA. It has always been believed that Hanmore sent those thugs to the cottage. Of course he denied it, and who was to argue with such a powerful man? However two months after the Learys had left for the USA the cottage was burnt down. It remained a ruin until old Hanmore returned from the war a wiser man. He rebuilt the cottage and offered it free of rent to a young Catholic couple. Not surprisingly they refused the offer, as did everyone else. The cot-tage fell into disrepair again until Sir Richard's fa-ther sold the estate. The cottage was sold separately to a strong Nationalist family named Keogh, who were known IRA supporters. In fact their only son, Liam, is active today. We have never been able to nail him, but we suspect him of committing several murders. He is a violent bastard. The Keoghs never lived in the cottage. Turned it into a sort of shrine to republicanism, and hold a service there every year on the date that the Learys were thrown out. It is sheer provocation in such a strong Protestant area, but that of course was the idea of purchasing the cottage in the first place."

"And the IRA want to rub Sir Richard's nose in the shit?" said Tim.

"Exactly." It may well not succeed, but what does it say of their commitment? Bugger all if you ask me!"

"I would tend to agree with you. But that doesn't mean they want him dead. You just said so yourself."

"Indeed I did, but I also mentioned the INLA. They would like nothing better than to kill him in the cottage. You see it would be very symbolic for them. But I think the INLA could be in danger as well."

Puzzled Tim asked, "You do? Why?"

Russell threw him a conspiratorial look "Let's assume that they have decided to assassinate Sir Richard. I think they will send at least two, maybe three gunmen. They seem to like working as a gang and they will reckon the IRA will have numbers on the ground. Also we cannot rule out the chance that one of the IRA negotiators might be INLA. There have been a lot of defections recently and some have certainly stayed within the IRA to spy. Okay, so now suppose we ambush these gunmen and rid ourselves of some very nasty and dangerous characters? If we are alert, and I accept a little lucky, we might succeed, and then at least if the talks fail we would have achieved something."

"Aren't you forgetting that you would be gambling with a man's life George and that you are light on the ground?"

"Indeed. But you are gambling with a man's life anyway. And consider the IRA's position. They don't want to see Hanmore killed on Irish soil, so they won't be too keen to let the INLA muscle in. In fact I suggest they might even help us. Not openly of course, but they might just stand by. Added to that we have the Scots Guards patrolling the Loch Neagh area and their commanding office, as I said earlier, is not under the same restrictions as the RUC. They pass the cottage every night and he has assured me they will help if they can. They are tough men near the end of their tour and would like to settle a few scores. And then my friend there's you and me! Neither of us beginners when it comes to a fire fight. I would say we have a pretty good chance if it comes to that especially if there is an IRA/INLA confrontation as well."

Tim shook his head. "My God this all sounds very iffy, especially your surmise about the IRA. I accept it must seem very attractive to you, but my prime task is to protect Sir Richard and I think any attack by us would put his life in even more danger."

"Very well: You are the boss. Then I think we should go for option two. We make a lot of noise about security and the IRA will call the whole thing off. Then your man goes back to London safe and sound."

Tim rubbed his chin thoughtfully. "Do we need to confront the INLA if they come to the cottage?"

"We must get to them first or they will surely kill your man. They won't be going there for a friendly chat over a drink; and commander if the IRA and INLA get into a fire fight where will your man be? Piggy in the middle I would say."

"You are right. So we either get the meeting called off or we prepare ourselves for a fight if the INLA turn up?"

"You have it in a nutshell."

"Well I don't think we should get this meeting called off—it is too important, and after all Sir Richard knows he's running a risk. Even if I told him what you have just told me I'm sure he'd say go ahead."

"So"?

"We go ahead. We say nothing—do our level best with the security we have on hand—and as far as I can see, pray bloody hard! But let me warn you George my duty is to protect Sir Richard above everything else. Eliminating a few of the INLA will not be my number one priority."

Russell nodded. "I accept that. But thanks for your support. Now I think it's time for us to go our separate ways don't you?"

Tim glanced at his watch. "My God you are right. Look at the time! I've been away too long from the Lansdown. I must be getting back immediately."

Russell leant across the table and touched Tim's hand lightly. "The meeting will be tonight mark my word. So no need to panic. You have plenty of time to get back to the Lansdown and be in position when the IRA makes its move. I will contact the Scots and ask them to be extra vigilant tonight. You have a radio?"

"Yes, and so has Sir Richard. All you need do is give me your frequency."

"Excellent. I will be switched on the moment we leave here. Any movement from the Lansdown and you ring me pronto. I won't be far away." He wrote the frequency down on his napkin and handed it to Tim before holding out a hand. "Good luck. Keep as invisible as you can, and ever vigilant; and rest assured wherever you are I will be close behind. Whatever we do we must not underestimate our enemy, they are a bunch of clever bastards and for sure they will expect a covert security job on Hanmore. But don't fret too much. I understand your concern for Sir Richard's safety. I have been a very lucky man in my life so far. If I fail, I will feel as bad as you."

Tim grimaced. "I very much doubt that!"

Richard had missed the warmth of Blanche's body, so he had slept badly. He had also dreamt too much. It had been a bad night. Now it was five in the evening and he was growing agitated and a little angry. Ryan hadn't shown his face all day and nor for that matter had Tim, although he'd had a call telling him the frequency for the radio. It was as if he'd been forgotten. He'd hoped that the meeting would be today but now he was beginning to wonder. He was not looking forward to spending another night in a strange bed alone and a slave to his conscience. He understood how a caged lion must feel. He wanted to go out, and breath in some fresh air, but he remembered Tim's warning. 'Someone might want you dead before the meeting, so take care.' Richard knew Ulster. The risk was not worth taking. His eyes darted towards the revolving door as he heard it's by now familiar swish. It was just another guest. Would Ryan ever come? He forced himself to sit in a chair and for some reason he began to think of the young woman. Was she Mary O'Neill? Was she out there somewhere, maybe only a street away? Did she ever think of him? Did she ever think of James and regret the moment she pulled the trigger? Did she regret not shooting him as well? It was irrational thinking brought on by intense anxiety and he shook his head violently. He didn't want to remember her. He heard the familiar swish of the door again. This time he resisted the urge to glance across the foyer and so never spotted the bearded Irishman until he was standing over him.

"Evening Hanmore. Getting worried I wasn't going to show?"

Richard jumped with surprise and eased himself out of the chair determined not to show his agitation to this aggravating apology of a man. "No, not at all," he lied. "I knew you would come when things were ready. Are we still on?"

Ryan nodded, "Yes we're on as you say. For tonight. Almost time to move now. You ready?"

"Give me a few minutes. Just got to go upstairs for my overcoat.."

Ryan smirked and took hold of Richard's arm. "No I don't think so. We go now."

Richard realised he had no choice. Swearing under his breath for his stupidity he reluctantly allowed himself to be led towards the exit. He should never have left the radio in his bedroom. As he walked out of the revolving doors he felt terribly alone.

Chapter Fifteen

TIM rubbed his sore eyes. It was over three hours since he had left the Europa and he was growing weary. He thanked his lucky stars he hadn't succumbed to a second drink. He did his best to stretch his tall frame within the confines of the car, and nearly missed them. As it was he spotted them late. They were already out of the hotel door and hurrying down the street before he picked up Richard's familiar back view. He swore silently as he gunned the engine, all the time not taking his eyes off the silver Subaru. He was lucky, the traffic was light, and he was moving by the time the Subaru pulled into the street. Christ why hadn't Richard alerted him on his radio! Had he forgotten to set his radio! Whatever there was no point worrying about it now. The adrenaline coursed through his body. His eyelids were no longer heavy. The waiting was over. Now he had to prove his worth. He tucked himself two cars behind them, not worrying too much if he lost them. Russell had assured him they would head for Gartree

Point, and although he wasn't sure of the exact location of the cottage he knew the area well. As he drove with his eyes fixed on the Subaru he worried what the next few hours would bring. He must be positive, time to caste off any lingering doubts and concentrate on the job in hand. He reached for his radio and called up Russell.

Richard sat in the front passenger seat cursing his incompetence. Leaving the radio in his room was one thing, but to underestimate Ryan could have been even worse. Ryan had thoroughly searched him before letting him get into the car. He'd have found the radio and what then! Alright he had no way of contacting Tim, but at least he was still going to the meeting. What might have happened was not worth thinking about. Nevertheless he was very nervous. Had Tim seen him leaving the hotel? The temptation to glance over his shoulder was almost unbearable. He consoled himself by the thought that Tim was a first class policeman and would be alert. Nevertheless it was hard not to fret. He glanced at Ryan smoking the inevitable cigarette, and decided he would have to watch him very carefully. He had moved quickly, giving him no chance to alert anyone. Now they were nearly out of Belfast and he had no idea where they were going. He felt it was time to ask the question.

Ryan pulled on his cigarette and blew the smoke towards Richard. "Can't tell you that Hanmore, but you will know soon enough."

Richard cursed under his breath. Why was the man being so evasive? What harm would it do to tell him now? Unless he threw himself out of the car he was a prisoner—alone and very apprehensive. But Ryan had already surprised him and he knew he'd get nothing out of him until the revolting little man decided to tell him. He swallowed his frustration and gazed out of his window at the wet streets, where people huddled under umbrellas or hunched against the persistent drizzle, hurried along the pavements. At a red light a car full of youngsters pulled up along side them and a pretty girl smiled at him. He raised a hand wondering if she would be the last pretty girl to ever smile at him. He swore under his breath. That was defeatist thinking and would get him nowhere.

By the time Ryan turned onto the A52 Richard had got his frustration and negative thoughts under control. A strange calmness seemed to envelope him and for the first time since arriving in Belfast he felt a jab of excitement at the thought of the confrontation to come. Yes, confrontation was the word, for without a doubt the IRA would be in a belligerent mood, demanding to know if the British Government were prepared to talk about a united Ireland. They would know already he would hedge, glance at his notes and suggest they talk about other things that were just as important. He would see their impatience and offer them a carrot like, 'But of course it could always be on any future agenda,' he would say with a smile. He shook his head. Well if they believed that then he'd know they meant business.

Ryan drove fast once he was out of the city and Richard continued to stare out of the window at the darkness knowing that sooner or later he'd see a road sign in the light of the car which would give him a clue to their destination. He was totally unprepared for what he saw. **CRUMLIN**. He went cold. This was home, what on earth were they doing going to

Crumlin? This was strong Protestant country. A most
unlikely place to have a secret meeting with the IRA.
In a worried voice he asked, "What on earth are we
doing in Crumlin?"

He couldn't see Ryan as he replied but he knew
he was smiling. The meeting is at Gartree Point."

"What! At the cottage?"

"You have it."

He didn't know whether to laugh or cry then.
This was some sort of sick joke. Did the IRA really
want to enter into serious dialogue if they chose a
place like this? All his new found confidence evaporated and he sank back into his seat. The bastards
were just playing with him and what better place than
the cottage? The car's lights were now picking out
familiar features which brought back so many memories. He felt tears wet his cheeks as he saw the ruined gates which led to his old home, long since de-
molished. Then came the shadowy outline of the
church where most of his family where buried and
where he'd been christened. He saw the outline of
the small cottage where his grandmother had spent
her last years in almost total exile. He even felt a
touch of the old bitterness towards his father. He'd
had no right to sell the Estate, so robbing him of his
inheritance and a chance to live on the island he was
just getting to love. His father's action had been the
reason for his obsession with Ireland and explained
why he was sitting in a car, heading for the place that
had shamed his grand father, to talk peace with a
bunch of killers who had unsuccessfully tried to kill
him while in office.

As they approached Loch Neagh the lights picked
out the mist hanging over the water. It was here that
he and his grandfather had spun for fish in the fail-

ing light of a summer's evening. On the way home
the old man would often recount stories of his life
and always end by saying in a voice tinged with sadness. 'I know I say this to you nearly every time we
walk back to the house boy, but I can't help wondering why such a beautiful country has to be so ill at
ease with itself.'

As Ryan drove into the mist he couldn't help
thinking nothing had changed.

"Nearly there, " growled Ryan.

He needn't have told him that. He remembered
every in inch of the road to the cottage—the small
white cottage now illuminated by the car lights. He
shivered, but not from cold. If the IRA had wanted
to make him feel uneasy they had succeeded. No
Hanmore had been inside the cottage for over thirty
years. Yet here he was about to walk through the door
to meet with the IRA. He couldn't help wondering
if he'd ever walk out.

Outside the cottage two armed men guarded the
four men and one woman inside. Three of them
were standing around the newly lit fire in the small
damp sitting room. The other two were sitting on a
threadbare sofa. There was no carpet on the wooden
floor and rat droppings were scattered about the
room. Keogh had placed seven old wooden upright
chairs, which he'd collected from other rooms in the
house, in a semi-circle near the fire. Mary had expected only Keogh and Kelly to be with her in the
cottage and the sight of the other two men walking
into the room a few minutes after she'd arrived made
her very nervous. She didn't recognise either of them.
She sat on the threadbare sofa next to Kelly and

wondered what was going on. She stared at Keogh's flushed face as he talked quietly to one of the strangers. He had ignored her the moment they'd arrived at the cottage an hour ago. He had been drinking ever since they had left her flat and she was convinced he was up to no good. She didn't trust him and wanted to challenge him. She wanted to ask him questions. But could she risk it? Would she be putting herself in danger? She had this dreadful feeling that the next few hours were not going to go the way she had hoped, and spent most of the night before on her knees praying for. She glanced at Kelly. Could she tell him of her fears? Shit, she had nothing to lose. So she said in a low voice, "I don't like this. I thought it was only us three who were going to meet Hanmore. Why are these two men here? I think we are owed an explanation." She held her breath, wondering what his reaction might be.

Through pursed lips he replied in a low voice, "I agree, but I don't think we will get one. What I can be telling you is that the two men are well known across the border. They are hard men, not men I would have said were inclined towards talking peace—at least not seriously. So perhaps we should try and get some sort of explanation from Liam and his two friends. Do you want me to......" The sound of a car cut him off in mid-sentence as Keogh waved everyone to silence. Mary felt Kelly tense beside her and watched Keogh walk slowly towards the door. This had to be Hanmore arriving. The silence in the room was intense.

When he reached the door Keogh turned and broke the silence. "Well it seems our friend from across the water has arrived. Now let us remember we do not compromise over anything. We send the bastard back to the mainland if he's not prepared to offer us a united Ireland, and as we know that's fucking unlikely we won't be wasting our time for too long. You can see I have brought in only a few logs," he added smiling at Mary. "So we don't want to be growing cold do we Mary O'Neill?"

She tossed her head contemptuously and was trying to think of an appropriate reply when they heard the front door open and felt a rush of air enter the room. Keogh once more signalled for silence. Mary blew out her cheeks nervously. This was a meeting she was not looking forward to! Jesus! It was the last thing she wanted. Would he recognise her? How would he react? Would it throw him into confusion just as it was planned? Her stomach churned. Did he have any idea of the danger he was in? Oh fuck why was she so worried—she hated the bastard!

He came into the room a little hesitantly, casting a nervous eye at those gathered there. Keogh gave him little chance to settle, greeting him with disdain. Mary stared hard at him as he stammered out a rather hesitant 'thank you' in his crisp upper class accent. She almost felt sorry for him. And then Richard saw her. She watched his mouth drop open and his eyes widen in surprise before he got hold of himself and gave her a weak smile.

Keogh had him by the arm and pulled him towards her, an evil smile on his face. "And you be knowing this young woman no doubt?" he sneered. "She's told us how much pleasure she got from killing your son. What surprises me is why she didn't kill you." And then he said, "I be hearing things about you Mary O'Neill from your old friend Seamus." Mary sucked in her breath. "Yes, indeed. He tells me your son is probably the product of you coupling with this man's son. Can you be denying that now!"

The last vestige of colour drained from Mary's face. She glanced at Hanmore and saw the shock written on his face. By God this was a bad situation! Her eyes fixed on Keogh's face. "Seamus Flanagan is a damn liar Liam Keogh as if you didn't know! I know who the father of my son is, but I not be telling you." She stood defiantly in front of him, daring him to argue.

There was a deathly silence in the room as they stared at each other and then he said, "It is of no matter anyway. We have more important things to discuss here tonight other than who you prostituted yourself with. Either way God will punish you in the end!

Mary smiled in her relief and looked at Hanmore. His eyes told her all she needed to know. He said to Keogh, "What may or may not have happened is of no concern to any of us tonight. It would make things easier if we tried to forget the past. I am only here to negotiate, not to listen to something that does not concern me or reasons why this young woman did as she did. Now if you don't mind I have had a longish journey with Mr Ryan here and would like to go to the bathroom before we sit down and talk. Can someone take me?" He looked at the gathered company and saw nothing but hatred in their eyes. He had no friends here and despite his outward confidence he'd been deeply wounded. Could he have a grandson! Could the mother really be in the room? He had to know! Would the girl understand or even care?

Keogh shrugged and looked at Ryan. But before

he could say anything Mary jumped forward and took hold of Richard's arm. "I will take him."

She'd understood!

Not waiting for a scowling Keogh's reply she led him out of the room. Once in the passage she put a finger to her lips. He nodded his understanding and allowed her to lead him to the bathroom. She switched on a weak overhead light to reveal a room almost totally devoid of anything to do with the necessities of a bathroom. No bath, no sink and just a hole where the toilet had once been. Mary pointed at the hole. "If you want a piss you must use that. So go ahead, but I'm not leaving. We have little time and I must warn you that I think you are in grave danger. I don't fucking know why I should care, except to say that I want peace on this island. Sadly I don't think Liam Keogh thinks the same way. He is up to something I'm sure. Certainly I would be surprised if he wants these talks to produce a positive result. You, of all people should never have come. Fucking stupid." Then with a shrug of her shoulders she added, "I have warned you—but there is little I can do to help you."

Richard nodded and pointing at the hole tried desperately to keep his voice calm. "I don't want to use that. I just need a little time to compose myself. Meeting you again has come as a terrible shock, and now this baby! Be honest with me please. Is your child my grandson? For God sake tell me the truth!"

"You have a grandson."

"Dear God!" His eyes misted over and she could see he was close to tears.

"You should never have known. We should never have met again. Why the fuck did you have to come!"

Richard looked at her small emaciated figure standing in front of him and wondered what was going on in her mind. What had driven her to kill James when she was carrying his child? He knew he'd never know the answers he so desperately sort for there just wasn't time. He gave her a weak smile and said, "Just one question. I suppose there isn't a chance I might see him before I go back?"

Mary's eyes blazed. "Not a fucking chance Hanmore! I may warn that you are in danger—I may not want you to die, because for some stupid reason I think you might bring peace to this island one day, but don't ask me to see your grandson! Get this into your head Hanmore I hate you. I only spared your life because I hated your son more!"

"Then why did you make love?"

Mary smiled. "Because I once thought I might love him. You see we both had a lot in common. We had hate in our hearts. But for some reason I can't explain I changed when he killed your daughter. For Christ sake my whole world turned upside down! I was supposed to kill you, instead I ended up by killing the father of my child! Shit, I don't know anything any more except for one thing—I want peace for my child. Now come on we must get back to Keogh or he will be growing impatient. I'm sorry. Yes, believe it or not I'm sorry."

Richard ran his hands through his hair, his mind in turmoil. He knew it was no good arguing—she'd made up her mind and it was what he'd expected. But a grandson! How was he going to concentrate now? And what had the girl said? "You are in grave danger." If that was the case he couldn't afford to be thinking of a small child. My God what a situation! He pulled his handkerchief out of his trouser pocket and mopped his brow before taking several deep breaths. "I'm ready so let's go." he said. It was meant to sound confident. To Mary it sounded like an acceptance of death.

Keogh was standing impatiently by the sitting room door as they returned. He growled, "About time Hanmore. Never takes me that long to have a piss." He pointed to one of the wooden chairs. "As I was about to say when you left sit there."

Richard lowered himself into the hard chair without objecting and looked at the men sitting facing him. They were not faces that filled him with confidence, especially that of Keogh, a man whose reputation had been well known to him when he'd been in government. In spite of the girl's warning he had to give them the chance. He pulled his briefcase onto his lap—pulled out several papers, and asked Keogh, "Would you like to begin?"

Bristling with unconcealed hatred Keogh jumped up from his chair. "Indeed Hanmore I would," he replied. "I will start with a question. "How much has your fucking lot got to offer us? Very little I suspect. Just another load of crap?"

Ryan interjected. "Now that's no way to start Liam."

Richard raised a hand. "It's alright Mr Ryan. I have known of this man and his family for years." He stared at Keogh. "It frankly surprises me that you are here to talk peace."

Keogh's eyes blazed. "If I had my way I wouldn't be here. But times are fucking changing and I have little choice. The word is we must be good boys and do as the USA and Sinn Fein tell us. So here we are. Some of us keener than others to talk to the likes of you." He almost spat the last three words out and glared at Mary. "So for everyone's sake let's hear what you have to offer us. I can hardly believe that you have any goodies in that briefcase that can persuade us to give up the armalite and the bomb. Especially as it is brought to us by a has-been politician with a rotting heart."

This time nothing was going to stop Ryan, and he leapt to his feet sweating profusely. "Now that won't do Liam. We cannot at this stage be so rude to our guest. I am chairing this meeting and I forbid you to be so confrontational. We are here on serious business, not to insult this man."

Keogh snorted disdainfully. "Sit down Ryan, before you shit on the floor. You are a lightweight in the Organisation and Sinn Fein is not in control here. The IRA will call the shots as was agreed. If you don't like that than I suggest you fuck off now."

Gasping for breath Ryan stood his ground. "But I don't think you are representing the views of the Army Council. You are introducing your own agenda."

"Oh Ryan you silly man," Keogh said in a sneering voice. "Of course I'm introducing my own agenda. The Army Council's agenda is weak and humiliating to the likes of me. So fucking shut your mouth you small man and sit down!"

This time Ryan buckled under the pressure and wiping his forehead with a blue handkerchief he collapsed back into his chair without uttering another word.

A smile spread across Keogh's face as he stood over Richard. "Good. Well at least that is settled." He tapped Richard's shoulder. "Our guest here." He turned to leer at Ryan. "Needs no introduction to any of you. We have all watched him on television over the years spouting lies about the IRA. He was

the Tory mouthpiece and used his ancestry to try to
fool us that he was the politician who cared about us
Catholics. By Jesus who did he think he was kidding!
Like his predecessors all he wanted to do was tread
us into the mud. Now let me be telling you a home
truth. He is here only because his Government is in
trouble at home. He comes in secret. A fucked up
old man. I don't think we should give him the time
of day. The British Prime Minister wants to save his
skin at the forthcoming election and that my friends
is the only reason why he's sent this 'has been'. It is
pure British cynicism and an insult to a downtrod-
den people." He waved disdainfully at Richard.

Unable to contain himself Richard jumped from
his chair. "Just a minute Keogh."

Keogh put one of his huge hands against
Richard's chest and pushed him back into the chair.
"Have the good manners to hear me out Hanmore."
Richard glowered at him, but stayed silent. "I think
it is fitting that we meet here in this cottage where
your grandfather meted out such terrible punishment on an innocent Catholic girl. I am sure my colleagues here will throw you out just as your grandfather did to her. Just thank your lucky stars that unlike the miserable couple you have somewhere to go
without having to depend on the largesse of someone else. We will send you back to the mainland with
your tail between your legs. Then we can get on with
the business of winning this war. Anyone disagree
with my prognosis?"

For several seconds no one spoke. Then very
slowly, with her heart in her mouth, Mary raised a
hand. "Yes me." She hardly recognised her voice.

Keogh moved across to her and fixed her with
an icy stare. "You disagree Mary O'Neill?"

"I do just that," she said defiantly, aware that all eyes were on her. "I think the least we can do is hear what Hanmore has to say. After all, contrary to what you have just told Ryan, I don't think the Army Council's agenda is a humiliation to the likes of us. And I think you have forgotten that we took a vote. Remember that Liam Keogh. So with that in mind I suggest we be sitting down and listen to what Hanmore has to say."

Keogh had difficulty in fighting back his anger. He had suspected Mary would cause trouble but her voice would be insignificant. There was no point in working himself up into a lather. He would have no trouble with the others, especially when, as he suspected, Hanmore told them he had little to offer. He decided to act quickly. He turned to Richard and asked, "Will you discuss a united Ireland?" He saw Richard's knuckles whiten as he gripped his chair and knew he had his man trapped.

Richard stared hard at the red face glaring down at him. He knew what Keogh was up to. For he knew damn well there was no way that such a delicate subject could ever be discussed at preliminary talks, if in fact it would ever be on any future agenda. It was brazen provocation—a way to end the meeting and throw him out. He did his best to smile and remain calm as he shuffled his papers and replied, "You have totally missed the point of this meeting Mr Keogh and I suspect deliberately. I'm not in a position at this stage to offer you anything. I am here only to see if there is any common ground between the two sides. But that does not mean that the subject cannot be discussed at a future date if we get anywhere tonight."

Keogh glared angrily at Richard. "Oh very clever Hanmore! And do you expect me to believe a word of it?"

Richard chose to ignore him and address the others in the room. "Gentlemen, please just listen to me for a few moments. You must know perfectly well at this time a united Ireland is not on the agenda. These are secret talks to see if we can talk. This is not a time for negotiations. This is a time to see if we can sit round a table in some sort of civilised fashion. So whatever Mr Keogh here would like you to believe, I came in good faith with hope in my heart and a prayer on my lips. Not much I grant you, but please don't doubt my sincerity. I love this island. Oh yes, I sense your antagonism and see the scepticism. in your eyes, but it is true. I speak from my heart when I say I would gladly die this very minute if I knew it would bring peace to Ireland. So I beg you don't throw out any chance however slim it might be. There is a new generation out there. For God's sake think of them."

Keogh jabbed him in the chest with a finger. "You talk rubbish Hanmore. The next generation will hate you as much as I do. And love Ireland? Jesus man, if you loved this island you would have moved the soldiers out long ago, and left us the island that belongs to us. I love Ireland. I fight for it. I would die for it. No. Please don't insult me by saying you love Ireland and would be prepared to die if it meant peace. Well I have news for you. You probably will die, but you won't get peace. I won't talk to you Hanmore. I would rather eat shit."

"And kill my children," Richard couldn't stop himself from saying.

Keogh raised his fist as if to hit him, provoking Ryan to gather his last ounce of courage and leap to his feet and push between the two men. "Oh for Christ sake, can't we be civilised?"

In the highly charged atmosphere no one except Mary heard the sound of voices as the front door was opened. Was she imagining it or was one familiar? She stiffened as the draft touched her face. Oh Jesus, it couldn't be! A cold finger of fear slithered down her spine.

Seamus Flanagan swaggered into the room an evil smile on his face and an AK assault rifle in his hand. "A good evening to you all," he said, before bowing to Ryan. "I'll start with you, you fucking little appeaser. You don't deserve to be called an Irishman. What did you hope; that by crawling up the Brits' arses you might be spared a prison sentence? Well I'll do that for you!" Without another word he shot him in the chest, the force of the charge throwing the little man several feet across the room before he collapsed onto the floor making strange gurgling noises. Frozen by surprise and fear everyone in the room stood and watched him drown in his own blood.

Keogh reached into his leather jacket and pulled out a colt .25. "Well by Jesus," he laughed, digging a boot into Ryan's corpse. "That's a good riddance. And what kept you Seamus? I was beginning to get a little trouble from one or two people. Hanmore here has got something of a silken tongue and your wee girl has some funny ideas."

Seamus replied, "What kept me Liam was the bloody weather. The usual road blocks which seemed more thorough than for some time. Could be something to do with what's going on here I suppose. Difficult to keep a secret these days eh Liam? But no worry, here I am, ready to help to negotiate with Hanmore and have a wee talk to young Mary." He gave her a nasty grin before turning to Richard. "A good evening to you Hanmore. At last we meet. Pity our meeting will be short. I would have liked to have had a long discussion with you about your murderous soldiers and your two faced politicians. But time is not on our side." He moved across to where Mary stood. "Ah my little girl. At last we meet again. I think you have been trying to avoid me. You shouldn't have done that to dear old Uncle Seamus, it makes him very angry and soon you will pay for your neglect. And as for that bastard son of yours, well wouldn't you like him to be brought up by me? That would be a good one little girl, wouldn't it? Especially as I suspect he's by Hanmore's fucking son!"

Mary's eyes blazed. She was scared, and her stomach churned at the thought of her son falling into Seamus's hands but no way was she going to give him the satisfaction of knowing he'd frightened the life out of her. Defiantly she replied, "I see you haven't changed Seamus, always spouting off threats and claiming to know things others don't. My son is my business and I will not be telling you who the father is. You lost the right to ask me such things after that night in your house. I gave up on you then Seamus Flanagan. I saw you then for what you really are. A madman, feeding on the blood of your victims. Look at you now; still just a ruthless killer. Do you know I believe you enjoy killing. Otherwise why shoot a man whose only crime was not to agree with you? And now you are threatening Hanmore and myself. You have no heart, no loyalty to Ireland, just loyalty to yourself and your killing. You changed me. I agree our cause is right, but I think the method to obtain it

is indefensible. I can see nothing wrong in at least
giving negotiations a chance. Jesus Seamus what are
you frightened of? That peace might just force you
to become an ordinary citizen with no gun to
terrorise people around you? Are you that pathetic
Seamus?"

Seamus chose to ignore her vocal onslaught. She
was a traitor—a woman gone soft—what she said no
longer mattered. He smiled at her and said, "I don't
fucking care what you think of me. I am right and
God is on my side." He ignored Mary's snort of disbelief. "And God will see your son being brought up by
a true catholic believer. Look at you Mary. You have
broken the Church's law. You may well have sweet-
talked your way onto the Army Council but I don't
kiss their arses anymore. They are traitors like you.
You vowed to fight and fight for freedom and now
look at you, pathetic! . So don't be fucking telling
me I'm in the wrong."

Mary watched him slowly raise his AK rifle. She
knew exactly what was coming but her reactions were
a few seconds too slow and as she dived for cover
behind the sofa his first shot shattered her left arm.
She cried out with pain and collapsed onto the sofa
watching helplessly as Seamus came towards her.

What saved her was Richard's intervention. Just
as Seamus was raising the AK to his shoulder, he
hurled himself at the Irishman's feet. Caught off
balance Seamus pitched forward onto the floor, his
rifle flying out of his hands. It was all the time Mary
needed. Although nearly fainting from the pain she
managed to get to her feet knowing she only had
seconds to save her life. Taking advantage of the
momentary chaos she stumbled from the room into
the dark passage with only one thought in mind. To

get back to her son before she bled to death. Breathing heavily and crying with pain she ran into the bathroom and with every ounce of strength she had left she hurled herself at the window she'd noticed when talking to Hanmore. The glass shattered and the rotten frame broke and she fell heavily onto wet grass gasping in agony. Only the adrenaline pumping through her body kept her going. She dragged herself to her feet and staggered into the darkness. She was gone before anyone in the room realised exactly what was happening.

It was surprise that saved Mary. Richard's intervention had given her those vital few minutes she needed to make her escape. Seamus was spitting with fury and he took it out on Richard. Swearing loudly he jumped up from the floor and grabbing his rifle swung round and struck Richard a terrible blow in the face with the butt. Blood exploded from Richard's shattered nose. "I'll deal with you later," Seamus shouted over his shoulder to the almost unconscious figure, as he charged out of the room, desperate to catch Mary. Worse for drink Keogh let out a roar of frustrated anger and turned his colt pistol on Kelly and Patrick. Before they knew what was happening he shot them both in the head as they stood rooted to the spot. He gave a brief look at the inert body of Richard to make sure he wouldn't be moving and shouted at the two men from across the border. "Come on! Let's be catching that fucking little girl!"

They stared open mouthed at Keogh's smoking gun and one cried out, "Jesus man, was that necessary?" Keogh looked at them with contempt. "Going soft boys"? And before they had time to draw their weapons he shot them dead. With a smile spreading over his face he turned towards the door just as a breathless Seamus returned. "The bitch seems to have got away. Jumped through the bathroom window. But she won't get far. She will bleed to death before she reaches her bastard son." Then he smiled at Keogh. "Well I see you've been busy while I've been away! Good riddance I say. And we still have Hanmore. Let's finish him and be on our way. There is nothing left for us here amongst all these corpses." He put a hand on Keogh's arm and said, "This has been a good night Liam. It will end any talk of peace for a long time if I'm not mistaken and we can get on with winning the war."

Keogh smiled and nodded as he reached for the half empty bottle of Bushmills on the mantle piece. "I'll drink to that," he said taking a long swig from the bottle before handing it Seamus. "What's more I think we will be thanked by many for what we have done tonight. We have proved we are true patriots!"

"To the Republic and victory!" shouted Seamus as he drained the bottle dry, the mixture of elation and the whisky combining to make him slightly drunk. "And now let's be finishing Hanmore and get out of this damn place!"

Keogh's reply was cut short by the sound of firing from outside. For a second his befuddled brain didn't register the danger, but as another shot rang out his mind cleared and he shouted, "Christ!" What the fuck is going on!" before lunging at the light switch.

"Shit!" gasped Seamus, blinded by the sudden darkness. "Who ever it is out there it certainly isn't Father Christmas to be sure! More likely to be the British army!"

Keogh swore loudly and hurling himself towards the door fell onto his stomach, his rifle at the ready and pointing down the dark passage. Feeling Seamus drop beside him he whispered. "To be sure it is someone who wishes us no good." He swore again as he heard a cry of pain. Shit what was happening? Not being able to see was unnerving. Who would burst through the door, one of his men or a fucking British piece of shit? He shrugged resignedly. The only way to find out was to wait.

Tim had heard the shots, then the sound of breaking glass and then more shots. He lay in some long grass not fifty yards from the cottage, soaked through from the mist and the dew. He was boiling with frustration and desperately worried. Watching Seamus Flanagan walk into the cottage had done nothing for his nerves. There could be no mistake, he'd have known that walk anywhere. God he'd never expected to come face to face with him again! His immediate instinct had been to run to the cottage, for Flanagan could only mean trouble, but realism had told him he'd die before he reached it. He had seen the armed men outside silhouetted by the light from inside the cottage. Just maybe he'd have risked a frontal attack before the arrival of Flanagan, but not now. He was trying to work out his next move when Russell dropped down beside him. "What kept you?" he asked urgently. "All hell has been going on in there."

Breathing heavily Russell gasped, "I got held up in Belfast. A suspected bomb closed the road. Had to take a long detour. Sorry."

"Well that detour may have cost my man his life! Seamus Flanagan arrived about half an hour ago and since then all has broken loose. Any sign of the Scots?"

"Not far behind. But perhaps we can't afford to wait? Do we have a chance on our own?"

Tim smiled in the dark. "Well the odds have improved! And I say we have no choice old friend. If Hanmore's still alive he needs us bad! We have delayed long enough. You on?"

"Of course."

Tim needed no more encouragement and flicking the FA 80 onto automatic he fixed his eyes onto the armed men silhouetted by the light from the open door. It was time to bolster his courage, pump some hate through his veins. If he were going to die he'd die shouting at the bastards. He heard Russell whisper, "Right I'm ready?"

"Then charge them man!" Tim whispered. "Make as much noise as possible. First target must be those two by the door.

"Understood," said Russell urgently.

Tim jumped to his feet yelling obscenities and charged across the open ground, all his pent up emotions spilling out. He could hear Russell shouting beside him. Luck was on their side. Lulled into a false sense of security by Keogh telling them that all enemy security had been neutralised, the two men's attention was focused on events inside the cottage. They turned slowly. It was a fatal hesitation. It gave Tim and Russell the vital seconds they needed. As one of the men shouted in alarm and fired a shot at random into the darkness they were shot before they knew where the attack was coming from. Immediately the cottage was plunged into darkness.

Tim threw himself through the open door and hit the hard floor, his rifle at the ready. He heard Russell land beside him. Their heavy breathing seemed to echo in his ears, and it dawned on him that if someone turned the lights back on or pointed a torch down the passage he and Russell were dead. He held his breath. Seconds ticked by. The cottage remained in darkness. He relaxed a little. Somewhere he heard a tap dripping. He risked whispering to Russell, "Don't move." He felt a tap on his shoulder. He'd understood.

Slowly his eyes grew more accustomed to the dark and he could just make out an opening at the end of the passage. He guessed it was a door into a room, and somewhere in that room there were some very nasty bastards indeed and almost certainly a rifle was pointing down the passage. The gunman or gunmen would be doing the same as himself and Russell, probably screwing up his eyes in the hope of catching a movement. It was an eerie feeling. When would the bullets come? He was certain it would not be long. He and Russell were sitting ducks in such a confined space, but there was nowhere to hide. And to move would almost certainly be courting death.

So it was the old waiting game. He was used to it. He and Russell had been trained for moments like this. They could wait forever, but it never got any easier. Nerves would be stretched. Courage would be tested. Always the enemy had to be forced into the first move. He knew Russell would be lying with his mini ruger rifle confidently tucked into his shoulder. It did him good to know he was alongside such a brave man. For it was almost certain that a man such as Flanagan was doing the same thing.

So they waited.

His eyes watered from the strain of searching into the blackness. Did he see a shadow by the door? He blinked. He couldn't be sure, but certainly it was not worth the risk of firing off a round. He longed to glance at his luminous wristwatch to see how long he'd been on his stomach. But there was always a chance that even such a minute light might be spotted and he would be cut in two by a hail of bullets. He resisted the temptation. His nerves screamed.

So they waited.

Cramp gripped Russell's left thigh. Tim heard him whistle in pain. Shut up you silly bugger. He held his breath, but nothing moved.

So they waited.

His rifle grew heavy. His fingers were growing numb. The damp from the bare floor was creeping into his limbs. The desire to move was almost irresistible. He knew Russell would be feeling the same. But if they moved they would be dead for certain.

Then he smelt it. The unmistakable aroma of body sweat. Pungent; tension induced. It was then that he knew he'd been right. Someone was very near, someone who wanted to kill him. Was he by the door? He thought he saw a movement. Yet again he could not be sure. But he had a feeling the stand off was about to end. He carefully edged towards the wall of the passage. Poor cover but better than lying in the middle. Then he heard the click. It seemed so loud in the silence. A round being pushed up the breach or a safety catch being flicked off. He braced himself.

The blast deafened him. He heard Russell scream. Shit! He pushed himself hard against the wall. Felt the rough plaster against his face, well aware that it was scant protection against a bullet. Another hail of

bullets ripped into the wooden floor, just missing his
left leg. The next burst might kill him. So bugger it
he'd die fighting! He fired at the doorway. Heard a
cry. Felt a surge of satisfaction. Fired again. Heard
the unmistakable rattle of a rifle falling on the
ground. He didn't move, even though he heard
Russell groaning beside him. That hurt. He counted
to ten. No return fire. Time to move. Time to
gamble. He leapt to his feet—nearly fell over because
his legs were almost numb—somehow recovered his
balance—ran towards the opening, firing a burst as
he went. He saw a shadow against a window. Fired
another burst. Heard the bullets ripping into flesh.
Heard the cry of death. Then he tripped over
something and measured his length on the floor, the
stench of blood invading his nostrils. As he lay
outstretched—defenceless for a second—the lights
came on. Half-blinded he rolled over prepared for
death. Standing over him was a soldier in combat kit
"Christ man," he croaked, "Am I glad to see you!"

The sight that met their eyes was horrifying. "Dear
God," exclaimed Tim as he surveyed the carnage.

"Shit," said the young officer, "Looks as if we are
a bit late." There were eight bodies spilling blood
onto the floor. "Which is your man sir?" asked the
officer.

Tim's eyes searched for Richard—saw him lying
by the sofa, congealed blood covering his left ear.
He rushed over and with a shaking hand he felt for a
pulse. He was alive! He shouted, "Quickly Captain,
over here. Sir Richard is alive."

The Captain stopped checking the other bodies
and rushed to Tim's side. "Is he dying?"

Tim gently rolled Richard over onto his back. "Maybe. It's hard to tell." He sucked in his breath as he saw Richard's damaged face. "Christ! Look at that! But I can't see a bullet wound, and his breathing is even. I'd say he had a chance but only if we can get medical attention to him pretty damn quick. The injury is serious. From past experience I'd say a rifle butt. Give me a hand to lift him onto the sofa."

Together they gently picked up Richard and lowered him onto the sofa. "Now captain the ball is in your court." Tim said urgently. "What you do next may well decide Sir Richard's fate. A man who has recently suffered a major heart attack needs a rifle butt in his face like a hole in the head. What are your options?"

"I can radio in for a helicopter. There is always one on stand by. That's probably the best option. Half an hour at the most."

"It could be too late, but we will just have to hope. Get on the radio now and tell the pilot to put his foot down."

"I'll do it straight away," said the captain, hurrying from the room.

Once he'd gone Tim examined Richard with more care. He was concerned that he was still unconscious but relieved that he could still feel a reasonably strong heart beat. A healthy man would probably survive, although bearing the scars on his face for the rest of his life, but Sir Richard could be different. He guessed it all came down to the length of time he stayed unconscious and whether his heart would stand up to the shock. It puzzled him why Richard hadn't been shot like all the rest, but he knew he might never know the answer. 'Don't die on me,' Tim thought. 'Please, please don't die on me.' He felt helpless. He'd just pray that Richard regained consciousness.

As there was nothing more he could do until the helicopter arrived he rushed out into the passage to see what had happened to Russell. He feared the worst. He found a soldier kneeling over him. "How is he?" he asked. The soldier looked up and shook his head. "Dead, I'm afraid commander. Took a belly full of lead. Must have died immediately."

Tim was not a man to cry easily. Four tours of duty in the province had seen to that. But he unashamedly shed a tear for Russell. He remembered the scream. Remembered he'd had to ignore it. It had not been easy. As he looked down on the soldier holding the dead man's hand he hoped he'd died without too much pain. Poor bloody sod. He'd given his whole life to the RUC and died doing a job he'd no need to be part of. His death would be hushed up for security reasons. It wouldn't do for the Government to be caught cheating on their deal with Sinn Fein, despite the duplicity of the IRA. There would be no commendation for him. Sometimes life stank. He touched the soldier on the shoulder. "Leave him now. He would like to be alone." The soldier dropped the already cooling hand and gave him a quizzical look. "But he's dead sir."

Tim knew he could never understand. "Just leave him soldier," he repeated. "Don't try to understand why." Once the soldier had gone back down the passage Tim knelt down by Russell's side and took a cold hand in his. "Forgive me George for dragging you into this," he said quietly with a lump in his throat. "You put your life on the line for me and Sir Richard." He released Russell's hand and made the sign of the cross on his forehead. "Rest in piece mate."

he whispered. Then brushing away the last of his tears he straightened his back and let out a long sigh. There was no time for sentiment in his job. It was time to rejoin the corpses.

The smell in the room made him gag. The captain was standing over a body. "Christ we hit a gold mine here tonight sir. Seamus Flanagan and Liam Keogh. We have been after them for a long time. Some good has come out of this evening. Two very dangerous characters will never give us any trouble again."

Tim looked at the young face flushed with success. God, how violence contaminated. "I don't deny that some pretty nasty characters have died here tonight," he said with a touch of anger. "But it should never have come to this. What turned a meeting about peace into a blood bath like this totally mystifies me. I will never understand this country. Violence has caused so much misery. Politicians have prevaricated and done very little. Millions of ordinary people have cried for the dead and yet when a chance comes along to perhaps end all the suffering what happens? They end up by killing each other. So more atrocities will be committed in the name of freedom. Believe me the death of Keogh and Flanagan, however welcome will change nothing. You may congratulate me on killing these two men, but out there are dozens more ready to take their place. You will still be shot at. The innocent will still die. Ulster will still bleed. And the politicians will still ring their hands in horror and be incapable of doing a bloody thing."

The captain shuffled his feet and looked sheepishly at Tim. "I'm sorry sir. I haven't your experience. I...." The sound of a helicopter overhead cut him short.

They rushed outside. The helicopter's lights cut through the mist and illuminated the field by the cottage. The pilot expertly landed his machine on the wet grass. He'd practised this sort of thing time and again until he could almost do it in his sleep. Before the rotors had even stopped, two medics jumped out and ran towards where Tim and the Captain stood. Tim nodded a greeting and hurried them into the cottage, talking as they went. "Several dead, and one badly injured man. We need to get him to hospital pretty damn quick"

Used as they were to the horrors that came as every day life in Ulster the medics sucked in their breath as they surveyed the carnage that met their eyes. One of them gazed at Tim a startled look on his face. "By God, someone has had fun here tonight sir."

Tim looked him in the eye. "You would never believe that this was the result of what was supposed to be a meeting about peace."

The young man, made cynical by his two years in Ulster, answered without a sign of emotion. "Nothing surprises me on this God forsaken Island sir."

Tim was sitting beside Richard in the helicopter when he regained consciousness. "Don't try and move sir," said one of the medics bending down close to his ear. "It won't be long before we have you in hospital."

Richard blinked an understanding to the strange face looking down at him. He struggled to speak. "Where…." His voice trailed away and the medic shook his head. "Don't exhaust yourself sir, we will soon have you in good hands." Then he added, "The commander is with you."

Richard turned his head painfully, his eyes closed "That you Tim? Good to have here." He tried to smile, grimaced with the pain, and mumbled a few incoherent words. Tim leant forward and took Richard's hand. "You heard what the medic said, don't try and talk, it will only exhaust you. Wait until you are stronger." Richard's eyes opened—only for a brief moment—but enough for Tim to see the panic in them. He sensed he was desperate to tell him something. He looked at the medic for guidance.

"If he's got something on his chest better to let him try and tell you. Any unease could quite frankly kill him at this stage."

It was all the encouragement Tim needed. Having got him this far there was no way Sir Richard was going to die. He put an ear close to Richard's mouth. "Speak if you want to," he said quietly. "If not let go of my hand." The grip tightened. Tim stayed very still and waited. He sensed the enormous effort Richard was making to speak.

"I, I have a......" His voice trailed off and Tim tried to encourage him. "You have a what?"

"A grandson"

A grandson! This was certainly news! But Tim knew he had to remain outwardly calm for he could see the tears in Richard's swollen eyes. "What's this about a grandson?" he asked gently.

"The girl. She told me. She was shot—don't know whether she's dead, but she's got a son and——." His voice faltered. "James is the father and she shot him!" His voice trailed off and he closed his eyes. Tim did not push him further. It was enough. The jigsaw was complete at last. The girl was Mary O'Neill and she'd shot Richard's son. And she was probably alive, for there had been no sign of a female body in the cottage.

Richard was struggling to speak again. "I want him Tim, do you hear. I want my grandson." He was silent for a few minutes, but when he spoke again his voice had grown in strength. "I want the boy and you will get him. This is the last favour I will ever ask of you."

Tim watched his eyes close and glanced at the medic, who bent down and took Richard's wrist. "Pulse still okay sir. But I think you should let him rest now, and with a bit of luck we may well get him back to the mainland alive."

Tim stared at Richard's white face, the shattered nose, the two black eyes and the trickle of blood oozing from his left ear. He looked a mess. "I hope you're right medic!" he said with feeling, "But I wouldn't like to bet on it."

He sat back in his seat and thought of what Richard had said. He was shocked by the request—it seemed so out of character, but he'd been very clear. There was no question of him not knowing what he was saying. Of course it could be done. There would be no problem in locating Mary O'Neill providing she was alive. The question was could he, Tim Roberts, become a kidnapper? For that was what Sir Richard was asking. But there was a moral issue here. Had Richard the right to take the child from her if she was alive? The answer had to be 'no'. Also it would cause more suffering. Surely it would be right to leave things well alone? And what would the Hanmores do with the child? Would they really want the responsibility of a baby after all the heartache they had suffered? It would be a child constantly reminding

them of their son. And yet he could understand how
Richard felt. Wouldn't he feel the same if he'd lost
all his children and suddenly a grand child had ap-
peared on the scene? He glanced at the battered
face of the man he had respected for years and knew
he could not refuse his request out of hand. He
needed to give it more thought when he was under
less pressure and not so bloody tired. He closed his
eyes and soon fell into an uneasy asleep.

He was woken by one of the medics urgently shaking his arm. "He's having a heart attack commander.
We've stabilised him for the time being but given his
past history and the state he was in when we found
him time is of the essence. But don't give up hope
yet. Not long before we land."

Tim felt a rush of sympathy for the man. He'd
suffered so much. First the heart attack that had
ended his career, and then the horror of his
children's deaths. Of course a lot of blame lay at his
feet, but what man deserved to be punished so
harshly, especially a man who had given many years
of his life in loyal service to his country? If he lived he
deserved better. Contrary to all his better instincts
Tim quietly sat down beside Richard, his face half
covered by an oxygen mask, and said, "if you can hear
me fight on. The boy will be with you when you recover."

Chapter Sixteen

THE pain throbbed in Mary's shoulder. She could feel the blood running down her arm. She knew she was losing too much blood and she could feel her strength ebbing away. How long had she got before her body refused to obey the signals coming from her brain? She touched the wound. Gasped with pain. She could feel the shattered bone. She knew she was in deep trouble. She thought about holing up until daylight in case Seamus had decided to search for her, but quickly discarded the idea. She'd be dead within an hour or two. If she was to live to see her child again she had to risk being caught and reach help. She didn't want him to become an orphan and perhaps fall into Seamus's clutches. So she had only one option. Struggle on and try to find help. One thing in her favour was her knowledge of the area. If she could reach Crumlin she reckoned she had a chance of survival. But every step she took was a struggle. Every minute that past was agony as her blood slowly ebbed from her body. She seemed detached from her limbs. Even worse her brain didn't seem to be focusing. She started to hallucinate, imagining she was seeing things, swerving all over the road she had no idea she was on. At last, her strength gone, she gave up the unequal struggle and collapsed by the edge of the road.

By the time the mail van drew up beside her inert body, half a mile outside Crumlin, she was unconscious and lying in a pool of her own blood.

Tim spoke urgently into the helicopter radio. Within two hours Special Branch in Belfast knew where Mary lived and the SAS were informed. Three hours after Tim's call four men were on their way. They broke down the door to the flat and in front of the terrified baby sitter, took the child from its cot. Six hours after the helicopter carrying Richard had landed the child was on the mainland, being looked after by an army nurse until further instructions reached her.

The postman saw her lying in the road. He rushed towards her, calm and resigned. It was not the first body he'd come across at five in the morning. It was unlikely to be the last. He saw the shattered arm and shook his head at the amount of blood on the road. He felt for a pulse, and found one. He rushed to the nearest house—woke the old lady whom he knew well, and rang for an ambulance and informed the RUC. He waited for the ambulance fearing they would be too late. But to his relief she was still alive when it arrived and once it was on its way he carried on delivering his letters as if nothing had happened. It was the way of things on his island.

Blanche was waiting at Stanstead. It was five twenty in the morning. She hung back as she saw the stretcher lowered to the ground, fearful of what she might see. She watched Tim following behind— saw him wave and smile, and knew at least that Richard was still alive. She hurried towards him and asked. "Is he very bad?"

Tim put his arms around her. "He's alive and that's a miracle on its own. But it's not looking good. The next few hours will be crucial."

Blanche gave a resigned little sigh and asked, "What brought the attack on?"

Tim explained the injuries. "But I don't think they were the only contributing factor. You see Blanche the talks were a failure." And then he gently took her hand and led her to the VIP lounge. "There is something I can only tell you in private."

Those people who were close to the lounge heard the screams and hurried on with worried looks on their faces.

Mary cried, cursing her immobility. An hour earlier a near hysterical girl had sat at the end of her bed and recounted the moment when four armed men had burst in and taken James. From what she had been able to coax out of the girl it did not sound like the work of the IRA. Besides what would they gain by abducting her baby? It was not their style. If they had wanted to punish her for the debacle at the cottage they would simply have come to the hospital, abducted her and summarily executed her. Nor was it Seamus. She'd watched with some pleasure on the ward television his body being removed from the cottage.

So she was left with one answer and it filled her with dread. It had to be Hanmore! He certainly had the contacts to organise something so awful as a kidnapping. But she had also seen on the ward television that he was hovering between life and death. If he survived, at best he would probably be an invalid. Surely neither he or his wife would want to be saddled with a baby? But however she looked at it, however much she tried to persuade herself otherwise, it always came back to Hanmore. So what the fuck was his motive? A last ditch attempt to rebuild a family? To be sure that was a possibility. Or could there be another reason, like revenge? Oh fucking shit! But the more she tossed and turned and cried into her pillow the more she thought it was the latter. It made much more sense. After all she knew he held her in total disregard and would feel that she was incapable of bringing up his grandson in the way he would want. Just because he was close to death or destined to be an invalid would not stop him. He wanted her child. Well fuck him. Whatever his motive, he had kidnapped her son. Once she was out of hospital she would have to go and get him back. But it would not be that simple. He was still a powerful man, with influence in all the right places. He could make sure she'd never set foot on the mainland. Well sod the bastard! James was her son and he'd find out that she was a resourceful girl. She wanted her child and no one however powerful was going to stop her. She'd kill to get him back, simple as that.

Suddenly the enormity of the situation hit her and she was overwhelmed by grief. Her baby should be by her side. She ached for him. She had nearly died, now she was confused, weak, and in considerable pain. Certainly in no fit state to leave the Mater Hospital for several more days. She wondered if the other ten women in the ward felt so desperate. She turned over and looked at them through her red rimmed eyes. Like her they were suffering in different ways from the effects of a bitter civil war. They were victims of domestic violence, IRA beatings, or bearing the scars of just being in the wrong place at the wrong time. She had had a dream to end such misery. What a fucking fool she'd been. How could she ever have thought that alone she could change a culture? Well fuck that! If she lived Mary O'Neill would be fighting only for number one. There would be no more heroics, no more impossible dreams. It would be just herself and her son. It would not be easy. The path was strewn with mines. She would be up against a powerful old man and probably the wrath of the IRA command. They would not forget the debacle at the cottage easily. She would never be trusted again. She would get no help from them. Her dream had well and truly died in the cottage.

The PM's face was pale and drawn. He sat behind his desk and stared at the three men sitting uncomfortably opposite him. Scarcely bothering to conceal his frustration, he asked, "What on earth went wrong gentlemen?"

The leader of the SDLP spoke first "We were ill prepared and ill informed. I believe the IRA High Command was genuine in wanting to open exploratory talks with your Government. What none of us knew was the extent of the INLA infiltration of their organisation." He threw an accusing look at the Secretary of State sitting next to him as if to say, 'Your intelligence should have told us that,' before continuing. "It had men placed in their top command structure who were hell bent on wrecking any negotiations however tentative. Believe me Prime Minister I would never have recommended the go ahead had I known the facts as we know them today."

The PM raised his hands in a gesture of complete hopelessness. "What's done is done. Nothing that any of us do can repair the damage. But gentlemen let me remind you of one thing. I trusted you. Listened to your advice, and acted accordingly. Now I must activate our emergency network and make sure the media do not get a sniff of what we were trying to do. It's keep quiet time gentlemen. Having let me down so badly I am sure I can rely on you to honour that request."

The two men on Tim's right just nodded, but he was damned if he was going to be made a scapegoat. Controlling his anger with some difficulty he said, "I'm sorry Prime Minister but I'm afraid I will not leave this room before reminding you that I expressed my gravest reservations for what I can only describe as 'your adventure.' I told you the mission was a grave risk, not only to your Government but also for the man you so recklessly threw to the wolves, and whom I might say has not received nearly enough sympathy here today." He glared angrily at the three men in the room before continuing. "Sir Richard lies gravely ill in hospital thanks to you persuading him to go to Ireland. In my view he was ill prepared and unfit. I told him this, as I did my superiors. I think you should acknowledge at least to us in private, that you were in too much of a hurry and therefore ill prepared. So I must tell you that I consider your proposed cover up to be immoral and indefensible. However I do not wish to be the cause of the fall of this Government or endanger any further secret attempts to talk with the IRA. I will keep my mouth shut, but I will not sleep easy in my bed for a long time. I hope that the same goes for you. Of course I accept I cannot talk to the leader of the country as I have done and remain a servant of his Government. So I shall resign from the Force as soon as I leave this room and try by God to live with my conscience." Tim rose slowly from his chair and nodded to the men staring at him open mouthed. "I'm sorry that I was forced to speak this way. And I'm even more sorry that your actions have forced me to resign from a job that has been my life. Good day gentlemen."

No one spoke as he stormed out of the room.

Chapter Seventeen

TWO weeks after his heart attack Richard was released from hospital. As Blanche pushed him down
the corridor towards the Range Rover she had difficulty in holding back the tears. A livid scar wound its
way across his left cheek. One ear still bore the marks
of bruising, and she had been told the shape of his
nose would never be the same again. He looked emaciated and fragile. In fact she couldn't help thinking
that he looked like an old man close to death. If this
was the case—and the doctors had told her it was a
real possibility—what on earth had she been thinking of when she took their grandson home to
Rosehall? Was it that she hoped it would revive
Richard's desire to live? Or was it desperation? (She
could not admit to herself that it might be revenge.)
Or a sort of trying to start another family and forgetting the past? After ten days she was still not sure.

Tim's news had badly shaken her and she'd
nearly lost control as she'd gazed at him in horror.
But now the shock of knowing she had a grandson,

and that the mother was the girl who had shot James was beginning to wear off. It was replaced by an immense joy, although she could not have put her hand on her heart and said she was easy with the situation. Sometimes when she lay in her bed at night she could not help thinking of the agony the mother must be going through. But she justified the circumstances by telling herself that the boy was getting the very best from life and the girl was only a murdering terrorist.

Now as she pushed Richard's wheel chair through the hospital doors and they thanked the hospital staff who had saved his life she was glad her conscience was clear. Their future was with the boy. But as they drove away and she eagerly waited for a suitable moment to tell him the news she felt an unexplained touch of panic. It was certainly not caused by any worry as to how he'd react—after all he'd more or less ordered the kidnapping—so perhaps it was fear of the future. Yes, that was it. Well there was no time to dwell on such dismal thoughts now. The present mattered now and she was happy. She glanced in his direction as the traffic eased a bit and judged it was time. In a slightly unsteady voice she said, "Our grandson is waiting for us at home." She heard his sharp intake of breath and felt him squeeze her arm. When she looked at him his battered face was doing its best to smile and for the first time for months she felt herself relax. Without a doubt young James was going to change their lives.

Almost unable to speak with emotion he croaked excitedly, "I knew Tim wouldn't let us down."

Briefly she thought of Tim. Poor man. His resignation from the Force, and loyalty to Richard had to be admired, but it had cost him a lot. The loss of his job had been a dreadful blow and she knew, in spite of his repeated assurances, that he was plagued by doubts over his action. From what he'd said to her she suspected he'd allowed sentiment and loyalty to over rule his better judgement; and that in his heart he felt he'd done the wrong thing. But she would never tell this to Richard. Never, and she knew Tim would be the same.

On arrival at Rosehall, Maria and Jose were standing by the front door, Maria holding the boy. "Oh dear God! Oh dear God!" was all Richard could say as he struggled to get out of the Range Rover. "Look at him! Just like James at the same age!" There were tears streaming down his cheeks as Blanche took his hand and gently led him towards his grandson. "When I'm better and he's a little older we will have a grand time together eh Blanche?" he said laughing.

She smiled at him trying not to show her sadness. She stroked his hand as he stood mesmerised by the sight of his grandson. "Of course you will Richard darling, and he will love you I know."

Richard leant towards her a little unsteadily (he was still used to being in a wheel chair), and said quietly. "I hope you think I did the right thing? Personally I have no doubt. The mother does not deserve him, even though I reluctantly admit she may well have saved my life twice. But she is a terrorist and has the blood of our children on her hands". His look challenged her, but for the moment she was happy to agree with him. There might come a time when she'd have to put her concerns to him but now was not the time. "You are right my darling.

Without a doubt you have done the right thing." She kissed him lovingly on the cheek. To have him home was nothing short of a miracle and nothing, absolutely nothing was going to spoil the moment. She took his arm and smiling up into his face led him into the house.

"I'm home! My God I'm home" Richard exclaimed as they walked into the hall. "When I faced those men in the cottage I was certain I was going to die. This is my second life. May God make it happier than the first."

"And you deserve happiness," Blanche said with a tear in her eye. "Don't you ever dare tell me again that you were a bad father. What's done is done, and as you say this is our second life. Let us never forget that. Few people ever get that chance."

When at last he was lying in their bed luxuriating in the feel of cool crisp linen sheets Richard was overcome by emotion. The whole day had been one of overwhelming excitement, a day he knew he'd never forget. He thought of Blanche downstairs feeding their grandson. He thought of James and Sarah and then much to his unease he thought of Mary O'Neill. Why did he have to think of her? But something nagged at his conscience. Had she survived? And if so was she wondering what had happened to her son? Was she distraught? His unease grew, driving out the pleasant thoughts of Blanch and his grandson and leaving him cursing his conscience. By the time Blanche joined him in the bed he'd made up his mind. "I think," he whispered in her ear as he held her close, "I have got to find out if the girl is alive. Tim will do that for me." He felt Blanche stiffen and had a feeling she'd been battling with her conscience as well. He put a hand gently over her mouth. He didn't want her to say a thing. He wanted to dream. Feel like he had done on their wedding night, touching her skin as he loved her, and feeling her body arch with excitement. He wanted to sleep peacefully in her arms, his mouth close to her breasts, knowing he'd wake up with her by his side. He wanted to push away the years and forget the tragedies that had beset his life. He wanted to forget the Mary O'Neills and the Seamus Flanagans of this world and the indecisive politicians who had never understood Ireland. All he wanted was Blanche lying by his side. What was the saying? Tomorrow was another day.

She walked out of the Mater Hospital dispirited, almost penniless, and longing for her son. Her arm throbbed constantly. A doctor had informed her she would never have full mobility in it again. Great! Added to that cheerful piece of news was the stark fact that within the next few hours she might be dead. Okay she hadn't been gunned down in her hospital bed or met by a hail of bullets as she walked out of the hospital. But she knew the rules, and although she'd had no control over the debacle at the cottage that would not be accepted as an excuse. Such a serious failure normally meant death, and she'd been given one life already. Her future looked bleak and she was in the mood to feel she'd be better dead anyway. Swearing loudly to no one in particular she hailed a cab. Fuck the bus! She might be short of money but she needed to be alone. She just wanted to get back to her tawdry little flat and shut herself away with her thoughts and mourn the loss of her son. Her bloody baby! Not fucking Hanmore's. What right had the man to kidnap her child! Without him her life meant nothing. She sat brooding as the taxi fought its way through the crowded streets wondering what she was going to do.

The driver's shout made her jump and she looked out at the graffiti covered walls of the flats. She felt a pathetic stirring of pleasure as she gazed up at her small window. The flat was all she had in the world now. It would be her refuge. She paid off the driver and walked slowly up the litter strewn stairs to the fourth floor thinking that perhaps she might put her head in the gas oven and end it all before the IRA could get to her. She was resigned to the fact that her son would be in good hands. Probably even have a much better life than she could ever give him. She let out a bitter laugh. Oh shit she hated losing! But then she caught sight of the blue push chair still resting against the wall of her flat. She froze and stared at its shabby fabric, clearly seeing her son sitting in it and grinning up at her. Her mood changed in a flash and her eyes filled with tears of anger. No! Why should the bastard have her son. She knew what she was going to do!

She was so overcome with anger and determination that she failed to register the unlocked door and did not realise anything was wrong until she walked into the small sitting room and saw the young man sitting in the chair pointing a gun at her chest. 'Oh shit!' she mouthed. No point in trying to run. No need for the oven. Within the next few seconds she would be dead and Hanmore would have won. She screwed up her eyes and braced herself to meet her death.

In the three hours that Aiden O'Brian had been waiting, he had bitten off most of his fingernails. He'd been to the toilet several times, and cursed the fact that he had been given the assignment. He had known Mary at school and would rather have been anywhere else but in her flat with orders to use the gun if necessary. He did not like being a messenger of death and certainly not to someone who he'd once had a school boy crush on. But he knew the score—his life would be worthless if he'd refused. He was beginning to hope that she might have done a runner when she walked in. He pointed his AK assault rifle at her stomach and said, "Hello Mary O'Neill."

She knew that voice! She opened her eyes. "Jesus! Aiden O'Brian! Where have you been all these years! Oh fuck they have sick minds!"

She looked pale and emaciated and Aiden couldn't help feeling sorry for her when he replied, "You can be saying that again! But you have a choice Mary." He pointed the AK at the ground. "I have a message for you."

"A choice Aiden O'Brian! By Jesus I bet I have! The bastards are noted for giving their victims a choice! So why waste time, just pull the trigger now or are you remembering those furtive kisses in the playground and going soft?"

Aiden smiled. "You always were a feisty girl! But I speak the truth. I really do be having a message. It is quite simple. Do as they ask or die now."

Mary allowed herself a smile. "Always an easy choice eh? They really are a bunch of bastards. Well let's be hearing it then."

Aiden cleared his throat. "The Army Council are very angry, very angry indeed, but they don't quite understand your part in the debacle. They are pleased that Keogh and Flanagan are dead and nor do they like the thought of Hanmore taking your child. So you have a choice even though they are inclined to think you fucked up. Some of the older hands even think you might be an INLA whore."

She stared at him boldly. "I'm no INLA whore Aiden. I wanted the talks to succeed. Coming face to face with Hanmore again was not easy, but I swear I wanted to at least talk about peace. That could not be said about Keogh or Seamus and believe me they would have surely killed me if I hadn't run." She pointed to her arm. "Just look at this. And who saved my miserable life? You will never believe this—it was Hanmore, God rest his miserable soul! One more shot and I would have been dead. I fled because I knew the talks were a shame and wanted to live for my boy."

Aiden gave a shrug of his shoulders. "I believe you, but it matters little to me. How very perverse that Hanmore saved you, and now you are going to have to kill him. Perhaps you should have done it the first time."

"Kill him!" Mary gasped.

"As I said you have a choice." Aiden stroked the AK and looked at Mary. "Well what's it to be?"

She looked at Aiden's small frame in its baggy blue trousers and black T-shirt and thought he looked totally harmless. And yet she knew he was desperately dangerous. IRA gunmen were not noted for their compassion. She smiled at him and said, "By Jesus you have surely changed Aiden O'Brian! Where has that irresponsible school boy with a big heart gone?"

His reply was abrupt. "My father died at the hands of a Protestant gunman."

She dropped her eyes to the floor. "I'm sorry to be hearing that. And you don't have to worry Aiden O'Brian I will kill Hanmore this time even though I thought I had given up violence forever. But no one takes my child. So go and tell The Army Council that he is as good as dead."

O'Brian looked relieved. "Your word is good enough for them. So now listen carefully. You will be armed and given money to cross to the mainland. "You will act on your own and God willing return here."

"I will not fail," Mary said, and then added, "And return to what, death? I will be no further use to them once Hanmore is dead. They won't want a girl who has turned her back on violence in their ranks. They are not ready to talk peace. I know that now. One day Aiden they will be forced to, but I can see now is not the time."

O'Brian couldn't meet her eyes when he replied, "Of course you will live. They gave their word. They would not want you to die now you have a baby."

Mary shook her head. "Oh dear God Aiden O'Brian, you do not know them well to be sure."

Chapter Eighteen

THE ferry carved its way through the quiet seas.
There was hardly a ripple on the water. The quiet-
ness and gentle roll of the ship lulling her into a
sense of peacefulness. How deceiving. How utterly
dishonest. She was heading into the biggest crisis of
her life. She shook her head violently. The sea was
lying. Underneath its calmness the currents ran dan-
gerously strong. Soon the ferry would be tossed about
like a minnow in a violent sea. She sensed it, and
knew it was a sign. The storm would soon engulf her,
and like the ferry, she would be at God's mercy. She
knelt down on the deck and prayed.

Ever since the horrors at the cottage the security
forces in Northern Ireland had been keeping an eye
on Mary, and within an hour of her boarding the
ferry word was passed to London that she was on her
way to the mainland. It was noted and filed. She was
not of much interest to the anti terrorist squad. But

it so happened that an eagle eyed officer who had worked with Tim Roberts saw her name and it rang a bell. He picked up the telephone and rang his ex colleague "Tim, I don't know if it's of any interest to you but that girl you mentioned to me some months ago is heading your way. To be frank she is not of much interest to us. Word is she has been dropped by the IRA after the debacle at the cottage, so not considered a security risk. However I remembered what you told me before you left us and I have a sneaking feeling you just might like to know. Perhaps she might pose a threat to your man? Now I can pull a few strings if you like and have her sent back to Ireland. Would you like me to take such action?"

It was what Tim had been dreading. She was on her way to get her child back for sure. He thought for a moment and then replied, "I'm not sure. Tell you what, I will consult with my man and then come back to you. And thanks Stephen, much appreciated."

"Well you have lots of friends here Tim. I felt it was the least I could do."

It was two in the morning when he rang Rosehall. The first time the ansaphone clicked in. The second time it was the same. The third time Blanche's sleepy voice answered. Tim quickly apologised and then asked to speak to Richard. "It's urgent," he said, anticipating Blanche's objection.

But no objection came. She knew Tim wouldn't ring at such an hour unless it was something very important. "I'll wake him. Just hold on for a few minutes." And then she couldn't stop herself from asking, "Is this anything to do with our grandson?"

Tim saw no point in denying it. "I'm afraid it is."

"The mother?"

"Correct. It looks as if she's on her way."

"Oh God. I always feared this. Hold on Tim I will go and wake Richard".

There was silence for a few minutes before Richard's unsteady voice came on the line. "She's alive then and on her way?"

"Yes I'm afraid so. She's on a ferry this very moment. A close friend of mine in the Force spotted a memo. She's been under surveillance only because I mentioned her name when I was debriefed after the cottage fiasco. Now the rumour is she's been kicked out by the IRA so she's of no interest to the Security Forces especially as they never knew she was involved in any activity here on the mainland. But you and I know differently don't we? So I need a decision Sir Richard. Is she allowed into the country or turned away? It is up to you. But before you answer just reflect on the fact that I don't think she would be coming here unless it was to get her child back."

"I agree."

"So what's your answer?"

Richard hesitated momentarily before answering. "It would be far better if she was dead, but as she's alive I think I have no alternative but to face her. I suppose she deserves that at least. So let her come. I feel confident I can deal with the situation. Let's face it her future must be pretty bleak. Perhaps I can persuade her that her son would be better off with us."

"And supposing you can't?"

"Then I will throw her out. One way or the other I intend to be rid of her and keep my grandson; make no mistake. She's done her best to ruin my life and I've had enough of her. So just tell me when would you anticipate her arriving here and leave the rest to me."

Tim suspected things might turn very nasty and that Richard was being naive to say the least. But he knew from experience that once he'd made up his mind Richard became very obstinate. It would be a waste of time trying to persuade him that he might find himself in a position not of his choosing and that at least he could have some security nearby. So he merely replied. "Let's assume she hires a car. The ferry gets into Stranraer around eight this morning. So say ten hours at the most. That means around late evening today she could be with you. Of course she could wait until the morning. Who knows. Whatever, for God sake be careful. I don't need to tell you how dangerous she could turn out to be."

"You most certainly do not! But thanks for your concern Tim, and for warning me. I will be ready for her tonight. Now you have done enough. Leave me to sort this mess out. It is not your concern."

"Very well, but that doesn't mean I won't be worrying about you. Please don't forget we stole her son from under her nose and you would be very wrong to underestimate a girl like her. She may well have no future but the boy is the only thing she has left. Desperate people take desperate measures."

"Stolen is the wrong word Tim. You mustn't think like that. We took the child for his own good so that he could have a decent life. A life that someone like her can never give him. And for God sake do you honestly think that after what she has done to my family she deserves any happiness? I certainly don't. And as for being desperate. Well I know that for heaven sake. I will be ready, I assure you."

Tim had no doubt they had stolen the boy but saw no point in saying so. Richard's mind was made up and nothing he said would change it. He said. "Okay then I will say no more. I will make the call. I only hope you know what you are doing."

"I have absolutely no doubt Tim."

"Then may God be with you and Blanche." Tim put the telephone down thinking he might have allowed another dangerous situation to develop. His loyalty to Richard was once again being put to the test. Here was an ill man taking on a proven killer almost certainly hell bent on getting her child back. How could such a man be a match for that? He should have the girl stopped. That would be the safe and logical thing to do in spite of Richard's wishes. And yet somewhere nagging away at the back of his mind was a small voice saying that the girl deserved the chance to face Richard. Just perhaps there was an outside possibility that he might change his mind when faced with the young woman begging for her child back. That would be the perfect result and allow him to sleep easier in his bed at nights. Tim was not proud of his involvement in the abduction. He bit nervously at a fingernail and played with the green telephone for several minutes before dialling the number he'd scribbled on his pad. The connection made he said, "It's me Stephen. My man says let her in." He was close to being sick as he replaced the receiver.

She felt depressed and cold as she walked off the ferry. She had stayed out on deck too long, but she had wanted to be alone. She looked around her, feeling uneasy. She had no doubt that Hanmore knew she'd landed on the mainland. A man who had the power to order the kidnapping of her baby, would certainly have the means of keeping an eye on her movements. And she knew perfectly well that Hanmore would be expecting her to come. She felt a chilly hand creep up her neck as she looked around her. Would she be stopped and unceremoniously dumped on the return ferry? Well sod the fucking lot! Whatever they tried she'd be back. She would reach him one day, be it take a week, a month or even years.

But a hand didn't touch her shoulder, followed by a voice asking her 'to step this way miss'. There were a few anxious moments as she imagined eyes watching her but every second that passed made her seizure less likely, and once she was standing in the Hertz office she began to think she might make it. For the first time since she had left hospital she felt her confidence growing. She might be followed, but what the hell? If she wasn't stopped by the time she reached Carlisle she reckoned she'd get to Hanmore and then only God knew what would be the outcome of the meeting. She took the keys of the car from the girl behind the desk and walked out of the office impatient to get moving.

It was raining hard as she drove out of Stranraer and headed south. The cloud was low and the roads glistened with dampness. Very slowly her fragile confidence began to wane as her tiredness grew and her eyes grew sore from staring at the black road in front of her. She had a gut feeling that the God she had so disdainfully cast aside all those years ago was not going to come to her rescue, and to her horror she began to think the unthinkable. By the time she was sipping a cup of tea at the Forton Service area off the M6 the reality of her situation had hit her and every last drop of bravado and confidence had drained from her body. What hope had she got! She stared into her empty tea cup and finally came to terms with the unthinkable. She had no future with her son. Her eyes filled with tears and her head dropped onto the table. What world had she been living in? How could she ever have imagined that she had a future with him or for that matter any future at all? She faced certain death if she returned to her country and almost no hope of getting James back unless she killed a man. And once she'd killed she'd be hunted like an animal until she was trapped. And trapped she would surely be for she would get no protection from the IRA and she had no friends to shelter her. She would be taking James out of a secure environment just for the sake of being able to love him for a short time. And when she died? The thought was too painful to dwell on. Tears rolled down her cheeks as she saw Hanmore triumphantly smiling at her, holding her son. He'd had no right to take him. No fucking right at all, but he was going to win because she had no future. She had no choice but to admit defeat and accept that James was better off with his grand parents. Shit, that hurt bad! Well she was damned if she was going to make it easy for him. But in the end she'd walk away and head out into a hostile world and put her life into the hands of God. "Oh fucking shit!" she cried outloud.

They waited. They drank endless cups of tea. The time slowly moved on.

They waited.

Morning turned into afternoon and then into evening. It grew dark.

They waited.

Their nerves at fever pitch. They ate nothing. They walked from room to room, Blanche terrified Richard would collapse. And still they waited. It wasn't until eleven minutes before midnight that the doorbell rang and their waiting was over.

Blanche opened the door, with her heart in her mouth. For a moment she gazed at the dishevelled figure of the slight girl standing in the drizzle holding what was obviously a handgun, before asking in an unsteady voice, "Mary O'Neill?"

"To be sure, that's me. I think you may have been expecting me." She waved a handgun menacingly, "I think it is time we had a talk."

Richard and Blanche sat on the sofa in the drawing room staring at Mary pacing up and down in front of them, the colt pistol held firmly by her side. The atmosphere was tense. Blanche couldn't stop staring at the slip of a girl, her unwashed hair touching the top of a faded brown bomber jacket, which met a pair of patched blue denim jeans at her waist. The hand that didn't hold the gun hung limply by her side and Blanche remembered that Richard had told her the girl had been wounded in the cottage. Too bad she hadn't been killed. Her face was white. Her eyes were sunk into dark sockets, and Blanche wondered how a girl like this could have ever seduced James. How she and Richard must have failed him. But then she didn't look the type who could plan so many deaths and then shoot her lover dead in front of his father. But as she spoke Blanche noted the cold, almost venomous voice and realised that within the frail almost urchin like body was a heart of steel, honed by years of violence and that she wouldn't hesitate to kill them both if necessary. Suddenly she felt very frightened, not so much for herself but for Richard. He'd been right when he'd described her as a dangerous and ruthless woman and at that moment Blanche became certain that Mary wouldn't leave without her son. She glanced at Richard wondering if he was thinking the same as her as he listened to the vitriol pouring out of the girl's mouth.

She was saying. "So fuck you Hanmore." I didn't fucking kill you, and what do you do? You kidnap my baby. Jesus man what were you doing? Did you think I would walk away and let you have him? Or did you think the IRA would put a bullet through my brain because of the episode at the cottage and that gave you the right to my son?"

Richard glared at her feeling threatened by the gun, but his voice was strong and dismissive when he replied. "Yes, I admit I thought you would be dead by now. But I have no regrets at taking the boy. James cannot be brought up in your world of violence. I know you have told me that you have turned your back on killing but I don't accept that people like you can ever change completely. He needs a stable upbringing, which you can never give him. And if I may say so, I think after what you have done to my family he should be mine by rights."

With her eyes blazing Mary replied. "Oh Jesus now I have heard it all! A stable upbringing! Jesus that comes rich from you! What stability did you ever give your son? Let me be telling you Hanmore, James was a sexual pervert if you didn't already know. He found me behind a bar and fancied beating me up. But things didn't work out that way because I was mentally too strong for him. I was an IRA sleeper waiting for orders and when he turned up and told me he was your son I felt as if God had sent me a gift from heaven. So instead of using me for his perverted desires I gained his confidence and before long had him eating out of my hand. Soon he was telling me all about his miserable childhood and how much he hated you. It was surprisingly easy to persuade him to kill you. What a propaganda coup that was going to be! I knew he'd do as I said but the IRA was not so certain so they set him a test. The result of course you know. It was his pleasure at the death of his sister that changed me. I had almost loved him for want of a better word, but such pleasure made me sick. To this day it still confuses me why I changed, given my upbringing. From an early age my life was one of violence. My father fought for a free Ireland. All his friends were the same. But my mother tried to persuade me there was another way. When your Sarah died I saw that other way whatever you may think. That is why I killed him and saved your fucking life. He was so evil. So fucking evil! And believe it or not I had come to feel that perhaps peace should be given a chance. With men like him around there certainly could be no chance! So, God help me I decided that you might be the one man who could help to bring that peace about. And how did you reward me? You fucking stole my son! You are no better than the men and women I have turned my back on!"

Richard opened his mouth to speak but no words came out. He just stared at the girl and shook his head.

Mary waved the handgun at him and smiled. "You're speechless Hanmore. You can't defend your actions. Why did you really take my son? Well, let me be telling you. You took him partly for revenge, to try and hit me where it hurt most. You succeeded there you bastard. But I also believe you took him because you knew you were dying and wanted Lady Hanmore here to have a life after your funeral. Ha, I see by your face that I have hit the mark! Well too bad Hanmore you're not going to get your way. I have every intention of walking out of this house to-night with my son and leaving you two to wallow in your misery."

Richard caught his breath, anger seething inside him and at last found his voice. "In that case Mary O'Neill we have a problem, for I have no intention of giving you back our grandson. Waving that gun at us doesn't frighten me for you know perfectly well if you kill us you will never get out of the country and then what will happen to your boy? So why don't you just leave the boy with us. Accept it is the best thing for him and go back to your beloved island without further fuss."

Mary stared at him; emotion threatening to over-whelm her. She had known her decision would be painful but now, inside the house where her son was sleeping and seeing Hanmore relishing in her pain she was sorely tempted to change her mind. Shoot the bastard, take her son, and take her chances. Oh shit if only! She stood up and waved the colt in Richard's direction. "You will not have my son! You are a heartless bastard and I have nothing but con-tempt for you. If you had an ounce of goodness in that rotting heart of yours you would hand James back to me now. But I can see that is not to be, so I must insist that you, Lady Hanmore, go now and bring my son to me. I have wasted enough time here listening to your husband's drivel. Go now before I kill you both and find my child on my own!"

Blanche's eyes narrowed and her voice was a little unsteady when she replied. "What choice do you leave me, waving that gun around? But by God if you were unarmed things would be very different." She rose slowly, almost painfully from Richard's side and moving past Mary she stopped and turned to face her at the door. "I won't ring the police or do anything funny. Please believe me I will get James and come straight back. You have nothing to worry about." Then with a note of desperation in her voice she added. "You won't kill my husband while I'm out of the room will you?"

"You have my word."

Blanche tossed her head. "Your word! My God that's laughable! However I have no choice but to believe you." She threw a swift glance at Richard before hurrying out of the room, not wishing to let Mary see the hatred that was disfiguring her normally soft features.

Once Blanche was out of the room Mary lowered the colt and dropped down onto the sofa beside Richard. She didn't know why, but she suddenly wanted the whole charade over and done with. She wanted to run from the house, curl up somewhere and die. Only then would the pain that wracked her body disappear. When she spoke her voice was devoid of all anger. "Listen to me for a few minutes Hanmore. I have something to tell you."

As he turned to stare at her she was close enough to see the damage to his face. He had suffered the injuries to protect her, and although her hatred for him could never completely die in some perverse way she felt that what she was about to do was paying back a debt. It made her decision just that little less painful. But she would never let him know that! She said in a quite voice. "I'm sorry you suffered those terrible injuries for me. I should be grateful for what you did at the cottage at great risk to yourself, but I'm not. Taking my child when I was in no position to protect him was a terrible thing to do however desperate you were. I am sorry that I was instrumental in the death of your son and daughter. I can't say it gives me sleepless nights but I accept it served no useful purpose. You may not believe this but I was genuinely hoping that the talks at the cottage would be a success. I was not one of those out to kill you or destroy the first tentative move towards discussing peace. I know the IRA High Command was genuine in wanting talks. The trouble was we had been infiltrated by traitors loyal to the INLA. The mayhem that ensued was not of the IRA's making. You are right about one thing. I should have been dead and will surely be if I return to Ulster. I have only been given a stay of execution because you kidnapped my baby. The IRA has no time for those who fail them and I was on my second life anyway having failed to assassinate you. This time I was supposed to finish the job. I was given a vague promise that I would live but I know differently. I have no future and therefore nor does James. My heart bleeds and I feel I am going crazy as I say these words, but you can have him. There by Jesus I've said it!"

Richard stared at her open mouthed. "But, but only a minute ago you were threatening to shoot us and take the baby!"

Mary smiled. "Oh I wanted to frighten you of course! But I was just saying what I would like to do. Make no mistake if I thought I had a future you would be dead and I would have my child. Take him Hanmore! Hold him to your rotten heart! Make him the respectable citizen that I would never do. Turn him into what ever you want! But never tell him his mother was a killer. I beg that of you."

Richard saw the tears in her eyes and knew what pain she was suffering but he felt no sympathy for her. She had been too much involved in ruining his life. He said quietly. "I will not say a word I promise. But I can never forgive you for what you have done to my family and nor do I care a damn what your future will be. But I know you must love your son like I did mine. Now we have both lost something precious to us both. Perhaps it is God's way, I don't know. Whatever, I think you have been brave in coming to your decision."

At that moment Blanche walked into the room carrying James. With a whimper of joy Mary jumped up from the sofa and ran towards her. Dropping the colt on the carpet she cried, "Let me have him, let me have him please." She was close to tears as she saw the small round face, the blue eyes staring in interest at her. He'd grown more hair since she'd last seen him and seemed considerably bigger. But he was still her baby and her stomach churned as she smiled at him.

Blanche pushed her away. "Just a minute. He's cold. He was asleep. Let me get a blanket for him." She moved swiftly over to the playpen and when she stood up she wasn't holding James but one of Richard's 12 bore shotguns which she'd hidden in the playpen as soon as Tim had rung. Her eyes blazing she waved it at Mary. "Now young woman experience for yourself the feeling of looking down the barrel of a gun. And don't make the mistake of trying to reach your weapon. You won't get near it."

Mary froze.

Blanche heard a shout from Richard and out of the corner of an eye saw him struggling to get up off the sofa. But she was shaking with anger, oblivious to everything except for Mary. She shoved the gun into Mary's stomach and hissed. "Now let me tell you something Irish girl. All my married life I have supported Richard. I have loved him for every second we have been together. I have stood by him when things have gone wrong and I have nursed him when he was ill. But one of my greatest joys was to give birth to our children. Of course like every parent we had difficulties, especially with James, but not until you came into his life did he become the evil young man who threatened to kill my husband. You were responsible for the road he took and you turned him into a murderous young man. Your hands were on the bomb that killed my daughter and for sure you would have killed my husband if you hadn't had to snuff out the life of my son. You did not save my husband's life, you have as surely killed him as if you had pulled the trigger that night in the library. You are a cold blooded killer, believing in a cause I frankly think stinks and I have nothing but the deepest contempt for your miserable existence. I am a gentle person, not prone to anger or hatred, but a deep hatred has been festering in my heart ever since I saw you in the library standing over the body of my son. You stand there bold as brass having come to our house uninvited and threaten our lives if we don't give our grandson back. Well for once you are not going to win, for I am going to end your miserable existence now and God will thank me for it."

In the back of her mind Blanche was aware of Richard shouting but nothing was going to stop her now. Mary heard the click of the safety catch being flicked forward and silently sent up a prayer to God. Blanche pulled the trigger with a smile on her face.

The force of the shot hurled Mary across the room to land only a few feet from Richard who was gasping for breath. Blood spurted out of a gaping hole in her chest and an eerie gurgling sound came from her shattered lungs. Blanche watched mesmerised as the body twitched for several seconds before lying still. The gun dropped out of her frozen hands and she began to shake uncontrollably. She had killed another human being. Something that she had thought she was incapable of. But as she looked at the body with its blood staining the carpet she found herself unable to feel any regret. The girl had ruined her life. Killed her children and had had the audacity to come to claim her grandson. She was justified in doing what she'd done. She shook her head in disbelief and vomited onto the carpet.

Only after she'd wiped the remains of the sour tasting liquid from her lips did she look at Richard standing over Mary white faced and with his hands clasped to his chest. "Blanche!" he croaked, "She was going to leave. . . . " His voice died as he crashed to the floor.

Within a second Blanche was kneeling by his side desperately trying to cradle his head in her arms.

"She was going to what, going to what!" she screamed as she put an ear close to his mouth.

"Going to leave...." The pain in his chest cut him off in mid sentence."

"Oh God no! She was going to leave us James!" Richard gave a weak nod.

"Oh no! I killed her for nothing!" cried Blanche. "Oh dear God I must live with that for the rest of my life! Oh Richard, Richard!" But he didn't respond and tears cascaded down her cheeks. "Don't you dare die on me now darling! Oh dear God, please, please don't let him die on me now! I will need him so much!"

But Richard didn't hear her. He was already dead.

EPILOGUE

SHE sat on the wet grass watching the flames from the bonfire twirling up into the black night sky. She felt it fitting that there were no stars or moon. It suited her mood. She was destroying all the memories. Richard's diaries, his clothes, all the letters from their children. Anything that would remind her of a troubled family. A vibrant family without a doubt, but who never seemed to be able to come to terms with each other's lives. She held a book in her hand. It had been Richard's bible. 'A history of Ulster.' With shaking hands she slowly began to tear each page from its binding and one by one she threw them onto the fire. As she watched the flames consume the pages she smiled. In her mind she was destroying Ulster. How she hated the very word. Dear God it had a lot to answer for. It had destroyed her family. Made her into a killer. She shivered as she remembered that terrible night still so vivid in her memory. The pages burnt, she hurled the cover onto the fire with a cry of pain, and did not move until she was sure the book had been reduced to ashes. She had completed her first task.

The second one would be no less painful. Tomorrow she'd arranged with the agents for the 'For Sale' signs to go up outside the gates. The white and red signs were in the stables, ready to be erected the next morning. It was time to leave. It would be difficult. The house had been her life with Richard. The house had been her children's home. The house had embraced her in its love. But it no longer held her in its spell. It was a place of too many deaths. She had to try and forget the past and build a new life. It would not be easy. If only she could have Richard by her side. Oh God how cruel life could be. It would be difficult to adjust to new surroundings, new friends, new life, without the man she'd loved for so many years. Richard was still with her, always would be. His premature death still haunted her, the memories of their life together always with her. She would not want it any other way. for Richard had been special.

Already she had made a positive move. A small cottage in Falmouth would be her new home with James, not far from where Tim had settled. What a man he'd turned out to be. Wracked by guilt at yet again arriving seconds too late to stop a disaster he'd dealt with the police. He'd explained to them that Blanche had shot Mary in self defence, and stayed with her until she'd been able to accept that what she'd done could not be reversed and she'd have to live with that. He would always be there for her. It was a great comfort.

She gave the dying embers one last look before slowly walking back to the house. She would climb the stairs, look into the room where Marie and Jose slept with James, and hearing their regular breathing would quietly shut the door behind her and cross the passage. Outside her room she would say good night to the dragons as she and Richard had always done. Once in her room she would pick up the only photograph she had kept in the entire house. She would kiss the glass, already smudged with her lipstick and fall exhausted onto the bed, her tears staining the white sheets as she clasped the frame to her breast. It was the nearest she would get to Richard until she died.

The End